FIFTH ESSENCE

A Reverse Harem Tale

Lovin' the Coven
Book 5

Jacquelyn Faye

∞ Untold Press ∞

Fifth Essence

A Reverse Harem Tale

Lovin' the Coven, book 5

ISBN: 978-1-945893-15-5

First Publication, June 2020

Published by Untold Press LLC
114 NE Estia Lane
Port St Lucie, FL 34983

www.untoldpress.com

PRODUCED IN THE UNITED STATES OF AMERICA

10 9 8 7 6 5 4 3 2 1

Dedication

I hereby dedicate this book to the Coven of the First Moon.

Not the one in these books, I mean the people in my reading group on Facebook. The fans. The ones who pimp my work every chance they have. They tell their families, their sisters, their parents. They read my ARCs and help me with proofs. I am truly humbled and amazed by them every damn day, and they make the joy of writing books so much better.

Bless your faces

Chapter 1

The dark elf in my doorway was lucky to be alive. The last thing in the universe I needed after the hellish nightmare I had endured in Faerie was a ransom note from the dark elves. They wanted me to marry the prince and so far, I had not shown interest, politely declined, and adamantly refused. Delron, the dark elf in front of me, had practically *begged* me to visit the unseleighe court, just to hear the queen's offer. They decided to up their game and *demand* that I come by holding my elven bodyguard hostage until I agreed.

My temper flared, as did my magic. Tendrils of magic flared out, aiming for the dark elf, and crackling in eldritch fire. Unfortunately, I couldn't kill him, *yet*. He had a message to deliver and I barely got them extinguished as they wrapped around Delron's skinny little elven neck. Coming into my house, threatening me with the life of my friend, was *not* the way to get me to do what you wanted. Ever. Just ask Chief.

I backed him against my front door and snarled in his face. Whatever the hell Dar had done to me in Faerie was trying to resurface. My teeth screamed in agony as my metaphysical fangs begged to rip open the soft flesh of his throat.

He saw his death in my eyes.

"Tell you what, *Delron*... How about you bring Jaeren back and I won't pay a visit to your court under these circumstances. Ask King Renlynn how pissing me off worked out for him. Oh wait, you *can't*. Because I fucking *ate* him."

His eyes widened in fear and he began choking, patting my arms and begging for breath. I let him go, not realizing, in my anger, I had lifted him from the ground. Even I gasped a little in shock.

"Please," he managed to choke out as he gasped for breath, rubbing his tender flesh. "All we wish...is for you...to hear us out."

"Kidnapping my friend wasn't a smart thing to do."

"I see that. We needed a bargaining chip."

"A life isn't something to be bargained with."

"You would not come..."

"You're right. But that option would be much better than me visiting and raining down destruction, the likes of which you have never seen. Do you understand? Bring Jaeren back." I enunciated each word slowly. "If you do, I will visit. If I have to come *get* him, I will fuck your shit up six ways to Sunday. Do you understand?"

"Yes, my Lady."

"Go."

I resisted the urge to kick his ass as he got up and ran out the door. Turning around, I nearly slipped and fell on the coffee and shattered mug I had dropped to threaten the dark elf at my door.

"I will clean it up," Candace said with a little squeak and ran for the broom and mop.

"Do you think he'll do it?" Yuki asked thoughtfully, standing next to Dar, Shea, and Jimmy.

"Did you see the look on his face? I bet the elf is back here within the day." Jimmy chuckled.

"He better be," I said and headed for the coffee maker. It had been a hell of a few days for me and my coffee reserves were dangerously low.

I had just set the mug into the machine when my front door burst open. Again. "Hi, Chief," I called out from the kitchen without having to see who it was. Everyone else knocked. He barged in like Josie in a candy shop.

He slid to a stop when he saw me, staring intently at my brewing coffee.

"Are you okay?"

I nodded, not looking up.

"Oh. Okay, then."

The machine stopped, and I reached down and picked up the mug, taking a sip before turning to him. "Sorry. Just had another visitor."

"The elf I saw running out of here? Want me to go shoot him for you?" It was sweet of him to offer, but I knew it was his attempt at a joke. Chief didn't shoot people. It was a serious character flaw.

"No. He has to bring Jaeren back."

"What the hell is going on?"

I opened my mouth to start talking but then I froze. Completely. I couldn't relive everything right now. Not this soon. I just couldn't.

You wish me to tell the tale?

Dar's soothing voice wrapped around my tired sorrow like a warm blanket. *Would you? I just can't right now. I need another shower. And my bed.*

It would be my honor. Might I borrow some clothes?

Sure. I think I have a dress or two in your size.

You wish to make jokes? He nosed me in the nether regions.

Sweatpants and hoodie it is. I laughed until I noticed Chief staring at the both of us. "Sorry. Dar is going to fill everybody in while I have another shower and a nap. It's been a shitty couple of days and the dark elves just kidnapped Jaeren."

"Seriously?"

"As a heart attack."

He did the absolutely worst thing he could have possibly done. He wrapped me in his arms and kissed the top of my head. I lost it, completely breaking down and turning into a sobbing mess. Everything that had happened, the pain, the suffering, the loss, came crashing down on me like a…building. He just held me until I got it out. All over

9

his shirt. There might have even been a rainbow or two as I pulled away and the sunlight reflected off my snot and tears.

"Sorry."

"Gonna change my name to Hanker Chief."

Not going to lie, there might have been a snot bubble blown, but it was his fault for being all sweet and cute, and making me laugh. "Thanks."

"That was kinda gross. Go have your shower."

"Thanks. Come on, Dar. Let's get you some clothes."

He followed me into my bedroom and waited patiently as I rooted through my drawers for pants, pulling out the largest, most stretchy pair I could find. Dar, in his demon form, wasn't gigantic, but still a lot larger than I was. We needed to take a trip to the mall to get him his own clothes.

"Here, these should fit," I said and held them out to him.

He morphed in front of my eyes into his new elven form. A form that was more-than-a-little-bit attractive when butt-assed naked. I pulled the pants back.

"What?"

"No."

"No, what?"

"You. I want to see *you*."

He breathed out a sigh. "This form is as just as much me as my natural form."

"But, you're my blue demon. And while you are very attractive in *this* form… I'm kinda on a 'I hate elves' kick right now."

"Oh."

"Plus, I want everybody to start getting used to seeing you in your normal form. There's no reason for you to be a dog all the time."

"It is rather limiting," he said and shifted again.

He was attractive in his elf form, but in his demon form… *Holy shiznit*. I'd always found him handsome, even with the horns. Something felt *different*. My body started visibly shaking as I fought the urge to reach out and touch him. All over. Even low. Especially low.

"Master?"

He could have called me Dot, Lady, or even Late-for-breakfast. Hearing him call me Master sent a shiver racing down my back that went for the reach-around.

"Dar..."

"I know you wish me to call you by your given name," he said with a soft sigh and stepped forward, reaching for the pants clutched against my chest.

I stepped back, wide-eyed.

"Are you teasing me now?"

Another step forward, and another step back from me, completely involuntary. My throat clenched as the fear of what would happen if he got too close hit me like a sledgehammer. In the groin. He thought I was teasing him. I was protecting him.

What really scared me was the utter lack of guilt. I wanted him and there was nothing to stop me from taking him but me. It wasn't because I was worried about the repercussions, I was afraid of hurting him.

He lurched forward with a smile on his face, his clawed hand encircling the soft fabric in my hands. As soon as mine had nothing to hold, they shot out and grabbed his horns. He was in my grasp and I launched myself at him, landing atop of him as we crashed onto the bed, and pressed my teeth against his throat.

"Master..." I couldn't see his eyes roll into his head, but I knew they had. I could feel the ecstasy running through him.

"You have kept the hearth fires warm, my beloved. I claim my prize." The words flowed through me, straight from somewhere inside me, someplace containing the beast.

"Master... Do not do this. You would never forgive me."

I shook my head and sat up, staring down at the horrified demon beneath me.

"What the hell is happening to me?"

"This cannot be."

"What, Dar? What can't be?"

"You are not D'lakii."

"A who?"

"What I am."

"So? I'm not horny and blue. Scratch that. I'm not blue. What does that have to do with why I'm hanging on to you like I can't let go?"

I felt him move beneath me. "Could you, um…get up?"

"Shit." I put my feet on the floor on either side of him, and lifted myself, offering him a hand.

Surprisingly, he took it, pulling himself up to his feet and letting go quickly. He practically jumped *into* the sweatpants, covering himself and backing away.

It is the fourth rite.

"The thing you did in Faerie to give me some courage?"

Yes.

Dar. What did you do to me?

It is like... It's not like, it is.

Is what?

I told you. A chance to mate.

This isn't a chance, Dar. It's a driving fucking need.

Well…you won.

What's the part about not being Dovahkiin?

D'lakii. Demon Lord.

I sat down on the bed. "Yeah. That."

There was a firm knock on the door. "Everything okay in there?" Chief's voice was only slightly muffled by the door.

"Peachy keen. Not feeling that well. Dar was just explaining why."

"Does it have anything to do with your vampire trying to make out with Candace?"

"What?" I walked over and flung open the door.

"Oh, no," Dar said softly behind me.

I charged into the living room. Josie was staring aghast at Yuki crouched over Candace, lips firmly pressed against hers. Candace was staring at me imploringly and shooting nervous glances at Josie, who didn't know *what* to do.

"Yuki!"

She ignored me.

"Yukina Abernathy, I command you to obey me. Stop this, now!"

My voice echoed with thunder. Literally. My sliding glass door instantly developed a hairline crack through it, and every dish in the kitchen either shattered or rattled. Everybody crouched low and held their hands over their ears and Yuki's back went rigid as she pulled away.

"Master?" My name came out as a whimper from her throat.

"What are you doing?" I tried to keep the anger out of my voice. I knew whatever was happening to her, it was more than likely *my fault*. Or at least Dar's.

"I don't know." She scrambled away from Candace and put her back to the short wall with the kitchen counter above it, hugging her legs and rocking in shock.

"Candace, are you okay?"

"Yes, Lady."

"Josie?"

"Why was your vampire kissing my fiancée?"

"Because of me. I'm not feeling well and it's spilling over on my… Wait. Hold the fuck up. Did you just say fiancée?"

"Uh. No."

"Yes," Candace said with a grin.

"Oh, my goddess! Congratulations!" I ran over to the both of them and scooped them up in a hug, momentarily forgetting about the sweet-toothed vampire practically crying behind me.

"Dot?"

"Yes, Josie?"

"While I appreciate the sentiment, you are changing the subject as to why fang-face was suckling my girl's lips."

"My fault. Let it go. Won't happen again." I turned to Yuki. "You are forbidden from kissing Candace ever again."

She nodded emphatically, not seeming too happy to have been doing it in the first place.

"Josie, too."

Yuki's shocked look turned to one of disgust. Her lip even curled.

"What's wrong with me?" Josie stared open mouthed at the vampire, hand on her hip.

"We're getting off topic here. Yuki, bedroom, now."

"Yes, Master," she said and took off, her movements too fast to follow.

"Seriously, you two. Congrats. I couldn't be happier."

Candace beamed and was still staring after Yuki.

Josie wasn't beaming. She was shooting daggers at Yuki. "Seriously? What is wrong with me? Did you see her lip curl like she was about to hurl?"

"Josie. Let it go."

She turned and stared at me. "You'd kiss me if you were gay, right?"

"No way. Not until you get that lip fungus taken care of." I turned and walked into the bedroom. Jimmy, Shea, and Chief followed me in. I thought about making them wait outside, but I really didn't want to be in the room alone with Dar and Yuki. It would seem Yuki and I were having difficulty controlling ourselves and it might take the three of them to spell us off Dar.

Jimmy shut the door behind us.

"Okay. What the hell is going on?" Chief put his hands on his hips and looked directly at me.

I pointed at Dar. "Blame him. He did some demon mojo on me while we were Underhill. In *fact*, I am going to relax and get comfortable on the bed while he explains to you all what happened. From the beginning," I added and stared at Dar when I said it.

"As you wish."

I walked over to the bed, fluffed my pillows, and sat back. Yuki curled up next to me, almost shaking she was so disgusted with herself.

"Thought you were asexual and that you didn't like girls," I couldn't help but tease.

"I am and I don't! At least I didn't think I did. But damnit, she was standing in front of me, the sunlight came in through a crack in the drapes and her lips were so shiny..."

"I'm teasing, Yuki. It totally wasn't your fault."

"Maybe I am gay?"

"Were you checking out my ass in the shower?"

"Yes. But in my defense, you have a very nice ass."

"Thanky." I patted her head.

Dar sighed again, now that our conversation was over, he hopped up on my dresser, ready to begin our tale of adventure and mishap in the land of elves.

I'd already lived it, so I closed my eyes and let the sound of Dar's voice lull me to sleep. It really was comforting, even more so than his mental voice.

Chapter 2

When I woke up, there was nobody standing around me listening to Dar's story. The lights were off, and moonlight filtered through my bedroom window, illuminating Yuki in a glowing aura as it reflected off her pale skin.

I guess I was more tired than I thought.

Dar, you still up?

Yes, Master.

Where is everybody?

Gone for the night. They bade me let you rest.

I have smart fellers.

For the most part, yes.

Do I detect a hint of jealousy in that statement?

Nay.

Uh huh. Where are you?

Lying on the couch.

Come here.

Is it safe?

Depends. How many legs do you have right now?

Four.

You are safe.

He nosed my door open, and slinked into the room, jumping on the bed and laying his head across my ankles.

"So how did the conversation go?"

They had not realized all you had been through. Even Shea, who was there for some of it, was aghast as I explained the events that followed the ambush.

"You didn't tell them I blew my hands off in stupidity?"

Should I not have?

"If they start calling me stumpy, you're grounded."

They would not. They were saddened by the pain you endured. Josie and Candace came in and listened to your tale, as well. Had the vampire not been by your side, she would have joined you. She shed many tears for you.

I sighed. Candace shedding tears over me was not a favorite pastime of mine. Yet, it seemed to happen with a great amount of frequency. I really needed a vacation. Someplace tropical. With daiquiris and cabana boys.

"And what did they say about the Fourth Rite?"

Little. Although, your friend James, did develop an extraneous glint in his eye.

"He would."

I suggest you ask them their thoughts on the matter, later. When I am not around.

"That might be a good idea."

The doorbell rang.

"Who is that at this hour?"

It is not as late as you think. Josie and her friend just retired. He paused and tilted his head, listening. *I believe it is the youngest of your lovers.*

Jason?

Yes.

I slid out of the bed, trying hard not to wake Yuki. She'd been through enough over the past week and the events of earlier didn't help, either.

The doorbell rang again a moment before I got it unlocked and open. Jason breathed a sigh of relief and stepped forward, wrapping me in his arms.

"Thank the goddess."

"I missed you, too," I said with a little chuckle, pulling away and letting him inside. "You just get out of class?"

"Yeah. And saw the text that you were home. Sorry, my phone was on silent or I would have come right over."

"No. Class is more important and I've been sleeping since."

"Did everything go okay?"

"No. Just do me a favor and don't ask. It's over. Mostly."

"Okay."

"Thank you, sweetie. Coffee?"

"Beer?"

"You staying the night?"

"If you want."

"Beer it is." I used the excuse of him not drinking and driving, but I was kind of hoping he'd stay. I didn't want to be alone and I didn't trust myself around Dar. Not until I figured out exactly what was going on and how the others felt about it. Out of all of them, Jason was the most comfortable to be around. He was completely undemanding. He didn't have Chief's overbearing demeanor, Jimmy's quirks, or Shea's need. He was just my Jason. Comfortable and sexy as all fuck.

"I just woke up, so see if there's something on TV to watch."

He nodded and headed for the living room.

Do you wish to be alone?

Nah. We're just going to have a few beers and relax. You're welcome to join us.

I am tired, and Yukina seems restless now that you are not there. I shall stay with her if you do not mind.

Not at all. Take care of her for me.

I shall.

"I need a bigger bed."

"Excuse me?"

I laughed as I handed Jason his beer. "Yuki and Dar have taken over."

"Oh. I can go if you don't have room."

I shut him up with a kiss. "Nope. We can just all snuggle. Or we can kick them out into Yuki's room, since Jaeren's not here."

"Did he stay in Faerie?"

I sighed as our conversation had fallen into the realm of what I hadn't wanted to discuss or think about.

"Somewhat. Kidnapped by dark elves. But that's all I'm going to say about that."

"Okay." He still looked worried, though. But he earned some serious brownie points by letting it go.

He was flipping channels and I fought the urge to reach over and grab the remote from him, just to put it on *something*. Anything was better than flip-flip-flip.

He was three-quarters through the whole rotation when he finally shut the TV off.

"Couldn't find anything?"

"Nothing better than sitting here watching you," he said with a shy smile.

I smiled at him and clinked my beer bottle against his. "Business management?"

"Um. Yeah?"

"Not how to pick up chicks or wooing the opposite sex classes?"

"Nope."

"How'd you get to be so good at it?"

"Kind of funny. Before I met you, I was *horrible* at it. One time, I walked up to a girl and asked her if she would like to go for a ham one day."

"Huh?"

"Yeah. I went to ask her if she would like to have dinner with me, and I asked her to go for a ham. One day. Most embarrassing moment of my life."

"And that didn't work?"

"No. She practically ran away."

"Good thing. Never trust a woman who wouldn't go for any type of pork product. Bacon is love. Bacon is life."

He chuckled and took a swig of beer.

"So, what is it about me that turns you into Don Juan Junior?"

"I just look at you and say the absolutely most truthful thing I could say."

"Jeez, Jason. Keep this shit up and you're going to make my panties melt."

"Damn it."

"Oh, the cross you bear, huh?"

"No. I was hoping to get them to burst into flames. That's how hot I wanted to get you."

He was close. "Unfortunately, with smoldering passion comes unbelievable wetness. No flames in these panties."

"Unless you consider your patch of flaming red hair…"

"Touché."

"Touchie?"

I laughed, downed the rest of my beer, and set the empty bottle on the table. "Is that what you want, Jason? Do you want to touch me?"

"I think you would be better off asking me, when *don't* I want to touch you."

One more word and my panties *were* going to spontaneously combust, wet or not. I reached down and slipped off my sweat pants, but kept the panties on, turning myself and putting my legs in his lap. He stared at me like I was a T-bone and he was me.

"Touch me."

His face turned red as he blushed, but he still put his hand over my stomach and made a lazy circle around my belly button.

"That's not where I meant."

"I know." He looked away, unable to meet my eyes. I wanted him even more.

"Don't you dare try to tease me right now. I need you."

He laughed softly and put his beer down next to mine and lifted my legs up. He stood for a moment while he kicked off his shoes and slid his jeans down over his boxers. "I'm not teasing you, I'm enjoying you."

"Hurry. Enjoy me faster."

He just smiled and lifted my legs up before sitting back down, turning toward me, and setting my legs down over his. "Is this what you wanted?"

"Whatcha doin?"

"This," he said and slid his fingers over the silky softness of my panties.

I gasped and lifted myself off the couch, getting a little closer and feeling the firmness in his boxers. "Yesss. That's exactly what I wanted."

His finger traced down the front of them, gently following the contours of my lips, grazing the flesh below and sending shivers of pleasure through me. Gooseflesh covered my legs and I reached up and grabbed my breasts through my T-shirt, giving them a squeeze.

"You are so fucking beautiful. And hot."

"You're already in my panties, no need for the sweet talk."

"It's not sweet talk. I just can't help but say aloud what I'm thinking." He was drinking me in with his eyes. All of me, not just the front of my panties.

He used his other hand to free himself from his boxers while he continued his gentle caresses with the other. Then he pulled the gusset aside. I half-expected him to thrust himself inside me, but he didn't. He gently lay his cock across my lips and covered himself with my underwear.

"Oooh." I shivered as his searing flesh touched mine.

"So hot, so wet."

"It's your fault."

"I take full responsibility."

"As you should. Now what are you going to do about it?"

He slipped his finger between us and gathered some of my wetness before spreading it over my panties, just above my already twitching clit. He began to make lazy circles around it, never quite touching and driving me insane. My breathing quickened as he began moving his hips. His cock slipping against my lips, trapped between me and my panties.

All I could do was make small noises from the back of my throat, not quite a moan and nowhere near a comprehensible word.

I let go of my breasts and lifted my shirt, pinching my own nipples and thrusting myself against him.

"Oh, fuck. I'm not going to last long. You're too beautiful and too wet. And you're turning me on way too much."

"You going to come in my panties?"

"Is that where you want me to?"

"Yes. I want to feel it."

He stopped teasing my clit and used his hand to cover us, pushing his throbbing cock against my lips as he began really moving his hips. The friction was driving me insane and the pleasure was exquisite.

"Oh. Wow."

"Yeah," he answered.

"Faster."

"Your wish is my command."

His velvety-smooth hardness was infinitely better than his fingers. His tip parted my lips, pushing upward and dragging slowly across my clit.

"Jason," I whispered. "Jason," I repeated. "Jason," I nearly cried. His name became a chant with every thrust of his hips. I opened my eyes and his face was just as contorted as mine, in pleasure.

"I'm going to…" He trailed off as I felt him throb against me.

"Jaaason," I shouted as it became too much, and I came against him, just before I felt a splash of scalding wetness cover me completely.

He let go with his hand and leaned back against the arm of the couch to catch his breath. I reached down and felt our combined wetness, soaking the front of my panties.

"Holy shit, that was amazing." I slid him across my flesh, still trapped and covered in come.

"Don't. I can't take any more right now," he said with a soft whimper.

"Oh. So, I shouldn't do this?" He was still semi-erect. Hard enough for me to slip him inside me.

"Dottt," he hissed my name.

I enjoyed the sensation of him filling me, throbbing inside of me, and just being closer to him. I didn't move, even I needed a few minutes before we even attempted to fuck.

"I love how you feel inside me."

"That works out good. Because I love being inside you. Next to you. Around you."

"There you go again. Quit being so sweet or I might have to eat you."

"That's my job," he said with a small chuckle.

"Oh? You'd eat me? Right now, covered in your goo?"

He blushed but didn't answer.

"You would?"

He nodded, slightly. "I couldn't think of a time when I *wouldn't* eat you."

"Is that so?" I took his statement as a personal challenge.

"What if I was covered in someone else's come? Would you eat me then?"

"Probably not Chief's, but I think so."

"Too close to home, huh?"

He nodded and gave me a grin.

"What about Jimmy's? Would you lick his off me? He'd like that, you know."

"Probably."

"Shea's?"

He averted his eyes and smiled.

"You would, wouldn't you. The thought kind of turns you on."

"A little."

"What is it about Shea? Even Jimmy has the hots for him. I think Chief might have a small crush on him, too."

"He's like a woman, with a penis. It kind of lowers your guard around him."

"Would you eat me while he had his penis in me? Would you suck on me while he was pounding inside of me?' I felt his cock twitch inside me. I gasped at the unexpected movement. "Somebody likes that idea."

"A little. Yes."

"Would you pull him from me and suck on it?"

"No. Probably not."

"Jimmy did," I said with a smile.

"What?"

I laughed, delighted to share the secret with him. He was probably the only person I would feel comfortable enough to tell it to. "The other night. We, all three of us, fooled around. Jimmy was on top of me, fucking me, and I was sucking Shea. I offered it to Jimmy, and he did."

Halfway through my confession, Jason started moving his hips, moving his now fully-erect cock inside me. "Oh, goddess."

"You're picturing that right now, aren't you?"

"Yes."

"Is it hot thinking of Jimmy sucking Shea's cock?"

"Surprisingly, yes."

"Want to know what else we did?"

"Yes."

I started rocking against him, both of us grinding him inside me. "Jimmy flipped us over, so I was on top."

"Yes?"

"Jimmy stopped sucking Shea and told him to fuck me, too."

"DP?"

"What?"

"Double penetration. It's an entire category of porn."

"You've seen a lot of this?"

"I live alone. There isn't much porn I haven't seen at least once."

"Wow. That's kind of hot."

"I can't believe you had a cock in your ass. That's kind of really fucking hot."

"Who said I did?"

"Didn't… Wait. You had both of them inside your pussy?"

"Yes."

He groaned and started moving faster. *Really liking that visual.*

25

"I was so full... And the feeling of them rubbing together inside of me was amazing."

Jason started grunting.

I bit my lip and enjoyed the feeling of him moving faster inside of me.

"Where did they come?" He asked slowly, between thrusts.

"Oh, they both exploded inside of me. It was literally pouring out of me."

That was enough to push him past the point of no return. Again. I was almost disappointed with his youthful...recuperative powers. He slammed himself against me and I felt him spasming inside me as he filled me.

"Aww. I was so close to coming." I chuckled.

"Your wish is my command," he said breathlessly, pulling himself out of me and getting up.

"What are you doing?"

"This," he said, pushing the table out of the way and turning me to face him. He knelt, yanking my panties to the side before diving in.

I threw my legs around his back and pulled him into me, his tongue removing everything from the outside and then driving up through my channel. I screamed his name as he sucked my clit into his mouth and began flicking his tongue over it. The orgasm I had been close to having kicked me to the curb and beat the hell out of me. I wasn't sure if it was multiple ones or just one that never ended. Either way, I didn't care. I couldn't care, that would have involved thinking.

"Wow."

"Did you like that?" He sat up and wiped his face off on the arm of his sleeve.

"Ugh. No. Absolutely hated that. I think. Maybe you should do it again to make sure."

At least he had the sense to know I was kidding. He gave me a happy grin.

"More importantly... Did *you* like that?"

"Coming twice with the most beautiful woman in the known universe? That was kind of a stupid question."

"Not as bad as asking me if I liked it."

"I see your point. But my answer is yes... It wasn't bad at all, and you made it much better."

The scream from my bedroom had us both on our feet and to the door without another word.

I gasped in shock.

Jason gasped in shock and then nodded approvingly.

Yuki had stripped completely naked and was lying on my bed, hand covering her sex and fingers buried within. Dar was on the floor in his elven form, spent cock in hand and orgasm splattered across his chest. I stared in shock, pushing down the jelly monster, and trying *very* hard to try and understand. They'd both gotten swept up in my orgasm, gotten naked, and rubbed one out. They weren't in the same bed and it's not like they had any control over the situation. I'd let them live.

"Looks like they enjoyed it, too."

I reached over and covered Jason's eyes. "Ya think?"

Chapter 3

"Hey, Darlin'. Where you been hiding?"

"Morning, Marge. Had to take a quick trip, just got back yesterday."

"Well, welcome back. Coffee and a Coke?"

"Please."

"I'm assuming you don't want nothing, as usual?"

"I'll try a coffee," Yuki said with a blush.

"Sure thing, kiddo." Marge resisted the urge to ruffle Yuki's hair, but I could tell she wanted to. She was reaching over slowly until she decided to draw her hand back, probably remembering that Yuki was a vampire. Marge was one of the only two humans in Cedar Falls who knew that fact.

"I'll be right back with your drinks."

I chuckled softly as she left.

"What?"

"She wanted to pet your head."

"Crazy old person did?"

"Marge. Her name is Marge."

"Why did she want to pet me?"

"Probably because you're so damn cute."

"Am not. I'm a snarling, angry, punkish vampire."

"I don't know. You looked pretty cute all naked and rubbing yourself next to Dar last night…"

She groaned like a wounded caribou. Half of the customers in the diner looked over at us. The other half probably knew better than to look. I'd been noticing looks and stares more often. Especially just walking down the street. Things were going to get pretty interesting in Cedar Falls if the rumor mill kept spreading tales.

"There it is. I was waiting for it," she huffed.

"Well, come on. It's not like I couldn't tease you at *all*."

"Please, don't. I am mortified."

"Why?"

"Because I don't do stuff like that. I mean I do, do *that*. Usually only when you're going to town on the boys. But that was the first time I'd ever done it with someone else."

"Look at the bright side. Your virginity is intact."

"Never said I was a virgin."

"Are you?"

"Yes, but that's beside the point. I might have had sex a long, long time ago."

"Just a feeling I had. No shame in it, especially if sex doesn't interest you. Does it?"

She opened her mouth to say no. "I don't know, anymore."

I chuckled softly. "Well…"

"Not with Dar. Even in elf form," she added distastefully.

"No?" I feigned surprise, the jealousy monster still rearing his ugly head. They were both my familiars… If anything ever happened between them, it would be pretty fucking awkward. I still wasn't sure how I felt about Dar, but the thought of Yuki even touching him made me snarly. If they did the deed, there wouldn't be a fucking thing I could do about it, we were stuck with each other forever. Or at least until I did something so stupid I ended up too dead to survive.

"No. It would be kind of like sleeping with…a cousin or something." She even made a little gagging noise. Thankfully.

"Ew," I said with a smile.

"Yeah."

"Well, if you ever need any advice… I'll find someone for you to talk to that isn't me, because I'm not exactly qualified…"

That caused her to chuckle. "True story."

"What you tryna say, Fangface?"

"That your relationships, while quite wonderous, are not nearly as vanilla as I would be."

"You calling me a slut?" I meant it as a joke, but she stared at me, almond-shaped eyes nearly in a perfect shocked circle.

"No!"

"I was kidding, Yuke. Calm your mammaries."

"What mammaries? And don't joke. Who you are had way more to do with it than you think."

"Who am I?"

"A true witch high priestess."

"But apparently, I'm not a witch, according to Jaeren."

"Well, here's your chance to do a little research." She nodded to the door.

I looked over my shoulder and smiled at Nana, who came strolling in with a youngish looking man in jeans and a flannel shirt under a jean jacket.

"Hello, Child."

"Hey, Nana."

She shot the guy a nervous glance. I guess I should keep the fact that she's my grandmother out of it for now. "Dot, this is Tim. He's going to be doing some renovations to my house."

"Hi, Tim."

He nodded without looking, completely infatuated with my grandmother.

"Go get us a booth, dear. I shall be along in a moment. I need to speak with my...cousin."

"Sure thing, Cathleen." He moved a few booths down and slid in.

"He's cute."

"But stupid. Amazing with his hands, though."

"Ew."

"I meant as a carpenter. You need to come by the house and see all that he has done."

"Why didn't you just use magic?"

"I did and restored it to perfection. However, the house was ugly when it was built. I wanted something a little different."

"Gonna have the elves paint the living room?" I snickered.

"You are an incorrigible child. I hope you understand this."

Yuki looked like she was going to shit a litter of bats, she was trying not to laugh so hard.

"I do. Sit for a moment. I need to speak to you, though."

"I am in a hurry, Child."

"It's important."

She sighed and slid into the booth with Yuki. Marge came over and brought our coffees, my Coke, and a cup of tea for Nana.

"Thank you, Marjory."

"You're welcome, Cathleen." She scurried away.

"Cathleen? Not Miss Blackwell?"

"Well, we were talking one day, and she was struggling with all of those nasty syllables. I took pity upon her and allowed her to address me by my goddess given name."

Uh huh.

"So, what did you wish to discuss," she said and took a sip of her tea.

"What am I?"

The cup started shaking in her hand.

"Nana?"

"I can…not. Do not ask."

I should have known. Even the goddess couldn't answer me. I don't know why I expected my grandmother to. At least she didn't pass out when I asked. A well-deserved sigh escaped my lips.

"How did you know?"

I blinked at her in surprise. "A little pointy-eared rodent told me."

"How did he find out?"

"From the simple act of tasting my blood."

She nodded. "I warned that misbegotten child of mine that you would find out soon."

"Not even the goddess could tell me."

That shocked the hell out of her. "You have been visited again?"

"Yes. Multiple times. She sent me to Faerie. I almost died. But I did get this," I said and lifted the gem I had gotten from King Renlynn out from under my shirt. The gem that had driven him insane and that the goddess herself had sent me to find.

Her eyes went even wider. "How? Where?"

"Do you know what it is?"

"No. But I have seen it before."

"Where?"

"Around the neck of your father."

"When was the last time you spoke to Mother?"

"Just yesterday. She called to accuse me of stealing her Yule gown."

"Did you?"

"Yes, but it looks much better on me. I was doing that old bat a favor."

"Well, you might want to hide it. We're going to have a visitor soon," I said and took a picture of the gem in my hand. I sent it to my mother with a quick text.

We need to talk.

"What did you say?"

I turned my phone to Nana, letting her read the message I had sent.

"I wish you luck, Granddaughter."

"Thanks, Nana."

And just like that, she and her tea left and went to sit with Tim.

"I take it you don't know who your father is?"

"Yuki, I don't even know *what* my father is."

"I thought I had it bad. I'm here. If you need a hug or something."

"After watching you molest that poor little fae fiancée of Josie's, I don't know about all that."

"Oh, my Night. Would you never, ever speak of that again?"

"Nope. I like it when you blush like that."

"I can't believe I did that. I mean, I've never *really* been attracted to anyone, but when I saw her…"

"She is cute. I'm not gay, but even I find her incredibly attractive. Kind of like Margot Robbie. Or Ruby Rose. I'd totally do them."

"Who?"

"Never mind."

"Wait. Isn't all this your fault anyway?" She narrowed her eyes at me.

"Don't know what you're talking about. But, if we were to blame somebody, it's Dar's fault."

"What did the dog do now?" Chief asked as he sat down next to me. I hadn't even noticed the door chime go off. I'll blame Ruby Rose for that one. She was rather distracting.

"He told you last night. The whole mating ritual thingy. It's kicked my sex drive into hyperdrive."

"So, I should thank him?"

"Or shoot him. It seems to be drawing my focus toward him."

"You're attracted to a German Shepherd?" He kind of gave me a half-disgusted, half-interested look.

"Ew! No." I slapped his arm. "That seems to be the only thing that's keeping me from rocking his plane of existence."

He sighed and held up a finger to Marge. She rushed over and set a cup of coffee in front of him. "You all want to order?"

"Burger and fries."

"I meant the ladies. I know what you want."

"I'll have the usual."

She looked at Yuki.

"I can't."

34

"That's right, Darlin'. I forgot. Can I get you anything else?"

"Not unless you have any blood behind the counter," she said with a chuckle.

"See what I can do."

Yuki stared after her incredulously.

"She gave me whiskey once. Don't be so surprised. It will probably be pig, though."

"Ew."

"Marge. Served you. Liquor?"

I looked at Chief, forgetting that what she had done was illegal. "No. It was um, amaretto *flavored* half and half."

"Uh huh."

"You give her shit and you will be cut off. It's just because you were being an ass that day."

"Oh. Okay. If it was my fault, I'll let it slide." He rolled his yes.

"Fucking Boy Scout," I mumbled under my breath.

"What was that?'

"I said, boy I wish they served trout."

"Sure you did."

"So. I found out something interesting," I said in all seriousness.

"What is that?"

Yuki kicked me under the table and shot me a glance. I laughed a little. She thought I was going to spill the beans about her and Dar. I winked at her. "The gem I got from the elf king…"

"Yeah?"

"Belongs to my father."

"I thought you didn't know who he was?"

"I don't. But Nana recognized it."

"How did the dark elves find it?"

"That's what I'm going to find out next. As soon as they return Jaeren."

"You think they will?"

"I think they better. If they know what is good for them."

"You're kind of scary when you're all ferocious. Just so you know."

"Scary hot or *scary* scary?"

"Little bit of both," he said and gave me a small kiss. My cockles were officially warmed. I blinked and gave him a goofy grin.

"Now you're just cute."

"Not so bad yourself."

Yuki kicked me under the table again.

You're going to make me puke.

Shut up. You're just jelly.

I am, kind of. She sighed wistfully.

"So, back to the Dar thing," he said. "How do you feel about him?"

"Dar?"

"Uh, yeah."

"Dar is…" I sighed, not knowing where to start or if I could stop once I started. "Dar. He's amazing, funny, loyal."

"Loyal is a quality for a dog. I meant as a man. Do you find him attractive?"

"Horns and all."

"Well, what's one more?"

"One more what?"

"Boyfriend. Lover. Whatever we are to you."

"You want to know what you are to me, Chief?"

"A pain in your ass?" He chuckled.

"Everything. Every single one of you. You mean everything to me."

I swear to the goddess, a tear rolled down his cheek. He coughed and started playing with his silverware, but a small smile forced its way out.

"So?"

"So, what?"

"What am I to you?" I wanted to strangle him.

"My high priestess, my lover. My girlfriend, my best friend. My reason for not giving up, and the closest I've come to being alive again for so many years."

My eyes squirted all over my face. I buried my face into his uniform covered arm. "You're the bestest, Hanker Chief."

"What he do now?" Marge set his burger in front of him but slapped his hand when he went to take a fry. "He deserve to eat?"

"Yep. I'll even buy him pie when he's done."

"Good boy," she said and shoved a fry in his mouth. "Bout time you wizened up."

"Fank you. Vose is hot!" He fanned his mouth, chewing the scalding bit of food.

"Here you go, sweetie," she said and set a mug of something in front of Yuki.

Yuki's eyes widened and she sniffed the air tentatively. "That's…"

"Sush, sweetie. Enjoy."

Yuki grabbed the mug and started drinking, making little ecstatic noises. I shot Marge a questioning look.

"A few of the others like to come into the diner… They uh, they gave us a supply of…*beverages* that we could serve so they wouldn't look suspicious sitting here doing nothing. They pretend it's coffee."

"Huh. That's kind of awesome."

"Yep. They even insist on paying us for drinking their own supply. Nice kids. Well, anyway. Eat up. You ever need a meal, kiddo. You can come here." This time she did reach out and ruffle Yuki's hair.

"Thank you!" She grinned and let her ruffle away.

My phone dinged.

I reached down and snagged it off the table.

There was a single message notification from an unknown number splashed on the screen. I frowned and set the phone back down on the table. Curiosity got the better of me, though.

There are moments in everyone's life. Moments that seem to happen in slow motion. Or moments that offer such clarity, that everything around you fades away. Moments that you are certain will change the course and direction of your life in a single instance. I was having one of those. My hand shook as I reached back down and gingerly picked my phone back up and slid my finger across the screen.

Greetings, Daughter.

My finger shook as I typed, *Hello?* I was about to hit send when it started ringing in my hand. My mother's familiar *Witchy Woman* ringtone blaring in the restaurant.

"Mother?"

"Greetings, Child."

"Don't greetings me. What the hell is going on?"

"I'm sure you have a thousand questions."

"A few more than that."

She sighed on the other end of the phone. "I am sure."

"No, Mother. You don't get to play this off. What the hell am I? Who the hell is my father? Why is he texting me?"

"He's contacted you, already?"

"Yes!"

"I am coming there. Do not contact him until I am with you."

The phone went dead in my hand. Not just the line. I mean the whole phone went dead and it wouldn't turn back on, even though I knew I had almost a full battery.

"Damnit, Mother." I set the phone back down and growled at it for good measure.

"You okay?" Chief nudged my leg with his.

"No."

"What's going on?"

"My father. He messaged me just before my mother called and then she magically zapped my phone. It won't even turn on."

"Why?"

"I can only assume she doesn't want me talking to him without her being here."

My grandmother got up from her booth and came back to ours, sitting back down with Yuki.

"Nana?"

"I heard."

"What is she doing?"

"I don't think that is the question you should be asking yourself. More along the lines of why."

"Because she and my father don't get along?"

Nana let out a bark of laughter. "Your mother does not get *along* with anybody. No, Child. This is much deeper than that, but do not ask me for specifics. Just know that the truth will come, in time. Be patient."

"My father texted me."

"I am surprised he knows how and that he was…free to do so."

"Can you at least tell me his name?"

"No. It is not my place, I am sorry. I shall leave that to your mother and *him*."

I snarled in frustration.

"Did you just snarl at me?"

"No, Nana. At everything."

She pursed her lips and nodded. "Can't say I blame you for that one. These are all things that you should have learned ages ago. Had he not disappeared, I'm sure you would have."

"He disappeared?"

"Again, this is falling into the realms of not my business to tell you. Sorry, Child."

"It's okay. Mother is coming."

"And I shall take that as my cue to leave."

"I don't mean this second."

"You don't know your mother as well as I. But here, take this. It has served me well, and I no longer have a need for it. You might."

She reached into her jacket pocket and pulled something out. When I opened my hand, she put it in it and

39

curled my fingers around it, whispering something in Irish I couldn't quite catch.

"There. It is now yours."

"What is it?"

"My broom."

"Nana!"

"Shush. At our battle with the demons, it served you better than me. You might find yourself in need."

"I don't know what to say."

"Yes you do."

"Thank you."

"You are welcome. See how easy that was?" She gave me an exaggerated wink. "Well, I must be off. Tim is going to service my plumbing."

"I hope to goddess you have a leaky sink."

"Not for long, dear."

Chief started choking on his hamburger. I started slapping him on the back as Nana stood and motioned for Tim. He obediently rose and followed her out the door. I opened my palm, stared at the rune covered twig, and smiled.

"You have a pretty cool grandmother."

I nodded at Chief. "It's the mother I need to work on."

Chapter 4

There was a for sale sign sticking out of the front lawn of my neighbor's house. Herb's name and phone number were on the sign. I didn't know which offended me more. The fact that my neighbors were selling their house, or the fact that Herb didn't tell me. I wanted that house, I just hadn't known I wanted it until I saw the sign in the front yard.

It was the couple who'd been staring at me from their front porch the other day. The ones who scrambled to get inside and away from me. They would be sorely missed.

I reached for the phone in my pocket, remembering its untimely demise as my fingers wrapped around it. "Hey, Yuki. Can I borrow your phone?"

She handed it to me without a word.

I dialed Herb's number straight off the sign while I unlocked my front door. He picked up on the fourth ring. "Hey, Herb."

"Dot?" Herb's voice sounded unsure through the phone, not recognizing the number.

"Yep. You're selling the house next to mine?"

He chuckled through the phone. "I should have known you would be interested. Are you interested?"

"Hell, yeah. It's gets a little crowded in here."

"I should have sold you a bigger house."

"You should have. But a second one will do nicely."

"You want to see it first?"

"Do I ever?"

"No."

"See. You answered your own question. Now answer mine. Did they bitch about me?"

"I also should have known that you were the crazy neighbor slut."

"What? They called me a slut?" Crazy I could live with, slut…

"Yeah."

"Wow. That…almost hurts."

"Sure, it does. You've been called worse by better people, I'm sure."

"True story." I sighed. They probably didn't appreciate the multiple men visiting at multiple hours. Plus, my bedroom wall was closest to their house. At least I wouldn't have to worry about that anymore. "Are they leaving town?"

"Pastor Thomas? No. They're moving into an apartment."

"He's a pastor?"

"Yep."

"No wonder he didn't like me."

"Actually, it was his wife who wasn't too enchanted with you."

That made me laugh. "Oh, well. Guess I won't be getting an invitation to the next church potluck."

"I can invite you, if you want."

"You're a God-fearing man, Herb?"

"More so than not lately."

"When the universe shows you what's really out there, you kind of need an anchor, huh?"

"You got it." I could almost hear him nodding his head in agreement.

"Well, if you ever need to talk about it, I'm your witch."

"Thanks, Dot. Not going to laugh at me for believing in God?"

"Hell no. I try to be tolerant of everybody's beliefs."

"Bet you wish more people were like that, huh?"

"Yeah. Saves us from getting burned at the stake."

"Well, I promise to give you a heads up if I hear anybody saying anything about large gasoline and torch purchases."

"Thanks, Herb. I'm sure the rumor mill is just grinding them out after the fiasco last week."

"You talking about city hall?" he asked after a pause.

"Yeah."

"I think you might be overreacting."

"How? I've heard the whispers. I've seen the stares."

"Not one person was seriously injured that day. Those who didn't chalk the whole thing up to a mass hallucination, just remember the good you did. Not one person has said anything condemning, to my knowledge. Trust me. Marge would have been the first to hear."

"So why is everybody so concerned about us?"

"You."

"Me?"

"Dot, this is a small town. You have been seen with no less than three boyfriends…"

"Oh. I'm the town slut, not the witch."

"Pretty much."

"I can live with that."

"Yeah. I don't think they burn people at the stake for that. Pennsylvania, maybe, but not New York."

I gave a little laugh. "Thanks, Herb."

"So, do you want the house?"

"How much?"

He told me the figure and I smiled. It was less than I had paid for my house. I guess having shitty neighbors was a plus.

"Tell them I'll take it."

"I'll let you know when."

"Thanks again, Herb."

"Always a pleasure, Dot."

I hung up the phone and stared at it, happy about the house, happy about the news that we weren't outed as witches *yet*, but I was kind of disturbed that the whole town thought I was a slut.

It could be worse. They could think I was dating Josie.

That made me feel a little better about myself.

"Thanks, Yuke," I said and handed her the phone.

"No problem. You going to get a new one soon? I don't have any friends other than you, anymore, but I don't think I could even live without one."

"Is there even a cell phone store in Cedar Falls?"

"Beats the hell out of me. Ask your boyfriend."

"Which one?"

"Does it matter?"

"Probably not. Could you text Jason for me? See if he can pick one up and drop it off. Let him know it's kind of important." And it was. I hadn't even had a chance to respond to the person claiming to be my other parent. The answers were in my grasp and I'd be damned if my witch of a mother was going to bind my hands.

"Sure thing, Boss."

"I like that better than Master."

"Sure thing, Boss." She chuckled as her fingers danced over the keys.

Josie peeked at me from around the corner. "Welcome back."

"Thanks. Been an interesting morning."

"All good?"

"No. I'll tell you after you get dressed."

"Kay."

What happened? Dar sat up on the couch, looking at me over the back. As soon as I had left, he had reverted back to doggy. At least there wasn't a hellhound on my couch. I had just bought the damn thing.

I got a text from my father, and a phone call from my mother. She wasn't too happy and killed my cell phone to keep me from talking to him.

And you automatically assumed it was out of spite?

Most things my mother does are out of spite, Darling.

You know there are mysterious circumstances regarding your sire...maybe she is trying to protect you?

Or herself.

44

If you always look for the worst, that is often all you will see.

Changing your name to "Fortune Cookie."

Wisdom can often *be found in confections. Take cheesecake for example.*

Good point.

Josie came plodding out of her room, Candace rubbing her eyes behind her and giving me a small smile when she saw me. "What happened?"

I sighed. I should have waited to tell Dar until they got in the room. I hated repeating myself, but I reiterated what I told him. Candace looked thoughtful, Josie seemed…Josie. "What?"

"I'm kind of jealous. Your father isn't human. He might be late to the party, but he's still around. I miss my dad." She frowned a little. "But I'm super happy for you."

"Let's just hope he's not an asshole. Going to have to assume he's already a deadbeat."

"Pshah. For all you know, he was locked in some celestial prison. Plus, do you think he could be any worse than your mother?"

"Or yours?"

"Not even going to bristle at that one. Or mine?"

Candace nodded emphatically. Her little fae head threatening to come loose.

"You don't have to agree that much, sweetie."

Wanting a change of subject… "So. When's the big day?"

"Next Samhain. So don't worry, you have quite a while to plan the bachelorette *parties*," Josie said with a chuckle.

"Separate? Or you both going to be ogling the strippers? And what flavor would you like? Dangling or non-dangling?"

"Why not both?"

I looked at Candace for confirmation. She seemed very unsure. I'd go with non-dangling strippers and just get a private show for Josie later. "We can discuss it further. I can't tell you how happy I am for you both," I said as my eyes got a little misty.

"Oh, sweetie. Thank you." Josie walked up to me and gave me a hug. The mist turned into a waterfall. I'd never in a million years thought she would be tying the knot before I did. "I can't believe you're getting married before me."

"Me neither. Not like you don't have a list of candidates."

"Meh. They'd probably get all jealous and demand rings, too."

I happened to look over at Dar. He was staring at me curiously.

What?

Nothing. Just surprised the little one agreed to marry your friend. Make sure she is doing so of her own free will. He gave me a mental chuckle.

I opened my mouth to broach the subject of the house next door but decided against it. It wasn't a done deal yet. When I had the keys in hand, I'd ask them their thoughts on the matter. There was almost a year before the wedding, I had time to get everything settled.

"Jason says there is a store, but wants to know which phone you have, otherwise...sim card...blah blah blah, techno nerd-speak." Yuki huffed and looked up at me.

"He really said that?"

"No. There was just a lot of big words. You want to read it?"

"No. Here," I said and pulled out my deceased cell. "Give him the model number."

Yuki took my phone and pulled it out of the case, typing in the model number off the back.

"Yuki?"

"Yeah?"

"Who pays for *your* phone service?"

"My Dad. I'm expecting it to run out this month."

"Take my phone, go meet Jason. Tell him to move mine, yours, and his to a business account."

"I don't really need one…"

"Shut your little fangy face and do as I say."

"Yes, Boss."

"Good girl."

She was out the door in a flash.

Dar looked up at me.

"You want a cell phone too?"

Hardly. I do not understand humanity's fascination with those devices.

"Obviously you have never played Candy Crush."

He huffed and lay his head back down on the couch. I sat down next to him and absentmindedly stroked his fur. Candace sat next to me and leaned against my shoulder. "You okay?"

She nodded against me. "Just glad you are home."

"I'm hopping in the shower," Josie said and headed toward her bedroom.

"Have fun. Don't get wet."

"That never gets old," she called over her shoulder. We'd been using the same line since we were kids. It had become almost a ritual.

I watched her round the corner. "She okay?" I whispered my question to Candace when she was out of earshot.

"Still angry about the Yuki thing."

"Yeah. I could see that. She does know it was my fault, right?"

"Yes."

"Just jealous?"

"Yes."

"I guess I can't blame her. I'd be jealous if someone kissed one of my guys, too."

"It is understandable."

"Did it bother you? Are you mad at Yuki?"

"No. I understand."

"That wasn't my question."

"No. It did not bother me. It bothered me that it hurt Josie."

"Yeah. I get that."

"I should go have a shower with her and make it up to her."

I chuckled softly. "Have fun."

"I shall." She got up and left Dar and I alone on the couch.

We sat in silence for a few moments. *Master?*

Yes?

Would you care to go...shopping? I smiled at the hopefulness in his mental voice.

We could, but I don't think bringing a dog to Walmart would go over so well.

I could take my elven form and wear something over my ears.

I hadn't thought about that. The thought of going anywhere wasn't exactly appealing, but maybe it would help me take my mind off things. "Okay."

Suddenly there was a naked elf sitting next to me. "May I borrow your clothes again?"

I sighed. He would probably be better dressed than most, but he would still stand out. They were women's clothes after all. But the less attention he garnered while trying to appear human, the better. "No. I'll have Jason bring you some of his. He needs to drop off my cell phone anyway. Would you mind waiting that long?"

"That is a good idea. May I borrow yours while we wait?"

"Please."

"You do not like seeing me without clothes." He didn't make it a question.

"That's the problem. I do."

"Ah. I shall change, then." He got up off the couch and I wanted so badly to reach out and just touch him. Anywhere. Everywhere. I waited until he was in my room before sighing and standing.

I walked over to Josie's room and lightly rapped on the door.

"Who is it?"

"Housekeeping, you want mint for pillow?"

Josie chuckled and opened it, standing there wrapped in a towel. Candace was just pulling off her shirt and didn't stop on my account. I tried hard not to look but failed miserably. "Can I borrow your phone? I need to call Jason."

"I don't have his number. Do you know it?"

Shit. "No. Crap."

"I have Yuki's," Candace said, grabbing hers off the dresser and handing it to me.

Jose cocked an eyebrow at her but didn't say anything.

"I have everyone's numbers for just such emergencies. It would be wise for you to, as well." She slapped Josie on the ass.

"Uh huh."

"Knock it off, Josie," I chided her, knowing she was half-playing.

"Just trying to make her feel guilty. She gets kinkier when you do that," she whispered conspiratorially, knowing full well that Candace could hear her. She got a well-deserved elbow to the ribs.

"You're sure you want to marry her?" I gave Candace a sad little look.

She nodded, stopped to think about it, and nodded some more. Josie couldn't elbow *her* unless she wanted to take out a tooth, so she just pouted.

"She gets kinkier when she thinks you are mad at her," Candace said and winked.

"Okay. Great talk, you two." I shook my head and headed back out into the living room.

Yuki picked up on the third ring. "I told you not to call me when Josie was around."

"What?"

"I'm kidding. I knew it was you."

"You better be kidding."

"I am, I swear!" She started laughing.

"Is Jason there?"

"Yeah. You wanna talk to him?"

"No. Just ask him to stop by his house. I'm taking Dar shopping and he needs some clothes. And a hat. If he wouldn't mind lending him some."

There was muffled conversation and she came back on the line. "He said no problem."

"Tell him I said thank you. How long are you going to be?"

"He's just signing everything now. We'll be back shortly."

"*Yokai.*"

"Were you trying to say 'roger' in Japanese?"

"*Hai.*"

"Congratulations. You just said ghost. Roger is *'ryokai'.*"

"That's what I said?"

"Give it up, Yankee."

The line clicked dead. I stared at it a minute to make sure. One thing was for certain, I needed to watch more anime.

Chapter 5

Hello? Are you there? I hit send on the same text as the last twelve I had sent. Dar, Yuki, and I were walking into Walmart and I almost ran into one of the metal poles they set into the concrete outside the doors to stop cars from driving into the store.

"Be careful, Boss," Yuki said and pushed me out of its path.

I saw the pole and shot her a look of gratitude. "Thanks."

She nodded. "The work of a familiar is never done."

"Just yesterday, I saved her from stubbing her toe." Dar chuckled to himself.

"Would you guys rather do little stuff like this or rescue me from other realms and assassins?"

"Assassins," they said simultaneously, nodding their heads. The effect was quite creepy.

"Sorry your job has been boring for all of twenty-four hours."

"Just kidding. Shopping barriers are more than enough danger," Yuki said and grabbed a cart after we passed through the sliding glass doors.

"Welcome to Walmart," the greeter said with a smile. He was human, but might have been close to my mother's age, judging from the leathery texture of his skin.

"Thanks. Glad to be here," I said and smiled.

"That's a first," he answered with a wink.

"Dar, grab a cart, too. We might as well stock up while we're here."

"On what?"

"The necessities. Coffee and beer."

"Don't forget, you're out of wine, too," Yuki reminded me.

"Yeah, but they don't sell that here. We'll have to go to a liquor store."

"Bummer."

"You need clothes?"

She shook her head but gave me that little blushing look that signaled she was full of shit.

"Fine. I'll just pick out some cute little dresses for you to wear."

"I could use some jeans. And underwear. Maybe a couple of T-shirts."

I looked down at her very worn shoes. "And shoes."

She looked down and gave me a resigned sigh. "Shoes, too."

I gave her a smile and patted her head. She was learning. "All right. Dar first, then we'll hit the women's section. Then get the rest."

"I do not know what size I am?" Dar was leafing through the jeans on the shelf.

"I'd say thirty-two waist, thirty inseam, and an extra large in shirts. Gotta fit those shoulders in."

"Help me?"

I chuckled and took pity on him, pulling out a few pairs and went down a size on a couple that looked like they would be a little baggy on him. An ass like that shouldn't be hidden behind curtains. Shrink wrap would be better. I stuffed the pile in his arms and pointed at the changing rooms, the attendant practically drooling at him as he walked over. "I'll find you some shirts while you try those on."

"Yes, Master."

The attendant blinked and stared at me open-mouthed.

I wiggled my eyebrows at her.

Yuki just laughed. "I'm going to go look, is that okay?"

"Sure."

She pushed the other cart across the aisle into the women's section. I kept staring at my phone, hoping for a response. Hoping for *anything*.

"How do these look?"

I tore my eyes from my phone, praising the Lady that I had. Dar was standing by the attendant's counter and looking over his shoulder at the mirror on the wall. She was clutching her heart and I wiped the drool from my chin. He was wearing the jeans and nothing else. The hat that had been covering his ears was gone and the cascading waves of brown hair he had tucked up under it was barely doing the job. Good thing she wasn't looking *anywhere* near his head.

I'd seen him in his elven form totally naked. There was just something about a shirtless man in jeans, barefoot, that just got the old juices flowing. He looked like he should have been on the cover of a magazine. Or standing in a field of wheat on the September page of a farming calendar. "Those…um… Those look good. Are those the thirties or the thirty-twos?"

"The thirties. The others would have required a belt. They kept sliding over my hips."

"Yeah. Go with those then," I managed to say.

The attendant could only nod in agreement.

"I shall. Did you happen to find a shirt?"

"Uh. I'll keep looking."

"Thank you, Master." He turned around and went back into the dressing room.

"Girl, where the hell did you find him, what did you do to get him to call you master, and does he have a fricking brother?"

"Oh, I went through hell to get that one. Unfortunately, he's an only child." *I think.*

"Damn. Kudos to you."

I made a mental note never to bring the other four into the store with me. Her heart probably wouldn't be able to handle it and she seemed like a nice lady.

"Thanks," I said with a grin.

Dar came back out, with two piles of clothing, and set the one on the counter. "My thanks," he told the clerk.

"Sugar, it was my pleasure."

"Come on, Dar. Let's find you some shirts."

It didn't take us long. We found Yuki and waited for her to finish picking out some clothes. She seemed hesitant but then I realized not much in the store suited her particular fashion sense. I'd make it up to her by taking her to the mall for a girls' day of shopping. She'd find more of a selection with chains and skulls there.

"Where to next?"

"Swing by the office supplies," I told her.

She looked around at the overhead signs and pointed us in the right direction. "You need stuff?"

"Crayons."

"Crayons?"

"Don't ask. Welcoming home present for Jaeren."

"If he comes home."

"*When* he comes home. I wasn't kidding when I said I would wreck their world if they didn't return him."

Yuki only nodded solemnly.

We would join you.

I know, Dar.

It kind of hit me, right then, when the moment of anger and protectiveness swept over me, that I realized how I felt about the stuck-up, condescending, statuesque elf. We had started out as enemies, but he was kind of growing on me. I wouldn't exactly classify us as friends, *yet*, but the foundations were definitely there. I wasn't kidding when I said I'd destroy an entire realm to keep him safe. If that wasn't a good foundation, I didn't know what the hell else was.

A sixty-four box of crayons, an entire ream of paper for him to draw on, six coloring books, two cases of coffee, two cases of beer, and thirty minutes in the checkout line later, and we were out the door. A very successful trip. I hadn't murdered anybody.

I'd closed the trunk and slid the cart to Yuki, who had offered to put it in the corral, when the air pressure around us dropped. I looked up, half expecting the somewhat-cloudy sky to start with a light dusting of snow. "Yuki hurry."

She looked over her shoulder and saw me staring at the sky.

I heard her gasp and push the cart the remaining distance while I stared at the swirling black clouds above us. "Get in the car!"

I nodded, still sort of mesmerized. Tornadoes weren't that common in Virginia and even rarer in upstate New York. I'd never seen one, let alone see one forming. Something about the whole situation felt *wrong*.

"Something's coming," Dar said from behind me.

"Yeah. The fricking Wicked Witch of the West. Come on, Dorothea and Toto. Get in the fricking car." Yuki almost sounded panicked.

"She is right, Master. Let us go."

"Afraid somebody is going to drop a house on me?"

"Or worse."

I nodded and turned, getting in and starting the engine with the key fob. We were all in and backed out when it fell from the sky. It wasn't a house, it was an angel. She landed in a classic superhero landing, knee to the ground and punching a solid crater into the asphalt in front of my vehicle.

"Fuck," I said deadpan and threw the car into reverse as I stared at her glorious, monstrously-sized wings as they stretched out and batted the cars parked in her landing zone backward into the cars behind them. People started screaming around us and running toward the store. "That's gonna make the news," I said and stomped on the accelerator, throwing us back away from her.

"Dorothea Blackwell!" Her voice boomed all around us, not unlike when I had yelled at Yuki to get off Candace.

"She knows your name," Yuki said fearfully.

"I noticed."

"She looks pissed."

I ignored her, spun the car away from the main entrance, threw it into drive, and gunned it. "Where is she?"

"Running after us."

"Not for long." I stomped on gas again after sliding out of the parking lot and heading back toward Cedar Falls. I was finally grateful we didn't have our own Walmart. At least the news of an angel crashing to earth wouldn't be town gossip for once. I fervently hoped three people being smeared across the highway didn't, either.

Looking in all my mirrors, I couldn't see her. "Where is she?"

"Flying behind us." Yuki was hanging over the back seat, looking out through the rear window.

"Gaining or losing?"

"Staying the same."

"Shit."

"Can you not go faster?" Dar was white knuckling the dashboard.

"No. You okay?"

"I do not care for…those creatures."

"Angels?"

"Forget what you think you know about them. Most of that is trash."

"So, not heavenly beings?"

"No more than the denizens of Gehenna. Simply from another plane."

"Great."

"As Gehenna is the lowest of the spiritual planes, it has the greatest negative energy. They come from the highest and have positive spiritual energy. We are natural enemies."

"Okay. Thanks for the lesson."

"You inquired."

"Not really. But, just to clarify, no heaven?"

"There are several of them depending on your gods of choice, but the heavens are not part of the spiritual world. It encompasses it."

"So, no hell?"

"Some places would make you think you were there. But no eternal damnation with a pitchfork-wielding devil stirring your soul in a cauldron of damnation because you didn't go to church every week."

"Good to know."

"Can you two concentrate on losing the thing with wings?"

I nodded at Yuki in the rearview. "Why is there never a tunnel around when you need one?"

"Make your own?" Dar looked over at me.

"Uh, yeah. Let me just whip one out."

"You opened a rift to the mortal realm in Faerie."

"Surrounded by limitless energy. Here… I don't have that kind of power."

"We will not lose that thing unless you try."

My energy reserves were full. The only thing I could do was give it a shot. "Fine. Take the wheel."

He reached over and grabbed it. "You can do it," he whispered calmly.

"She's attacking! With a big fucking spear!"

"Fuck me." I held my hands out on front of me, aiming my intent above the road in front of us.

"No. Do not open a hole beneath us, we will fall! It's why you dropped part of this world into Faerie. Open one in front of us."

"I thought we needed to go down."

"Up, down, does not matter. This realm was all you knew. Now you have been to Faerie. You can take us there without dropping us from the sky."

"Sure. I'll just take your word for it."

"Trust me, Master. You can do this. Picture the clearing in your mind."

I gave it my best shot, ripping a hole through reality right in front of the car… and screamed as my car started bouncing across the unpaved, un-mowed grasses of Elfhame Autumn Glade. Unfortunately, we were nowhere near the clearing where the portal was and it was apparently night time in Faerie.

"I did it!"

"Close it!"

I flung my intent to the wind, severing my tie to the rift behind us. It slapped shut with a clap of thunder as I slammed on the brakes, sliding across the dew-covered grass. Even with the portal closed, we covered our ears as the angel's scream rang through.

"She sounds pissed," Yuki said with a throaty laugh.

"Great. We're safe. Now how the fuck do we get home?"

"Well, I would not suggest driving through the gate. It would be more difficult getting your vehicle out of the basement of the bar," Dar said, looking around.

"I was picturing the clearing, where the hell are we?'

"I do not know. The only places of the elfhame I saw were with you."

"Well, I guess we could drive around and ask someone for directions," I said and looked around. We were in a field of grass nestled between two large hills, replicas of where we were in the mortal realm, without the highway between them. "Wait."

"What?" Yuki leaned closer between the two seats.

"We're where we were in the mortal realm, just in Faerie. Look around you. It's a geographic match."

"So if you keep going about ten miles and then head south…"

"We can go back closer to the house," I said.

"Hopefully we don't end up *in* a house."

"Yeah. That would suck."

"Better than sitting here waiting for the elves to notice us."

I nodded and gave the car a little gas, turning us around and heading in the direction we'd been going when we came through the gate. I reset the trip function on the odometer. Being a shitty judge of distance, it was the only way to know when we were getting close to town.

"I'll pop us back out before we head south. Hopefully there won't be any cars in front of us."

"Good plan," Yuki said and patted my shoulder.

"Wouldn't call it good, but it might work."

We sat in silence, everyone watching for anything that might hurt the car or us, while I slowly watched the odometer *finally* climb its way to ten miles. I stopped the car and gave a little prayer to the goddess that we would emerge unscathed.

"Look around you."

"Yuki, we're in the middle of a field."

"Look not in this realm, Daughter. Use your eyes and intent. Focus. What do *they* see?"

Yuki's eyes were glowing golden in the mirror. Apparently, Candace and I weren't the only ones who could be inhabited by the goddess. "Greetings, Lady."

"Hello, Child."

"I see grass and a starry sky."

"Now think of your world as you do."

I knew better than to question her. If she said I could do it, I could. After about a minute I was ready to give up. Until I saw a set of red glowing lights pass right by us at about sixty miles an hour.

"Oh, shit. That would have been bad."

"Now you have your reference." She kissed the back of my head and I felt her presence leave.

Yuki made spitting noises. "Why am I kissing your hair?"

"You said you loved the way my shampoo smelled and then started making out with the back of my head."

"What?" She pulled away. Even Dar started laughing.

"Just kidding. You were visited by the goddess. She showed me a new trick."

She shuddered. "I think I'd rather have a shampoo fetish."

I moved the car over about twenty feet from where I had seen the tail lights pass us. If we had come out where we were, it would have been in the middle of oncoming traffic.

"You could see the mortal realm?" Dar was staring at me incredulously.

"Yeah. We were in the westbound lane. That could have been bad."

He nodded.

"Okay, here goes nothing," I said and pulled the magic from around us, leaving my already filled reserves alone, in case we needed it when we got back to New York.

I opened another rift in front of us but didn't move until I saw grass and not asphalt on the other side. Breathing a sigh of relief, I slowly rolled us through, closing the door behind us.

"You did it, Master." Dar sounded genuinely impressed. We were just beyond the shoulder of the road. No cars and no angels were in sight.

"Let's go home."

Chapter 6

"You did what?" Chief was rubbing the lower half of his face with one hand in shock. The other hand was on his hip, just above his belt.

"Took a detour through Faerie. We were being chased by an angel."

Chief had been parked at my house when we pulled in the driveway. It was almost like he had a sixth sense that magically alerted him when weird shit happened to me. "Why were you being chased by an angel?"

"I don't have a clue. She looked pissed, though. That was enough for me."

He just shook his head, rubbing the bridge of his nose and blinking several times in frustration. "Only you."

"Tell me about it. Want a coffee?"

"Sure."

Yuki and Dar were bringing the bags of clothes, coffee, and beer in. We never made it to the liquor store, though. I was going to be stuck with coffee, not wanting to venture out again so soon. I just hoped my shields and wards were enough to keep the angel at bay.

Chief followed me into the house. Candace came out of her room, crying. "What's the matter?" My heart broke seeing her cry. Especially since it wasn't over me for a change.

She shook her head, sniffled, and rubbed her nose.

"Candace?"

She frowned, ran across the room, and wrapped her arms around me.

"What's wrong?"

She shook her head against my chest.

"Give us a minute, Chief. Help yourself to the coffee."

"Not a problem."

I ushered Candace into my room. "Josie?"

She nodded.

"What did that brainless wonder do?"

"It was not her. It was me."

"Start over. What happened?"

She sniffled. "We were in the shower…"

I steeled myself for the details, wanting to be an attentive listener, but not really wanting to know. "Yes?"

"We were…" She sighed. "We were being intimate."

"And?"

"I couldn't help it. Knowing how jealous she had become, it was all I could think of. I began to worry and worry and worry. It drowned out everything else."

"What were you so worried about?"

"That she would not be able to get over the thing with Yuki…and leave me."

"Sweetie," I said in relief and wrapped my arms around her. "All you did was get kissed by Yuki. Trust me, making love to you was probably the only thing on her mind."

"I know. But then I did the unthinkable."

I chuckled. The unthinkable for Candace was probably cooing too loud. "What, did you call her Yuki?"

I'd meant it as a joke. I said it without thinking about it at all. When her eyes widened and the tears started streaming, my joke wasn't funny at all. She had done exactly that.

"Oh, shit."

She nodded and started wailing, falling over and collapsing into a sobbing mess on my bed.

"Candace, I'm sorry! I was joking, I didn't know that's what had happened!"

She couldn't even talk.

I'm a fucking idiot.

Yuki came running into the room "What did you do to her?" She looked fierce and overprotective.

"Nothing! If anything, *you* did."

"Huh?"

"Nothing. Never mind. You go in the other room, just in case Josie comes home."

"What did I do?"

"Nothing. Seriously." *Candace accidentally called Josie, Yuki,* I told her.

Oh. Oops.

Yeah. Not good.

She storm off?

I'm guessing.

I'll leave you to clean up your mess, then.

Damn you and your sultry Japanese lips. Wrecking homes already.

Not funny. Seriously though, tell her I'm sorry when she can talk again.

I will. Entertain Chief. Not with your lips though, please.

You're hilarious.

I turned back to the sobbing part-elf on my bed. "Okay. Knock the tears off, Candace. We'll fix this."

"How," she managed to say between wracking sobs.

"I'm going to text Josie, right now."

"You will?"

"Yes. It's my fault this happened at all. I'll fix it."

She wrapped her arms around my waist and hugged me dearly. As if her life depended on it. From where she was, I'm sure it felt like it did. "Thank you, Lady."

"Come on. Let's get you cleaned up and some coffee into you."

I pulled my phone out of my pocket and motioned Candace toward the bathroom. *Get your ass home, now,* I texted Josie as I followed Candace into the bathroom.

No. I need a little time.

I sighed at her response. *This isn't a request. You're being stupid, she's being stupid, and all of this is my fault anyway.*

No, it's not. It's that damned vampire with the loose lips.

Yuki is as innocent as Candace. One more word and I'll vaporize your disco ball and fuzzy pink rugs.

You wouldn't dare.

Try me, biotch.

On my way.

"She's on her way home, sweetie," I told Candace, grabbing a washcloth from the cabinet. She hopped up and sat on my bathroom counter while I ran the rag under some cold water. "Now, when she gets home, and for the rest of your life, I want you to quit worrying about what happened with Yuki. Can you do that?"

"I will try."

"Do or do not. There is no try." I even did a horrible impression, trying to make her laugh. Failing miserably, I should have known she had never seen the movie.

"Thank you, Lady," she said as I started gently wiping her eyes and face.

"You're welcome. You are family, this is what we do."

I probably should have kept it light hearted and not gone for sappy. She started crying again.

"What if she leaves me?"

"She won't"

"But what if?"

"You'll still be part of my family. But, you're over-reacting. She's not going anywhere."

"Promise?"

"I do."

"Okay." She nodded.

"Now go lie in my bed. I'll talk to Josie when she gets home and then you two can kiss and make up. Say it with me now. Joe." I motioned for her to repeat after me.

"Joe?"

"Zee," I said and nodded.

"Zee," she repeated with a little smile.

"Good. Now don't screw that up again, okay?"

"Dear Lady, I won't. Ever."

"Good girl." I followed her into the bedroom and got her settled, leaning down and kissing her on her forehead.

"Thank you, Dot."

My heart swelled with pride. She'd finally used my name. "You're welcome, sweetie." I left the room and shut off the light, closing the door behind me.

"Everything okay?" Chief handed me a cup of coffee.

"I love you, man."

"I love you, too." He leaned in and stole a kiss before I could take a sip. I blushed and gave him a goofy grin.

"Can I get one more of those? I missed you."

"You can have as many as you want." He kissed me again, after taking my cup and setting it, and his, down on the counter and wrapping me in his arms.

It was a good thing I was wearing socks. Otherwise, he wouldn't have anything to knock off with that kiss. I melted in his arms and I was truly digging his new aftershave. Even when he pulled his lips from mine, I curled into him and just breathed in the scent.

"Are you sniffing me?"

"Yeah. You smell good. Damn good. Like really damn good."

"Uh… Okay."

"Why is that weird? I like your new aftershave and you're giving me grief?"

"I'm giving you grief because I knocked the bottle off the counter and it shattered in my bathroom and I haven't made it to the store to buy any more yet. I'm not wearing anything but soap, and I haven't showered since this morning."

"No way."

"Way."

I moved my nose to his neck and practically dragged it across his flesh like I was snorting a line of cocaine. Or at least what I pictured it would look like. Witches didn't do drugs. Spells had a tendency to spontaneously cast if we didn't have control over our magic and intent. I smoked a joint once and turned Josie's hair into a bag of Doritos. They had a nice crunch but tasted like Aquanet. She'd been less than impressed. Especially after she tasted one.

"You smell like...steak, sex, and home."

"Dot?"

"Don't worry, I'm not going to eat you," I whispered into his ear but then licked his neck unconvincingly. He tasted even more amazing than he smelled.

"Do you mind if I grab one of the beers you just bought?" Dar's voice pulled my face from Chief's neck.

I looked over my shoulder at my blue demon in tight jeans and an extra-large T-shirt that stretched across his muscled chest.

"Wow. You clean up nice," Chief said.

"Thank you, William."

"My beer is your beer," I said and moved Chief out of the way of the refrigerator. I couldn't help it, I checked out Dar's ass as he bent over and ripped the box open. When I looked up, Chief was staring at me and trying not to laugh.

"Getting a good look?"

"It's kind of amazing in jeans, isn't it?"

"I don't know. I'm not staring at it."

"Well, you should. It's impressive."

"Not into guy butts."

Dar must have realized we were talking about him and pulled his head out of the fridge. "Uh. Sorry?"

"Don't be," Chief chuckled. At least he was handling it well.

Dar headed back to the living room. I hated seeing him leave, but I loved watching him walk away. Seriously.

"You okay?" Chief whispered the question in my ear.

"Something is wrong with me."

"Something more than the usual stuff?"

I turned my head and narrowed my eyes. "You're going to get all witty and shit when we were being romantical?"

"Um. I mean what's wrong, sweetie?"

"Better. I mean I am… Well, I'm usually feeling frisky, but lately it's been like woah."

"Like sniff people's necks and stare at them like they're a burger?"

"Yeah."

"So horny it spills over on your familiars and causes them to make out with other people?"

"Yeah."

"So horny it drives you insane at restaurants and causes embarrassing moments?"

"Well, that was hungry more than horny, but kind of the same thing."

"Don't know what you're talking about. Seems like the same old awesome Dot I fell in love with."

"If there wasn't a fae girl in my bed with severe emotional trauma right now, I'd totally drag you in there and have my way with you."

Ding dong.

"Fucking doorbell…"

Chief chuckled and let me go. "You expecting someone?"

"It's most likely Josie. I told her to get her ass home and she probably forgot her key." I walked over to the front door and unlocked it, flinging it open to give her a disgusted look.

Delron fell through my door, an arrow piercing his chest, perilously close to his heart, and slash marks covering most of his body.

"You're not Josie," I said, confused.

∞ ∞ ∞

"He going to live?" Chief didn't sound overly concerned.

If I were being honest with myself, I didn't like how much magic it was taking to heal his wounds. It was almost like they had been coated with something to keep him from healing. I needed more power.

"I can heal him, but it's taking *way* more power than it should be. I don't think it's because he's an elf, but I'm not sure. Can you text Shea and ask him to come over?" I stared at the wound and concentrated, feeling bad for having to kick Candace out of my bed, but my room was the largest and had the most room to work. Plus, I had towels and a sink close by.

"Sure thing," Chief answered. "Uh. I don't have his number."

"This is fucking insane. Everybody in this damn coven better have everybody else's number in their damn phone by the end of the week or I'm going to start zapping tender parts."

"I have it." Candace got up off the bed where she had been sitting, watching with concern. She ran to her room to get her cell.

"You're right. I'll get with Candace and get everybody's number. Start a group text or something, just in case of emergencies. Like this."

"Good." I frowned. "It's like the arrow and whatever cut him were covered in acid, and it's still eating his flesh."

"That's kind of gross. Who would use weapons like that?"

"Uh. Just a guess, but I'm going to say dark elves."

"His own people did this?"

"I'm guessing."

"I hope you're wrong. For Jaeren's sake."

"Me, too."

"I texted him," Candace said as she padded back into my room.

I prayed he would have an answer, because I was running out of juice quickly. A moment later, he solidified out of the shadow in the corner of my room. "What is wrong?"

"His wounds aren't healing!" I was starting to panic. If he died, there was no hope for Jaeren. I didn't want to waste a good box of crayons.

He came around the bed and inspected some of the lower wounds on the elf, letting me continue to pump healing magic in the arrow wound by his heart. Getting the arrow out without causing more damage had been almost impossible and used a good portion of my power. "I sense no negative magics."

"Well, it shouldn't be this damn hard to heal him. There has to be something."

Chief moved closer and put his hands on my shoulders. I half-expected him to pull me away from my patient. I gasped a little in surprise when he started feeding me power as only he could. "That help?"

"Yes! Much. Thanks, Chief."

"Welcome," was all he said and gave me a little squeeze.

Shea reached down and touched the wound, bringing his finger to his mouth and tasting it. He made a face and spit the blood out on my floor. If he knew what it was, I would forgive him for the grossness factor of spitting on my floor.

"Waste water."

"Like sewage?"

"No. It is the venom of a rift wight. When they bite you, the wound never heals and you waste away to nothing, becoming a wight yourself. Like the venom of a brown recluse with ghostly effects."

"Is there a cure?"

"The combined power of a team of healers, perhaps," he said sadly and cast Delron a pitying glance.

"We need to get him to Faerie. I could heal him there."

"If he were to step one foot in the court of light, he would be killed within moments of being seen. I fear it would be the same if he returned home…"

"Shit."

"Yes. An impasse."

Thoughts fluttered through my brain and a vision of my car bouncing across Faerie settled in the forefront. "If we can't bring him to Faerie, I'll bring Faerie to him."

"Wait, what?" Chief did start to pull me back this time.

"Lady that would be inadvisable," Shea managed to caution as I used my left hand to claw a hole through the veil beside the bed. It was strange seeing the purple liquid part beneath my fingers, floating like a gaping wound in my bedroom, but I didn't hesitate and shoved my hand through the tear.

Limitless power was literally at my fingertips. Chief was physically blown back away from me and left a dent in the wall behind him. Shea scrambled away and Candace began floating beside the bed.

"You have finally realized what you can truly do, even in this world." Candace's voice took on a familiar, otherworldly tone.

"Greetings, Lady," I said without looking up from Delron.

"Greetings to you, Child."

"Is this okay? I'm not in trouble, am I?"

"No. Not in trouble. I just wish to advise you that you have now drawn even more attention to yourself. What you have done," she paused to motion to my arm hanging into another realm, "has not gone unnoticed. Your visitor today will have been the first of many. Now is the time to find your father."

"I'm trying. My damned mother stopped me the first time."

"She fears for you."

"I know. But she should know by now, I can be just as stubborn as her."

"She knows quite well," my mother said from the door of my bedroom. I didn't have to look over my shoulder to see her. I'd have recognized her voice anywhere.

"Shit."

The goddess chuckled. I was glad she found my family dysfunction funny. "Greetings, High Priestess of the Coven of the Black Well."

"Greetings, my Lady," my mother said reverently.

"I shall leave you to your task, Daughter," she said and reached out and stroked my cheek before Candace collapsed to the bed beside me. At least she didn't drop her to the floor.

"Daughter, might I ask what you are doing?"

"Healing the dark elf who kidnapped my elf, but he's got some kind of poison in his wounds, so I had to tear a hole in the veil between worlds to access the power of Faerie to heal him. You know. The usual."

"Might I ask how?"

"When I'm done," I said and concentrated on the wound, *finally* able to concentrate. As long as my mother stopped talking. Using the power at my disposal, I literally *burned* the poison from his wounds, watching as it evaporated in plumes of black smoke. They were making my eyes water, but hopefully not damaging to anyone's lungs. Wight poison smoke probably ranked right up there with asbestos.

When the venom was gone, the wounds healed almost instantly, and Delron came to with a sucking noise as he took his first deep breath since he had collapsed in my doorway.

"Lady?"

"You're safe, Delron."

"You have my thanks, as well as my apologies."

"Rest for a moment while I speak to the others. Just answer me one thing, is Jaeren safe?"

"For now."

"Okay. One step at a time. Rest and I'll be back soon."

"Thank you."

"Shea, keep an eye on him? Please?"

"Yes, my queen."

"Oh, you need to stop saying that." I leaned closer to him. "Especially in front of my mother."

"Yes, my queen," he whispered back with a small smile.

"I can still hear you both."

"Of course you can, you're part bat," I mumbled under my breath.

"What was that, Daughter?"

"I said, I love your hat."

"As I am not wearing one, I shall assume you are hallucinating. I shall be in your kitchen. You do have tea, do you not?"

I looked over at Candace. She gave a quick nod. "Of course, Mother. Help yourself."

I got up from the bed and turned around, nearly running into Chief who was magically fixing the damage he had caused to the wall.

"Sorry about that, Chief. You okay?"

"Yeah. Your drywall, not so much."

"Didn't know it would have that much kick. Forgive me?"

He looked over and smiled. "For being so damn beautiful? I think that can be arranged."

"Sweet talkers. The lot of you." I leaned over and gave him a kiss before heading to deal with my mother. While I wasn't looking forward to dealing with her, I was looking for some damn answers. Hopefully, she would be able to give them to me.

Chapter 7

"Where is it, Daughter?"

"Where is what, *Mother*?"

"We've been over this before. Watch your tone, young lady."

I sighed, grabbed a clean mug from the cabinet, and set it in the coffee maker. If I was about to deal with her level of bullshit, I needed caffeine. Or wine, and we were out of that.

"You didn't answer my question."

"Mother," I said and held up my hand until the brewer sputtered the rest of my patience potion into my favorite cauldron mug. I graciously took a sip and breathed a sigh. "You never answered mine. Where is what?"

"The gem you sent me a picture of."

"My father's gem?"

"Yes!" She slammed her empty mug down on the counter. She was still waiting for the tea kettle to boil, thankfully.

"Safe."

"Give it to me."

"No."

"Daughter!" She was practically wailing.

I'd had more than enough. "Who is my father?"

"I can't."

"I didn't ask what he was, I asked *who* he was. Give me a name at least."

"Aodh," she managed to stammer. "He has many names, but that is the one he gave me."

"Aodh?"

"Aodh."

"You say it like that's supposed to mean something to me."

"You asked me for a name, and I have given it to you. You have the gem, you need to give it to me."

"No."

"Daughter. I am doing this for your own damn good. I know you don't believe me, but it is the truth. That gem is not what you think it is."

"What is it?"

"Insanity and death."

"I've seen that, but it doesn't seem to be bothering me," I said and pulled it out from under my shirt.

Her eyes, as soon as they gazed upon the red facets, narrowed as she reached a hand out for it, shaking like some sort of drug addict.

"Mother?"

Her hand stopped, but the haunted look never left her eyes, nor did the gem ever leave their sight. My mother and I might not have gotten along, even at the best of times, but my heart broke when she started sobbing.

I shoved the jewel back in my shirt and wrapped my arms around her. My mother crying as I held her was something I would never have expected to see, not in a thousand years. She pulled away when the doorbell went off. Again.

"I'll get it," Chief called out softly.

"Thanks."

Mother straightened herself and began frantically wiping the tears from her eyes. I knew why a moment later, when Nana came strolling into the kitchen.

"Nana?"

"Greetings, Child."

"Why are you here?"

"To act as mediator."

I nodded my thanks to her when my mother turned around to finish wiping the moisture off her face. "Greetings, Mother."

"Hello, Daughter," Nana told her with a sad smile, even though she couldn't see it. "The past has finally caught up to us. It's time to for her to know the truth."

"We can't."

"We must."

"No. I mean we can't." My mother turned back around and gave her a fearful look. "Don't you think I've tried? I am physically unable to do so. He is the only one who can."

"Alright. Hold on, both of you. Go sit in the dining room. I'll make tea."

They both nodded and headed for the dining room table. Dar padded up to me, back in his canine form. *I shall keep an eye on the elf, as well. Give you some privacy.*

Thank you.

He took off toward my bedroom, nearly trampling Candace as she came out. I lifted the kettle off the stove and shook it, adding more water before setting it back down to boil.

"Sit, Lady. I shall make the tea."

"Thanks, Candace."

"I'll get going, unless you want me to stay?" Chief raised his eyebrows questioningly.

"I do, but go ahead. I'll fill you in later," I said with a slump, sighing and not looking forward to the family reunion in my dining room.

"Call me if you need me."

"I will."

He gave me a tight hug and kissed me once more on the lips, before heading for the door. He turned and waved one more time. "Good luck," he mouthed and pulled the door open.

Josie was standing there, not moving and looking like she was either pouting or unsure if she should come inside. I felt bad for forgetting her and Candace's problem. I stuck my hand out and motioned her in with my finger, narrowing my eyes.

She shook her head.

"Josephina Barton, you have three seconds to stand before me before I destroy your *signed* New Kids on the Block poster."

Her eyes widened and she practically ran into the house.

"Come with me."

I noticed she refused to look at Candace, and Candace wasn't looking up from the kettle on the stove. I hoped she realized it would never boil staring at it like that. "Be right back, Candace."

She just nodded.

"I'll be right back," I called out to Nana and Mother as we passed by the dining room. "Have a bit of drama in every room today."

Nana nodded; Mother frowned.

I led Josie into her room, the only unoccupied one at the moment. Moving out of the way, I let her pass me and closed the door behind us.

"Dot, save it. I'm sure you have bigger problems to deal with than Candace and I."

"Since you two are my family, you couldn't be more wrong."

"She called me Yuki, Dot."

"I know. She told me, or rather, I told her. I'd meant it as a joke."

"I don't know what to do."

"I'll tell you what you're going to do. You're going to forget about the whole damn thing," I said and motioned for her to sit on the bed. I pulled her rolling chair from her desk and sat down on it, facing her. "She wasn't dreaming of Yuki while you were making out."

"Uh...pretty sure she was."

"No. She wasn't. She told me exactly what happened. The whole time you were fooling around in the shower, she was panicking that you were going to leave her over the stupid kiss that had nothing to do with her to begin with."

"I'm not leaving her! I was just pissed off."

"I know that. You know that. But think, Josephina. Think about how horrible of a life that girl has had up until now. Of course she was afraid you were going to leave her, and running out the door as soon as she *accidentally* screwed up wasn't the brightest thing you've ever done. If you had stopped and *talked* about it with her, instead of jumping the gun, you would have known that and saved her and you a lot of tears and pain!"

I'd meant to calmly lecture her, but I was more than a little pissed off. Candace invoked maternal instincts in me that I didn't know I had. I kind of wanted to take a shower and wash them off me.

"She was?"

"Yes!"

"Oh, crap. I shouldn't have given her shit before it happened. I'd meant it as a joke, but it was kind of therapeutic. I fucked up."

"You think?"

Josie sighed and covered her face with her hands, shoulders lifting and falling as the tears came. "I'm a horrible person. I should have known. I'm used to dealing with people who always seem to have ulterior motives, but I should have realized she would *never*. What am I going to do?" She pulled her hands away from her face. "Please tell me I didn't just wreck the best thing that has ever happened to me?"

"Of course not." I opened the door. "Candace, come here, please," I called out to the kitchen.

When Candace walked, it was quieter than a whisper of a breeze. I nearly chuckled when I heard her feet shuffling across the floor.

"Yes?" She peeked around the wall.

"Come in." I closed the door again after she entered the room. "Tell this doltish oaf that you still love her," I told Candace.

She looked at Josie and nodded, eyes as wide as they could go. "I do."

"No, Candace. *Tell* her."

"I love you. I love *only* you."

"And you, Josie. Do you love Candace?"

"With all of my heart, soul, bits and pieces."

"Congratulations. Now quit being stupid, the both of you."

"Wait. Did we just get married?" Josie started laughing between sniffles.

"If you want to be. I now pronounce you dolt and oaf. You may kiss the elf." I patted Candace on the head and left the room, closing the door behind me and sighing.

One problem down, twelve-hundred to go.

My grandmother and mother were quietly sipping tea at the table, trying not to look at one another. Basically, they were both looking to their left until I came back into the room.

I snagged my coffee and plopped down on one of the dining chairs, careful not to spill any out of the half-full mug. "So. Where were we?"

"Your mother thinks it's a bad idea for you to be exposed to your father's gem."

I nodded at Nana. "And it would appear to be safer with me than with anyone else."

"Daughter… It is evil."

"No, it is not. I can feel it. It is power, yes. But like any power it can be used for good *or* evil. I'm sure my father didn't use it for evil. The elf that came upon it did."

"I'm not so sure he just happened by it. It might have been an effort of Aodh's to smuggle it out of his prison," Mother scoffed.

"Wait. What? He's in prison?" Every single image I had built up about my father in my mind shattered in an instant. I was the daughter of a convict.

She sighed and nodded.

"Where?"

"I cannot say."

"Please?"

She shook her head. "Just as I cannot tell you *what* he is, nor can I tell you where he was, or why he was there."

"So, for now, all I have is his name until he shows up."

"Your father is like death. He will always come, eventually."

"That's kind of morbid."

"So is your father."

"Great."

"He is that, too. Especially between the sheets."

I made gagging noises and set my coffee down on the table while Nana cackled, and my mother wiggled her eyebrows.

Why couldn't I have been adopted like a normal witch.

Something occurred to me. "Your story about accidentally meeting my father in another city for a one-night stand… That was just a heaping, steaming pile of minotaur shit?"

"I'm afraid so. I thought it would be a good excuse to stop you from asking too many questions. We were married for ten glorious years before his incarceration. Did you honestly think I would allow myself to be impregnated by a single tryst? That is not how witch physiology works, Daughter."

"I always wondered about that part, finally chalking it up to wanting a daughter and using him as a donor."

"Hardly. He donated *many, many, many* times."

"Ew. I don't need figures."

"Good, because they would be quite large and I know how complex numbers hurt your head."

"Nobody knew you were married? Nobody saw this mysterious husband of yours?"

"He did not live in Ashville with us…"

"Where did he live?"

She started shaking her head, fighting the compulsions she was under not to give me any information that might give me a fucking clue to what he was.

"Never mind. Forget I asked."

She breathed a sigh of relief.

"I'm just going to have to find him. I'll get the story from him."

Mother's eyes widened, but Nana nodded in agreement.

"Any idea where I should start looking?"

They both looked at each other before turning and leveling their gazes at me. "Who had the gem?"

"Former King Renlynn of Elfhame Autumn Glade."

"And how did he happen upon it?" This time Mother asked alone.

"It was sent to him as a betrothal gift from the Unseleighe Court of Willowmere. The same court who wanted me as a bride to their prince."

"You were approached?"

I nodded at my mother. "Practically accosted."

"What happened to King Renlynn?" Nana asked curiously.

"He had an adverse reaction to my hands in his chest, ripping out his heart."

She chuckled. "You little heart-breaker, you."

"Maybe you should start at the beginning, Daughter. Tell us what has happened."

So, I did. It took me three-and-a-half cups of coffee to tell them the story in its entirety. It was worth it to see the looks on their faces. When I got to the part about the angel, my mother gasped and seemed almost frantic. "What?"

"Since they have come for you, I can at least share that it was they who imprisoned Aodh."

"Did you say Aodh?" Shea's voice broke through our conversation.

We all turned and saw him, Dar in his blue demon form, and Delron standing just outside of the room, listening to my story. My mother practically snarled at the dark elf before turning to my little half-dark elf. "Hello, Shea."

"Greetings, Madeline," he said and bowed to my mother.

"You know the name?" I practically bounced in my chair.

"Yes. I know it."

"Who is he?"

He opened his mouth and his eyes rolled up into the back of his head as he collapsed to the ground. Gasping, I shot out of my chair, but Dar picked him up gently and brought him into the room, setting him down in the chair beside me.

"That would have been too easy, Granddaughter."

"Thought I was finally catching a break."

"No. If you wish to learn about him, you will have to seek him out yourself. My suggestion would be to travel to the unseleighe court. Rescue your elf, firmly reject the marriage proposal, and find out what they know about Aodh."

"You don't think they know who Dorothea is, do you Mother?" My mother almost looked fearful as she asked. "Do you think that is why they wish her to marry the prince?"

"I would not put it past them," she said and leveled her gaze at a very uncomfortable looking Delron.

"I know not. I merely was acting upon the wishes of our queen. What she knows, or does not, is beyond my scope," he said and lowered his head in apology.

"Why did they attack you?" I wanted to know.

"I delivered your message about destroying our court if they did not release Prince Jaeren. It was not met with a positive response." He sighed.

"Sorry, Delron."

"Do not be. I did not want to abduct the prince to begin with. I strongly advised the queen against it and was met with a similar, but not as enthusiastic, punishment. She would risk an all-out war with Elfhame Autumn Glade to bring you to her court."

"If it is an outright war she wishes to risk, you should bring one to her door. She might be more cooperative," Nana mused aloud.

"What?"

"Instead of travelling to the unseleighe side of Underhill, venture to the seleighe side. The princess seemed very reasonable, from what you told us. Tell her that her brother is being held prisoner. March to the unseleighe side with an army at your back."

Even my mother nodded appreciatively at my grandmother's cunning strategy.

"I do need to rescue Jaeren. It is my fault he is being held captive," I said guiltily. But I would make it right. Even if I had to crush the dark elves myself.

Chapter 8

I thought my mother would go home, but she informed me she was staying until things worked out. Thankfully, she had already checked into Farrell's Motel. My house was full and there would be a fifth ice age in Gehenna before she stayed at my grandmother's house. She even had her own rental car. I was almost proud of her.

Delron, on the other hand, was a completely different issue. I couldn't send him home, I couldn't check him into a motel. I was stuck. With another elf. That I didn't want. But until I had the house next door, he would be staying in Yuki's room. Purplylocks was bunking with Mama Bear again until further notice. At least she didn't snore. Or breathe.

Putting my back to the front door, I sighed, happy my mother and grandmother were at least gone. Just in case, I reached down and twisted the deadbolt before heading for the kitchen. I needed a beer or five. Before I even made it to the fridge, I spotted the extra bottle of elderberry wine that Shea had given me as a gift. All thoughts of *cervesa* went away.

"Shea, want a glass of your wine?"

"I would. Thank you."

"Dar?"

"I will try some."

Grabbing the bottle off the counter, I pulled the drawer open and grabbed the corkscrew. Shea was behind me before I turned around. He was quieter than Candace when he moved. I squeaked in surprise and almost dropped the bottle.

"My apologies, Lady."

"Gonna put a bell around your damn neck. Here. You get to play sommelier, while I go electrocute myself to jump start my heart." I shoved the bottle and corkscrew in his hands and leaned against the counter.

"I truly am sorry." I noticed the small smile on his face.

"No, you're not."

"No! I really am!" He blinked at me in surprise.

"Then why were you smiling?"

He blushed and looked away. "Because I made your heart race. It made me happy."

"Lord and Lady, you are going to kill me with cuteness. Next time just touch my butt or something. I'd prefer it if you didn't make my heart race by scaring the bejeezus out of me."

"As long as I have your permission..." He chuckled wickedly and set the bottle down on the counter, pulling his blade from somewhere inside his clothing. He moved so fast I couldn't follow his movements.

I reached over and touched his chin, turning his head toward me. "You are always welcome to touch me." I leaned forward and kissed him gently on his lips. "You don't have to wait for permission."

He nodded and the smile that had been on his face a few moments ago was nothing in comparison to the grin that had taken its place.

Grabbing three glasses, I set them down in front of him, just as the cork popped from the bottle. He poured the three glasses full, handed one to me and grabbed the other for Dar. We had killed the bottle already and I wanted to weep.

"I really need to go to the liquor store. This is the last of any wine in this house."

"I shall get you some."

"No, you won't. I am perfectly capable of restocking my wine."

"But you do not have the ability to shadow walk to my cellar in Ashville. I have wines that would make you happy, wines that would make pain fade, and wines that would make you blush. Please, allow me."

"Just a couple of bottles!" He *really* wanted to, I could tell just from looking at his face. The least I could do was drink them with him. "Thank you."

"My pleasure," he grinned again. In all the years I've known him, I saw him smile more in the last few minutes than I had my whole life. But, in my defense, I'd also gone almost my whole life with only catching glimpses of his face. At least I didn't have to fight him to take his damn hooded cloak off while he was in my house anymore.

Dar was on the couch, I plopped down on the seat next to him and Shea headed for the loveseat after handing Dar his wine. "Where are you going?" I pointed at the seat next to me. "Unless I still smell?"

"Like sunshine and lavender."

"The lavender is my body wash. The sunshine is your imagination."

"Nay, Shea is right. You do smell like sunshine."

"You, too, Dar?"

He nodded with a chuckle, tearing his eyes from the television. "We are not joking. Have you ever been outside and stared up at the sun and closed your eyes? That warm smell all around you when you do that. That is what you smell like."

Shea was nodding.

"How would you know, Mr. Shadowboy?"

"You cannot find the shadows without the light that casts them. I honestly think that is what drew me to you in the first place. Even a moth, who lives in darkness, will seek out the brightest flame."

"Even if he gets burned," I said dryly. I didn't do well with compliments, and between the two of them, I was going to gush to death. And not in the fun way.

"To bathe in your glow, would be a small price to pay," Shea said and his mouth curved in a little seductive smile.

"Somebody's getting laid tonight." I stared at him blankly, taking a sip of wine.

At least *he* had the decency to blush. Dar just chuckled.

"You shut up. You're almost as bad as he is, when you're not insulting my intelligence."

"I have done no such thing. Not for days. You impressed me in Faerie, once you stopped blowing appendages off. And getting knocked unconscious. Oh, and dying."

"Fine. I get your point. I'll be more careful."

"That is all I ask."

Yuki passed by us, carrying an armload of clothing and heading for my room. "Take as much space in the closet as you need, roomie."

"Thank you, Boss. Wait, you're not going to make me sleep in there are you?"

"Not unless you kick me in your sleep."

"I'm more worried about you." She rolled her eyes and walked away.

I took another sip of my wine, and Shea leaned against me, putting his hand on my leg, tracing the patterns of my leggings with his fingertips. I snuggled a little closer, enjoying the sensation and the closeness.

"Do you wish to be alone?"

I looked over at Dar and shook my head. "No."

He nodded and focused back on the television.

"You wanna snuggle, too?"

He turned his head and cocked an eyebrow. "Probably not the best of ideas."

"Why?"

"I am in my true form. Contact…might be a bit awkward."

"I hate to break it to you, but it's not just physical contact."

"I know. Would you like me to shift forms?"

"Why would I want you to do that?"

"Ease the burden?"

"There is no burden, Dar."

86

"But you find me attractive in this form. If I were in my canine–"

I shut him up with my lips. Even still, he stared at me in shock, wanting to mumble something. To ensure his silence, I stuck my tongue in his mouth. A moment later, I was kissing air.

Opening my eyes, I saw him crouched on the ground and staring at me, breathing heavily. I could almost feel his heartbeat from where he was.

"We cannot!"

"What? Why?"

"Can you not feel it?"

"All I feel right now is how much I care for you and the beating of your heart."

"You *can* feel it."

"Which part?"

"My heart."

"Yes. I just said that. Kind of freaky, but kind of nice."

"Kind of dangerous."

"Huh?"

"What happened to asking the others?"

"Chief said yes. Jimmy wants video. Jason wouldn't care. Shea?"

He smiled and nodded. "Dar has my blessing."

I turned back to Dar. "Unless you don't want me?"

"You do not understand…"

I narrowed my eyes. There was something he wasn't telling me. "What? What don't I understand?"

"We… I did not think it would affect you, but it has. I hadn't realized, I mean I kind of did, but…fuck."

"Come here. Sit down."

"I shall take the loveseat." He sat down across from us and rubbed his face.

"What are you not telling me?"

"The Fourth Rite."

"Yes. You're my prize. We've been over that."

"But you are not d'lakii."

87

"So, you're pulling the racist card? I'm not good enough?" I was starting to get pissed.

He sighed, reached across to the coffee table and grabbed his wine, downing it in a gulp. "You misunderstand."

"Then explain it to me."

"I shall check on Yuki," Shea said and got up.

"I can't," Dar said sadly.

"You better."

"Dorothea, please?"

Oh, no, he didn't. "You will explain. You will tell me what the fuck is going on *now*. Do you hear me?" There was a rumbling in my voice, but no claps of thunder.

Dar began to whimper. "You will hate me."

"No. I won't." I stood up, set my now empty wineglass on the table and crossed my arms.

"The Fourth Rite…"

"Yes?"

"Is not just a challenge for a rite to mate."

"It's not?"

"No. It is a mating ritual. Once complete, you do not claim your prize…you become a mated pair…"

"Huh?"

He sighed again and looked at me imploringly, wanting me to make the connection I wasn't getting. "Mated pair… Think matrimony, Master."

Where I had liked him calling me Master before, suddenly I didn't find it so attractive. "Husband and wife?"

"Yes."

"You fucking asshole!"

I turned and left. Or I tried to. Wanting the sanctuary of my bedroom, I stormed toward my door. One moment he was behind me, calling my name, and the next, he was in front of me, blocking my way.

"Move!" This time my voice did thunder.

He moved to the side. "Please! Let me explain!"

Something in his voice stopped me. It was pain. "This had better be good."

He paused and drew in a breath, collecting his thoughts. "To tell you the truth, and I swear that it is, I did not think it would have an effect on you."

"Bullshit. You knew it would drive me to kill Renlynn."

"You are right. I thought it would make good motivation, but I did not think it would have the *d'lakii* effects on you. You are...very much like us. Minus the horns and blue skin. When your talons and fangs grew, when your eyes turned to black... I almost panicked. That should not have happened." He paused to let me digest what he said. I did and still wasn't impressed, or in a forgiving mood.

"Is that it?"

"May we sit and talk?"

"No."

He nodded. "Master, I swear upon my essence that I had no intention to bind myself to you in that way. When everything was said and done, I truly wanted to believe that it was you who wanted me, not an after effect of the rite. I can't even begin to tell you how sorry I am. When I saw how you have been acting, I tried to convince myself that it was anything but what it was. I even tried to blame your behavior on the gem you now carry."

"Nope."

"I know." He hung his head. "Then, when you kissed me on the couch just now, I felt it. I knew, without a doubt, that if we went any further that the bond would be complete. I worried what would happen to you just from the familiar bond. If we consummated the rite..."

"Well. No chance of that now."

"As you wish," he answered and nodded. "I shall... I'll–" It was all he managed to get out before the tears, blood red tears that looked purple against his blue skin, began to leave ruddy lines down his cheeks. I wanted to wipe them away. I wanted to kiss them away. But I also wanted to punch him in the face. I knew how I felt about him, but now I wasn't so sure that the feelings were my own.

"I hate you."

"As you deserve to."

"No, Dar. I don't. If you had never performed that fucking ritual, I would be standing here now, knowing how I felt about you. Now, I don't know if the feelings are even mine. You have no idea what that is like."

"Being bound to someone without their consent? You're right, *Master*. I wouldn't have *any* clue about that."

"Sarcasm? You're going with sarcasm?"

He sighed. "What would you have me do?"

"Sarcasm is never the answer."

He wisely said nothing, but the look he gave me spoke volumes. Like Encyclopedia Britannica volumes. One through thirty-two.

"Fine. I bound you, you bound me. But at least, my bonds didn't involve feelings!"

"Are you stupid?"

"What the fuck did you just ask me?"

"Are you mentally deficient?"

That feeling of wanting to punch him in the face became more than a feeling. In fact, I smiled when the knuckles of my right hand shattered against his jaw. The pain was worth sending him crashing into my kitchen. At least he didn't dent my new fridge.

The door to my bedroom opened. Josie and Candace's door opened, and they all came pouring out. At least I couldn't see Shea and Yuki behind me, and Delron had the sense to stay in his room.

Dar got up off the floor and snarled at me. "You wish to fight? Why? Because you know you are just as guilty as me?"

"What the fuck are you talking about?"

"You do not think your little bonds forced feelings on me? You think you are innocent?"

"Yes! What the fuck are you talking about?"

He looked behind me. "Yukina. Tell her."

"Tell her what?"

"How you feel?"

"I think you're both insane."

He narrowed his eyes at her. "Please."

I heard her sigh behind me. "Fine. He's right."

I looked at her over my shoulder. "About what?"

"When you bound us. There were…feelings…involved."

"Like what?"

"Love."

"What?"

"Love."

"I heard you, Yuki. What the fuck are you talking about?"

"I love you."

"Uh, thanks?"

She shook her head. "Not in a sexual way, and these feelings didn't develop over time. I'm saying the moment I tasted your blood, I was in love with you. We have a need to protect you, but it's also a want. And while I *need* to be by you, I also want to. Always. Does that make sense?"

It made a lot of sense, and that was the problem. I was being a hypocrite again. I hated being a hypocrite, it made me feel like a politician. "Yeah." I walked past Yuki and Shea, into my bedroom, and shut the door behind me, locking it.

I stripped and threw back the covers of my bed, crawling between them and burying myself in their warmth. I'd had enough world for the day. If it needed anything else from me, it could kiss my lily-white ass. As I lay there, cocooned away from reality, the incessant knocking started.

Not even remotely wanting to talk to Dar, I tried Yuki instead. *Who's knocking.*

Shea.

Tell him I want to be alone.

The knocking stopped.

"Remember how I told you I had a wine that could make pain go away?"

I lifted the cover off my head. Shea was holding out a glass of wine in front of my face. "Yeah?"

"I thought you could use a glass."

"I drink that, and the world goes numb-numb?"

He chuckled. "No. You will still feel, you just won't care."

I grabbed the glass from him and motioned to the other side of the bed.

He shook his head, smiling softly. "I just wanted to give you that. I know you want to be alone."

"I did. But then you went and did something sweet for me. Now I don't want to be alone."

"If you are sure," he said doubtfully, but walked around the bed and sat down, putting his back against my headboard and tucking his knees up by his chin.

I sat up, not having the ability to drink wine lying down. It was probably a good thing I couldn't. I might never have gotten out of bed again. "Thank you, Shea."

"You're welcome, my Queen."

"Why do you call me that?" I took a sip of the dark red liquid in my glass. I nodded appreciatively at the taste, not too dry, not too sweet. Kind of like me.

"Because you are."

"Nope. Not royalty. Just a Dot."

He sighed. "You are far from just anything. You are extraordinary."

"At screwing up."

"You are upset. You often belittle yourself when you are. It is very…frustrating."

"Then explain to me. Why do you think I am extraordinary? Why do you think I'm worthy to be your queen? They better be damn good ones, because I have a million reasons why I'm not."

"You have been visited by the goddess *numerous* times. Most high priestesses will go their entire very long life without a single visitation. That, in and of itself, should be more than enough to convince anybody."

"Or I screw up so badly she has to help."

"You sealed a portal going through all the realms to Gehenna, banishing hordes of demons while using a firetruck as a weapon."

"I got lucky."

"You faced an entire kingdom of elves, practically alone, just to find a clue about your father."

"I died."

"You saved an entire clan of vampires from an evil creature, just because they asked for your help."

"Got bit pretty bad. And poisoned."

"Your coven was broken. You healed them and gave them a sense of purpose, while rooting out an evil and saving lives."

"Didn't save them all. And I got blowed up."

"Everybody loves you."

"Everybody?"

He nodded.

"Are you saying you love me?"

"I am. And I do."

"So, what you are telling me, is you call me queen because you're biased."

"I may be biased, but you're difficult."

"I am."

"Is there no way to cease your aimless self-depreciating rambles?"

"You could kiss me."

"I could?"

I set my glass of wine down on the nightstand. "You should."

"I shall." He moved forward, getting on his hands and knees, crawling to the end of the bed. While I had a superb view of his ass in leather pants, he was going the wrong way.

"Um, Shea? My lips are up here." I pointed to them.

He looked over his shoulder at me and gave me a grin. "Silly Queen. You did not specify where I should kiss you."

"Well you passed *all* the fun parts."

"I took it as I should kiss you everywhere."

"Oh."

He pulled the cover off my legs, leaving most of me still under the warmth of the blanket. I knew about foot fetishes, but up until that moment I never understood the pleasure of having someone gently kiss your toes. A soft moan escaped me as my toes spread.

He gently ran his lips over the top of my foot, backing up slowly as he worked his way to my ankle, up along my calf, and finally, my knee as he lifted my leg from the bed. Turning around he moved between my now open legs and lay on his stomach, staring up at me adoringly. I wanted to close my legs and keep him trapped there forever, he was so frigging cute, sexy, beautiful, sweet, and most importantly…mine.

"You are so beautiful," he whispered and placed a gentle kiss on my thigh. Then another, and another, and another, working his way upward toward his goal.

"You are, too."

"May I be handsome?"

"Oh, you're that, too. But you are beautiful to look at. Even a male lion can still be beautiful."

His smile was my reward. As were the dozens of tiny kisses he was placing all over my skin. I lifted my other leg off the bed and spread myself for him.

When he reached the top of my thigh, he kissed the crease between my leg and lips, gently and lovingly before he began to taste my skin with the tip of his tongue. My breath caught and my back arched. "Mmm, Shea."

I felt his warm breath before his lips found my open wetness. He kissed the entrance and let his mouth trail up, pushing back my hood and sucking my already swollen nub between them. His tongue glided across it and my lazy pleasure turned into a burning need.

94

"Fuck, that feels good."

"This?" He used the tip of his tongue and dipped inside me, dragging my own moisture up and using it to make my clit slick. His tongue danced around it, letting the edge lightly caress my flesh. It was ecstasy. I spread my legs open further and he scooted closer, bringing his arms under my legs and back over my thighs. He gave my most sensitive spot one long last lazy lick before dipping back down and forcing his tongue inside me.

His nose was in the perfect position to keep rubbing me while he began to slowly thrust his tongue in and out. "Oh, fuck." My hips began to quake against his face, which only drove him inside me further. "You're going to make me come."

His lips slid into a smile against me as I started to groan. My fingers found my own nipples and began teasing them gently. His right hand let go of my thigh and slipped beneath me. I bucked as his finger collected the juice that had escaped his mouth and dripped down. Half expecting him to slip it inside my ass, I cooed as his fingertip slid over the opening, wetting it and letting the sensitive flesh push me over the edge.

I let loose with an expletive that lasted the length of my orgasm before collapsing back into my pillow and grinding myself against him, shuddering and smiling.

He placed one more gentle kiss on my clit and smiled up at me before resting his head on my thigh. "Thank you for dessert."

"That's quite the sweet tooth you have."

"With as sweet as you taste, I would be more akin to a bird draining the nectar from a flower than a child with candy."

"Now I want you to pollenate said flower. Come here."

"Did we just unwittingly make a bird and bee joke?" He chuckled softly, the vibrations sending shivers through me.

"Yours might have been unwittingly. I totally meant to wittingly do that."

"You did, did you?"

"Yep. I deserve more kisses. Much higher. And I want you in me."

"You do." He slid off the end of the bed and pushed his trousers down, stepping out of them. His loose shirt completely hid him. I almost mewled, I wanted to see him so bad.

"Hurry," I said with a cracking voice.

Instead of undoing the multitude of buttons, he untied the cuffs and lifted the shirt off his head. I smiled as he came into view. All of him. The tattoos only added to his statuesque appearance.

He crawled back between my legs and trailed kisses up my stomach, over each breast, and at the bottom of my neck. I felt the tip of him nudge my opening as he softly growled at my neck and playfully nipped my flesh. I laughed and pulled him against me and gasped as he slid inside. He was as surprised as me. His playfulness faded as he hissed in pleasure. "You are hot around me. So warm and wet."

"Not so bad yourself, Mister."

There was a flash of light as all his tattoos ignited at once, casting blue light across my room and making the walls almost glow.

"Woah."

He lifted his head and looked at his arms. "They are all glowing."

"Yeah."

"Every day, something new."

"Yep. Life is never boring around the old Dotmeister."

He chuckled and kissed me while he curled his arms under me, gripping my shoulders and pulling himself even further into me. He started slow and steady, but the longer we kissed, the faster his hips moved. I stopped kissing him when the pleasure became too much and I started moaning in time with his thrusts.

"Too fast? Too hard?"

"Hell no. Fuck me harder, Shea."

He lifted himself off me and knelt, the tip of his cock still inside me. He drank me in for a moment and then reached down under my legs and hooked them with his arms, pulling them up as he leaned forward. When he drove himself back inside, his name became almost unintelligible as it flew from my lips.

The position he had put me in was driving me insane. His cock curved upward and with the arch of my pelvis he slid across the tender area just behind my pubic bone. I started shaking. My eyes rolled in my head. I fought to keep consuming oxygen while I screamed his name repeatedly. My whole existence centered around the orgasm rolling through me, shattering me. With one final grunt he slammed himself against me and I felt him twitching inside me as he came.

"Thank fuck," I managed to whisper as he slowly lowered my legs and put his head against my shoulder.

"What?"

"Just glad you came," I answered, breathlessly.

"Me, as well."

"I don't think I could have taken much more of that and lived. Write that position down. That was pretty fucking amazing."

"No need. It shall be engrained in my memory, forever."

I smiled next to him, still unable to open my eyes.

Still inside me, he pulled the comforter back over us as we lay there and slowly drifted to sleep.

Chapter 9

When I woke, I was alone. I could almost still feel him in my arms, on my chest, sleeping peacefully. Smiling at the feeling, I stretched lazily and got up to find my clothes.

Then the whole night before came crashing back, and the last place in the universe I wanted to be was in the kitchen with Dar. Panic began to seize my chest. I hadn't been totally in the right, but I wasn't in the wrong, either.

"Fuck."

Welcome back.

Morning, Yuki.

Just morning, not good morning?

You're brave, talking to me before coffee.

Just wanted to let you know it's safe to come out of hiding.

Was it not safe?

Dar went for a walk. No need to be an ass about it. She abruptly severed the mental conversation. I winced from the whiplash. It was the first time either of them had done it to me.

"I guess I was being an ass."

Yes. You were. And I can still hear you. Vampire ears, remember?

"Oops." I sighed and pulled on my hoodie and sweatpants, throwing on some warm fuzzy socks for good measure.

Taking one last deep breath, I headed into the center of my own home, still feeling unwelcome. Yuki was standing in the kitchen, brewing a cup of coffee.

"Is that for me?"

"If you want it."

She reached up and pulled another mug out of the cupboard. She hadn't been making it for me. I frowned. "That's okay, I'll make it."

"Suit yourself."

"Okay, Dar I get. Why are you pissed off at me?"

"Gee. I don't know. Probably because I was up all night consoling your *other* familiar."

"No."

"No what?"

"No. You don't get to be pissed off at me. I fucked up, but more importantly, he fucked up worse. He did some mumbo jumbo on me and practically made me his wife."

She pulled the mug out of the machine and set it in front of me. "I'll give you a couple of minutes to realize just how fucking hypocritical that statement was."

She left without brewing herself another mug.

I stared after her, wanting to tell her she could go suck the clots from a dead baboon. I wanted to, but I didn't. Arguments can swing in two directions. Either you are completely right, and the person you were arguing with comes to realize that fact and humbly comes and apologizes for being in the wrong. Or, you realize you were completely fucking wrong, and don't want to admit it, end up packing up all your stuff, and living in a yurt in Central Asia to avoid apologizing to the person you wronged.

I saw some nice yurts on HGTV...

"Fuuuuuuuuuck!" I was overly loud.

Yuki spun around, looking for an enemy. Josie and Candace shot out of their room at my outburst. Even Delron came out of Yuki's room, blinking in the bright sunlight.

"What?" Yuki practically shouted her question.

"I'm an asshole."

Josie scoffed, grabbed Candace and went back in her room.

Delron sniffed the air and stared at the mug in my hand. I pointed at the machine behind me. "Help yourself."

"You're now just realizing that?" Yuki was being snide. I didn't know she knew how.

"Yeah. Well, sometimes it takes a crabby-assed vampire to point out the error of your ways."

She smiled and nodded, not even bothering with looking indignant.

"How the hell do I fix this?"

"Say it with me now...I'm sorry, Dar."

"I will. Where did he go?"

"As soon as you went in your room, he shifted into dog and started pacing around the house. Shortly after your first orgasm, he started pawing at the door. The mind blowing one caused him to shift back."

"Shit."

"No, he rubbed one out while crying."

"He did what?"

"What did you think would happen? You have no idea what happens to *us* when you're getting *your* jollies. In tears, he sat on the couch and got his rocks off."

"You're kidding... Please, tell me you're kidding."

"I wish I was."

"What did you do?"

"Angrily got mine off. If I didn't think the goddess herself would have come down and smote me, I'da kicked down your door and slapped the shit out of you. There's cruel," she paused and held out a hand at chest level. She reached up with her other hand and held it about a foot above her head. "And then there is what you did to Dar last night."

"Fuck."

"Yep. That's what you did."

"I didn't even think—"

"That's just it. You don't. Ever."

"You're lucky I deserved that," I said and sighed, putting my mug down and sliding down to the floor, back to the counter. I probably would have stayed there until my flesh rotted from my bones in a couple hundred years, but the burning need to make things right kind of overwhelmed me. "How do I fix this?"

Yuki sat down beside me. "Apologize to your friend, Dot."

"I'm sorry, Yuki."

"Your other friend."

"I know. I was apologizing to you, too."

She nodded and leaned her head on my shoulder. "I won't pull any punches. Seeing him like that last night broke my heart. Good thing I really don't need one."

"I suck."

"I know."

"So, apologize. What else should I do? Think he'd like flowers?"

She chuckled. "He'd probably just eat them."

"Steak! I'll buy him steak with *I'm sorry I'm an asshole* branded into it."

"That might work. Just be honest. And non-judgmental. You know he would *never* do anything shady or anything that would intentionally hurt you."

"I know."

"And don't you dare fuck him."

"Pardon?"

"If you have sex with him now, it would probably feel like a pity fuck. Wait. I'm not saying not ever. I'm saying not right now."

"How'd you get to be so smart. You're like a supernatural relationship therapist. Dr. Phil Maholin."

She lifted her head and shook it, trying not to laugh. "Nobody's filling these holes in, thank you very much." She finally let out a little chuckle and got up, offering me a hand. I took it and wrapped my arms around her when I got up.

"Thanks, Yuke."

"You're welcome."

"When do you think he'll be back? I don't want to wait too long to tell him what a douche nozzle I was."

102

"He's in Josie's room, hiding under her bed."

"He's what?"

"Hiding under the bed."

"Why?"

"I told him to. Figured it would be easier to talk if you thought he wasn't here and so he could listen in and know how you really felt."

"You're a little fucking shit."

"Yep. But I haven't hit my growth spurt yet." She grinned. "You can come out now. The jig is up."

There were a few scratching sounds and then the creak of Josie's door as it swung open. His paws bounced across my hardwood floors all the way from the hall to the kitchen, where he slid to a stop and sat, looking up at me with those damn puppy eyes.

Yurtsforsale.com. I wonder if that's a thing? I squatted down, putting my eyes closer to his. "I'm an asshole. I'm sorry."

Steak?

I laughed and cried at the same time. Craughed. Dropping to my knees, I threw my arms around his neck and hugged him. Until he pulled back.

Not joking. Steak.

There will be steak. And wine. And more apologies later. You were still wrong to do what you did, but you did it for all the right reasons. Me, I'm just dumb. Big old hypocritical dumb ass. Forgive me?

If you forgive me.

I already have.

He licked my fucking face. If he were a demon, or an elf, I'd have been all over that like white on rice. I just happened to not like doggy drool. *That's enough of that. Unless you turn blue. Then, knock yourself out.*

Shall we pretend that the previous evening never occurred?

No. What doesn't kill you makes you stronger. As friends, lovers, mates, or whatever. We'll keep last night in our memories, so it doesn't happen again.

So stupid, and yet so wise. He was lucky his German Shepherd eyelid winked at me.

"Not my fault. I was dropped as a child. Knowing my mother, it was probably on purpose."

He shifted without warning, putting his blue popsicle right in my face. "I'm sorry," he said with a chuckle and backed up a little.

"Sure, you are." Naked or not, I stood up and hugged him. His arms wrapped around me and I felt something wet on my neck.

"Are you crying?"

"I'm not if you're not."

"Good call." I lay my head on his shoulder and just stood there, breathing him in. He always smelled a little spicy, but it was one of the first chances I had to really get a good whiff. He smelled like cinnamon.

"Well, this is awkward. I'm taking a nap in your bed," Yuki said and left us standing in the middle of our kitchen.

I lifted my head and looked around. Delron was long gone, too. I hadn't even heard him leave. "I live with a bunch of ninjas."

"Ninjas?"

"Surely you've seen ninjas on TV."

"Yes, but I fail to see the… Oh. I get it. Because everyone in your home is stealthy."

"Yep."

"Not Josie, though. I've heard quieter horses. Every time she gets up in the middle of the night to pee, I search in vain for a lost pack of wildebeests. They look tasty."

"I could go for a wildebeest steak right about now, too. How about I buy you lunch?"

"Steak?"

"Steak."

∞ ∞ ∞

The parking lot of Bunyan's was almost empty. I guess they didn't draw a big lunch crowd, but the price of steak probably was a big deterrent. Dinner was one thing... Lunch was another. Either way, I wanted a big juicy T-bone, medium raw.

I looked over at Dar. One thing we had forgotten to buy at Walmart was a hat. He kind of looked like Axl Rose in his elf form with the bandana wrapped around his head to cover the tips of his ears. In his younger years.

"You know the safe word?"

"Chimichangas."

"And what do you do if I say the word?"

"Get you the fuck out of there."

"Good boy."

"Please stop using that expression."

I pulled into a spot, doubting my sanity. Meat and I...we were like long lost lovers tossed naked into a vibrating kiddie pool full of Spanish Fly flavored Jello. Dar had assured me that I would be fine and that I should learn to start controlling my urges. I thought he was just trying to get me back for making him whip up a fresh batch of blue-baby batter on my couch while he was pissed off at me.

"You ready?" I asked, hoping he would say no.

"For steak? I always am."

"Remind me to buy a cow and a freezer."

"That is a good idea. We can thaw it out and frolic in the flesh of the slaughtered."

"Yeah. I don't like steak *that* much." That's what I *said,* but the thought... I blushed and coughed, popping the handle on my door.

"Hi! Welcome to Bunyan's!"

"Chimichangas."

"Pardon me?"

"Do you have chimichangas?"

"Er. No, but we have soft tacos!"

"That'll work."

"Just the two of you?"

"Yep."

"Right this way!" She grabbed a couple of menus from the wood holder by her little hostess stand and headed toward the back. I was starting to think that the entire staff at the steakhouse was medicated. There couldn't possibly be that many happy people in the entirety of Upstate New York.

"Here you go. Chelsea will be right with you."

"Oh, goddess, no."

"Pardon?"

"Just thinking about those soft tacos," I said with a fake smile. She ate it up.

"They're super nummy!"

"I bet she is, too," Dar muttered under his breath.

My inner jealousy monster snarled in rage. Dar must have caught my look. "I meant as a meal, Master. Not in the other way."

"Oh. Okay. I'll allow that."

"I assumed you were referencing the chimichangas at the door as a joke?"

"Yeah. I forgot how happy their wait staff is at this place."

"I was just noticing that, as well."

"Do you think they're medicated?"

He stared at me.

"No?"

"You cannot tell?"

"Tell what?"

"They are not human."

"Oh. That explains so much. What are they?"

"I do not know. Some sort of fae creature. They are heavily glamoured."

"Huh."

Dar was glancing over the menu. "What is the cut of meat you brought me the last time?"

"Prime rib?"

"Yes. That. It was very good."

"What I usually get. Tenderest meat."

He wiggled his eyebrows at me.

"But sometimes I love a good bone."

"You do?"

106

"I do. Love ripping the meat from it with my teeth as I hold it in my hand."

He winced.

"That will teach you to be pervy."

"My apologies."

"I was kidding. Perv away."

"You like it?"

"I do. You may not have noticed, but I have the humor of a twelve-year-old school boy."

"Is that why you enjoy James' company?"

"Um. Yeah. That and he's hot. And sweet. And excites me."

"I often watch Yuki's expressions while you are out with him. I can tell."

My face became the same shade as the red pleather booth we were sitting in. "You two have gotten quite close."

"We are both your familiars. It is only natural."

"So, because you're both tied to me, you became masturbation buddies?"

He lowered his menu. "My apologies. When you are being inundated with amorous waves of pleasure from your master, sometimes it becomes…overwhelming."

I felt bad. I hadn't meant it to come out snarky. "I wasn't complaining, and I understand."

"You are not jealous?"

"Believe it or not, I am. Just…keeping it inside. It's a miracle," I said with a little bit of surprise in my voice.

"But the hostess…"

"Off fucking limits. No. Don't even joke."

"Interesting. It must be the bond we share."

"Huh. Maybe. But if you ever fuck Yuki, I will kill you both. Just a heads up."

He chuckled and went back to his menu. "I do not think you have to worry about that. She shows no interest, nor has she ever."

"How do you know?" This time I did mean it to be snarky.

107

"The opportunity rose early in our relationship." He motioned to me and him. "She was in the throes of your passion. I offered to help her, and she declined."

"That was very generous of you."

"It was. While she is charming, she is no you."

"I don't know about all that. If I were gay, I'd be into her."

"You would?"

"Definitely."

"What about Candace?"

"Me or you?"

"You, obviously. I do not wish to find my manhood severed."

"Smart boy. Candace is just adorable. Everybody loves her."

"She is fae blooded, but I do not believe it is sidhe in her blood."

"No?"

"No. The power feels…different."

"Huh. Whatever it is, I doubt she even knows."

"Most likely not."

We ended our conversation when Chelsea walked over to the table. "Hi! I'm Chelsea. I'll be taking care of you tonight. Oh! Welcome back!"

"Hi, Chelsea."

"Know what you want to drink?"

"Beer, please," Dar said over the menu, trying not to look up at her with his elven eyes.

"Bottle or draft?"

"I am not picky. Whichever."

"Bud it is. And for you?" She turned to me and her appearance wavered. Ears elongated, as did her teeth. I blinked and refocused, her human seeming reappearing and solidifying.

"Um. Yeah. Wine, please. Red."

"Cabernet, zin, or pinot noir?"

"Zin."

"We have–"

"Whatever. As long as it's red."

"I'll bring you my favorite! It's absolutely *zin*ful!"

I debated throwing my steak knife at her retreating back. There was evil in the world. And then there were puns. "I saw her for a moment. Long ears and pointed teeth," I mentioned to Dar when she was out of eye and earshot.

"I suggest not making her angry."

"Tell her to stop with the puns."

He chuckled. "What is the difference between a T-bone and a porterhouse?"

"Thicker cut. Go with the porter if you want the bone."

"I shall. It sounds delightful."

I flipped over the menu and set it down. It was the first time I had ever seen the back of the menu, I had always just assumed it was blank, or a kiddy menu. The only thing on the page was an advertisement for their house special steak. The Babe. Sixty-four ounces of lean ox steak, bone-in and served with au jus.

"Dar."

"Yes, Master?"

I pointed at the back of the menu, unable to take my eyes off the description. "Look."

"Oh. That sounds superb!"

"Shall we?"

"Oh, we shall."

"You get a T-shirt if you can finish it."

"Free clothing. I almost feel guilty."

"Me, too."

Chelsea came back with our drinks. Dar took a swig of his beer while she opened up her order book. "What can I get for you?"

"We'll both have the Babe, rare with no sides."

"You're going to split it?"

"No. We both want one."

She stared at us in open-mouthed shock. Glancing around quickly, she leaned in closer. "That is almost four pounds of meat. Each. Are you sure?"

She dropped the act and acted more human than she had since I had first met her a week ago. I nodded emphatically. "Have the T-shirts ready. I'm a size small. He's an extra-large."

Being that close to us, I noticed her nostrils flare as she scented the air around us. "Oh. You're not…"

"Human?"

Again, she stared at us in shock. "Yeah."

"Nope."

"I see. I'll have your orders out shortly. Would you care for anything else?"

"Better bring us some napkins. Things might get a little messy."

She chuckled and gave us a wink, heading off to put our orders in. I watched her as she sashayed away. She seemed almost happy.

"That was unexpected."

"What was?"

"That you outed yourself and me to a total stranger."

"What? That's Chelsea. I've known her for over a week, now."

"She could be a soul sucking lamprey for all you know."

"There's no such thing. Is there?"

"Not lampreys, but there are things out there that would devour your soul, yes."

"Well. I'm trying to get everybody to play nice in this town. And no bodies have showed up, so they can't be all that dangerous. Just putting some feelers out there."

He shrugged. "I am not judging. Just cautioning. It is only my job to keep you safe."

"Keep me from blowing parts off and all that?"

"Yes. I did not say I was good at my job."

"Meh. I'm hard to kill, anyhoo."

"Thankfully."

"Not everybody would share that opinion."

"I do not understand why. You are quite charming."

I snorted into my wine. Thankfully I hadn't taken a sip yet. Just blew a couple of bubbles. But then, I sighed. "I'm sorry."

"What for?"

"Being such a bitch lately."

He took a swig of his beer. "You have had many reasons. Life has not exactly been...easy lately. I understand."

"But it doesn't give me an excuse to treat you like shit. That's what I feel horrible about."

"It was my fault. I should have been truthful with you from the start, but I feared your reaction."

"You knew I would be a bitch."

"No. I knew you would be angry. I only prolonged the inevitable and made things worse."

"Yeah. You shoulda told me in Faerie."

"It had been a long day."

"True story." I said and toasted him with my wine glass. Curiosity got the best of me. "So, what exactly does consummate mean? Like, full on penetration? Are we free to fool around? Can you put it in me if you don't come? What are the rules here?"

He stared at me in shock. "Uh... I'm pretty sure it means sex until completion. Are you willing to chance it?"

"Are you?"

"What do you mean?"

"What do you mean what do I mean? Would having me as a mate be so bad? How do *you* feel about it?"

He actually paused to think about it for a moment. He finally cracked a small, sexy smile. "I could think of worse options."

"So what does being a mated pair entail? You better not say mutual exclusivity."

"No!" He held up his hands in defense. "Nothing like that. D'lakii mates...become stronger. Share power. Fighting one of us is an arduous task. Fighting a mated pair would be suicide. Your attacks become coordinated. We would become a truly formidable force of nature."

111

"More than we already are?" I winked at him to lighten the mood and was rewarded with a smile.

"Here you go!" Stepford Chelsea was back. At least she had our food.

"Oh, sweet mother of gastrointestinal salvation. That looks amazing." I wasn't kidding. I was drooling. Thankfully I had a napkin on my lap.

Even Dar shuddered as the four-pound slab of meat was set in front of him.

"Need anything else?"

"Yeah. If you could keep everybody back while we eat, that would be great."

"Safer that way?"

"Don't want anybody to lose a hand."

"Okay. I like you."

I blinked up at Chelsea's confession.

"Not like that, silly!" She slapped my arm. "You were all bitchy and scary the last time you were in here. You're a lot nicer today."

"Yeah. Sorry about that. I was starving and trying not to eat the guys I was with."

"I don't blame you for that one. That Chief is dreamy. He yours?"

"Yeah. So was the one next to me. The other was an ex, though. You can have him if you want."

"The one with the accent?"

"Yep."

"Bless you!" She practically danced away.

"Wait! You're not going to eat him, are you?"

She turned around and wiggled her eyebrows.

Oh, well. Steak!

I grabbed my knife and fork and cut off a chunk. The steak was about four-and-a-half inches thick and I'd wondered how they cooked it so fast. They didn't. They seared it to bloody perfection. My hand was shaking, and I almost stabbed myself in the lip with my fork as I took that first bite. I huffed as the meat touched my tongue. It had the flavor of a beef steak, but the texture wasn't quite the same, and it had just a hint of gamey flavor that seasoned it far better than any spice would have.

"Oh, my goddeth. Vith it tho good."

Do not talk with your mouth full.

Thowwy.

He sent a mental chuckle and looked around. Instead of using his utensils, he picked his slab of meat and bit into it, tearing a hunk of flesh off and chewing it happily. It seemed much more efficient and a hell of a lot more fun than having to cut bite-sized pieces off.

I tried it.

Dot went bye-bye.

Gripping the ends tightly, I growled softly as my teeth pierced the bloody, soft flesh and tore a mouthful away. I didn't chew it, either. It went down whole and filled my tummy with protein and happiness.

That is much better. This is how meat should be eaten. He smiled at me from across the table, his eyes going black even in his elven form.

Your eyes...

Yours, too.

I feel alive.

"Can I get youuu...oh my. Let me know if you need anything else!" Chelsea practically squeaked, put a stack of napkins on the table, and left us to our meal. Dar chuckled softly.

We ate in silence, giving each other meat filled smiles as we polished off our meal, not even pausing to drink. Dar finished first and dropped his gnawed bone on the now empty plate. But I wasn't far behind. There was a particularly tasty piece of grizzle I'd been trying to pry loose. It had been totally worth it.

As I was setting the bone down, my world came to a screeching halt. Jimmy walked in through the front door and a smile was creeping up on my face...until a blonde woman walked in behind him, standing a little closer than she should have been as they talked to the hostess.

Chapter 10

"What is wrong?" Dar immediately sensed my distress.

Jimmy.

What is wrong with James? Dar was facing me and couldn't see toward the door.

Nothing. Yet.

I watched as the hostess seated them in a booth and ducked when Jimmy looked around. I wasn't sure if he had seen my car in the parking lot, or if he was just checking out the restaurant for anybody he knew. He probably didn't want it getting back to me that he was having lunch with a hot blonde.

Oh, Jimmy. Jimmy, Jimmy, Jimmy. You chose the wrong restaurant today, my friend.

"Can I get you guys anything else?"

I'd been so focused on boring a hole through Jimmy's skull with my dagger-vision, I hadn't heard Chelsea sneak up on us. "Just the check, please," I said without taking my eyes off the scene unfolding across the restaurant.

"Everything okay?"

I finally tore my eyes from my Jimmy and nodded politely at Chelsea. "Yeah."

"Okay. I'll be right back with your check and T-shirts." She smiled and grabbed our empty plates, heading back toward the kitchen.

Dar turned around and looked over the back of the booth. "Is Jimmy with that woman? Is that why you are staring?"

"Yeah," I whispered, unnecessarily. They were far enough away I could have banged Dar on the table, and they wouldn't have heard. If Jimmy laid so much as a finger on the woman, the theory might actually get tested.

"Do you wish to leave?"

"Wild horse demons with barbed chains couldn't drag me away."

"Why does it always have to be about demons?"

"Sorry."

"Do not be. I find it funny."

"You're distracting me."

"Would you like for me to spice up their lunch date?"

"It's a date?"

"Is it not?"

"I don't know. I'd like to give him the benefit of the doubt, but the angry monster inside me wants to bite him in places he wouldn't want to be bitten."

"This is James you are talking about. He might like it."

"True. What do you mean by spice?"

"I could turn into a hell hound and render the flesh from her bones as James watched in horror."

"Too spicy. Got anything medium or mild?"

"I could do the same thing, but instead of mutilating her, I could do it to his vehicle…"

"We'll call that Plan B. If it turns out he *is* on a date with that…woman, you are cleared for launch."

"Roger."

"I should ask my mother if she knows any good impotence spells. Or, I could spell her skirt to smell like carp. I got Josie with that one in high school."

"Carp?"

"It's a fish."

"You did this as an attractant?"

"Deterrent. You see… Wait. Never mind. Fish smell gross."

"Ah."

"Maybe I'll just turn them both inside out."

"Would that not be a little permanent?"

"So would cheating on me."

"Do you not have four lovers?"

"Shut up with your logic. Jealousy is lawless. He touched her hand!" I nearly shot out of the booth, but Dar quickly stopped me with a hand on my arm.

"Do not do anything rash. It might have been a simple gesture."

"Gonna gesture my foot up his ass if he does it again."

"Again. This is James. He might enjoy–"

"Shush. I'm concentrating. That would distract me."

"My apologies."

"What can I do? Hmmm."

Jimmy threw his head back and laughed heartily. He was having way too much fun. The blond gave him a goofy smile, whispered something across the table, and my boyfriend nodded at her. His voice, much deeper and stronger than hers, carried across the restaurant and bored into my skull. "I missed you, too. And I love you, too. Sorry it took so long."

My heart stopped. Icy veins of anger, betrayal, and hatred gripped my heart and tightened relentlessly. My vision went from red to black.

Chelsea stopped at our table again and dropped off the check and our T-shirts. "I'll be right back to pick that up. Just need to go take their order real quick." She motioned toward my boyfriend and his lunch date.

A flash of inspiration struck. A flash of wicked, delightfully evil, inspiration.

"Chelsea, do me a favor?"

"Sure. What do you need?"

"Do you have a pen?"

She reached into her pocket and pulled one out, holding it out proudly in front of her. I took it from her and stared at it, focusing my intent. An intent to release a spell when it was dropped. A spell that wouldn't harm my soon-to-be-ex-boyfriend, but would get my point across while hopelessly ruining his lunch tryst.

"*Pléisiúr,*" I whispered to the harmless ball point pen and let all my rage and intent settle upon its innocuous white plastic before handing it back to Chelsea. It wouldn't go off in her hand, my intent had been clear. "The gentleman whose order you are about to take. You will remember him from last week. That's my boyfriend. Would you do me a favor and just accidentally drop this pen in his lap?"

"Did you just spell it?"

"Yes."

"You're a witch?"

"Yes."

"Cool. It won't hurt him or make a mess of the restaurant? The boss would kill me."

"Nope. The mess will be localized to the inside of his pants."

"Oh, my. He's not going to shit himself, is he?"

"No! Damn. I wish I had thought of that first. No. Just drop it and watch the fireworks."

"Fireworks?"

"You'll see. And there's a hundred buck tip in it for you for doing it."

"You should have said that first. I wouldn't have asked any questions." She chuckled evilly and headed their way.

"Should I turn around and watch the show?"

"You'll be able to hear it. Act natural."

"I shall do my best."

Chelsea introduced herself to Jimmy and the skank. She waited until they placed their drink order and then let the pen roll over the back of her hand...

An evil grin crept up my face in sync with the tumbling pen. It struck the table and bounced, and my grin was replaced with shock, but it must have landed in his lap. I couldn't see most of him, just the back of his head until it tilted back, and a groan escaped his lips as he looked up at the antlered chandelier suspended above.

He started convulsing as my magic concentrated on firing every nerve ending in his lap, sending electrical signals to the pleasure centers of his brain. "Fuuuuucck," he called out, and every other customer in the restaurant turned and stared in his direction. Even Dar stood and turned, kneeling with one leg on the bench beneath him.

"Uh, Dot…"

"Huh. Musta poured too much juice into my spell."

"Don't cast angry?"

"Something like that."

We watched with growing concern as Jimmy continued shaking and shouting obscenities for over a minute. Even Chealsea began to back away as Jimmy's lunch date got up and stared at him in absolute horror…and disgust?

"Why does she look grossed out?"

"I have no idea," Dar answered. "Usually humans look upon sexual pleasure with interest. She does not look like she will be ordering food."

"That would suck if they were related or something…"

Dar's head turned and he cocked an eyebrow.

"Oh, shit. Maybe I should have found out who she was first. But I lost it when he said that he loved her, too."

"You mean like how sometimes family members express themselves to one another?"

"Fuck. Fuckity fuck, fuck fuck."

"You might wish to check upon your lover."

"No. No way! Let's get out of here." I frantically started waving at Chelsea. She noticed the movement out of the corner of her eye and practically ran over to our table.

"Is he going to be okay?"

"Once the magic runs its course. Here. Pay our bill so we can get out of here!"

"Right away."

She ran to the bar, the closest credit card machine and started frantically punching buttons just as Jimmy fell over sideways. His legs were sticking out of the booth into the aisle, still shaking. I knew he was still alive because he was cursing and clawing at the top of the booth.

Hurry, I mouthed at Chelsea. She pointed at the machine and shrugged.

"He is going to end your existence. If he ever stops orgasming."

"Give her a hundred-dollar tip. You sign my name. I'll be out in the car," I said and started sneaking toward the door.

"Dorotheaaaaaaaaa…" Jimmy turned my name into a curse. He knew who was responsible without seeing me. I should have used a different spell.

I ignored his plea and kept heading for the door, my head tilted low. I glanced over to make sure I hadn't been seen and my eyes locked with a very angry blonde woman.

"Red hair?" She looked down at Jimmy.

"Yessssss!"

She curled her finger at me and pointed at the floor in front of her.

Busted, Dar's voice rang in my head.

Shut up.

I trudged over to the angry blonde and the convulsing boyfriend. Slipping into the empty booth next to theirs, I kneeled on the seat and looked over the edge. "Oh. Hey, Jimmy."

"Why?"

"Um. Not really sure. Seemed like a good idea at the time? You okay?"

His convulsions slowed to quivers and he stared up at me, a tad bit angry. "What. What were you…thinking," he said with one last spasm. The front of his jeans was completely soaked. The scent of semen and steak filled the air. Not the most appetizing of combinations. He started to sit up and I reached down to offer him my hand, but he looked at it suspiciously.

"April fools?"

"It's December."

"Smile, you're on candid camera?"

"Show went off the air decades ago."

"It made a brief reappearance in the Nineties."

The blonde coughed, still standing away from the table.

"Dot, this is my cousin, Sherry. She's my lawyer."

"Cousin."

"Yes."

"Oops."

"Dorothea Blackwell, sit down."

"Uh... I got Dar with me, and you're not really supposed to have dogs in restaurants..."

"The bill is paid, Master. Here is your T-shirt." Dar walked up to us, quite human. Elvish. Whatever, he only had two legs.

"Thanks, traitor."

Jimmy looked apologetically at his cousin. The lawyer. Not his girlfriend. "Sherry, how about we skip lunch today?"

"That sounds like a good idea. I'll start with the Fire District depositions after the weekend. Call me if you need anything. Oh, and Jimmy, no woman should ever have to watch her cousin make that face. See you, sweetie."

"Thanks, Sherry."

"Dorothea? Pleasure meeting you," she said and walked around me, avoiding looking at me, as well as touching me. I didn't blame her. I suddenly didn't want to touch myself either. I closed my eyes and groaned internally like a wounded caribou.

"Since my *cousin* graciously drove me here, would you mind taking me home? I need a shower. And a cigarette."

"She forgot she drove you here, didn't she?"

"Probably not. She's human. Witch stuff freaks her out," he said and got out of the booth.

"I'm really sorry."

He just nodded.

"What do you need a lawyer for?"

"I was let go from the fire department. Permanently."

"Oh." I didn't know what else to say. Instead, I let it go. He would talk when he was ready.

He didn't speak to me the entire ride to his house. Dar just sat in the back seat, smirking at me in the rearview mirror relentlessly. When I pulled into the driveway, I put it in park and waited for him to get out. He sighed heavily.

"Thanks for the ride."

"Jimmy…"

"Yes, Dot?"

"I'm *really* sorry."

"Me, too."

He got out of the car and shut the door. It was official. He was pissed. Angrier than I had ever seen him. Jimmy didn't get angry, he got horny. I guess he got it all out of his system in the restaurant.

I was starting to fear an end to our relationship when he stopped halfway to his door and turned around. I rolled down the window. "I'm not mad," he called out. "Just hurt. You should know me way better than that, and it kills me that you didn't." He turned around and finished walking to his front door.

And I watched him go.

He had his hand on the handle, key inserted when I grabbed the door handle. For the life of me, I couldn't open my door. My heart wouldn't let me. I'd screwed up so bad, and I knew it. It seemed to be my modus operandi lately. If I got out of the car, I would end up just begging for forgiveness and it wouldn't mean shit. I *needed* to make it up to him.

"You're really going to let him go?"

"Yeah. I was a complete twat waffle. I'll let him cool down before I beg him not to dump my stupid ass."

"That might not be a bad idea. He didn't look like he was in a forgiving mood."

"I don't think he was lying. He isn't mad. He's hurt."

"Next time, get the whole story before you blow somebody's crotch up."

"You getting in the front?"

"No. It is not that far."

"Hey, Dar?" I put the car in reverse and backed out of the driveway with a wistful sigh.

"Yes?"

"Thank you for forgiving me."

"Hard not to. You are a victim of your own stupidity. The quicker the others realize that, the happier they shall be."

"Gee, thanks."

"You are welcome."

We were pulling into the driveway when I finally asked Dar what had been bothering me the entire ride home. "He will forgive me though, won't he?"

"He loves you. You need to trust him, and the rest of them, more."

"I know. Tell the little green bitch inside me that."

"I'm telling you. You need to be in control of all of you at all times. Just like the hunger. When she surfaces, take control. Do *not* use her as an excuse."

"But she's so… Gah. You're right."

"Of course."

Chapter 11

I was using my need to recruit an army to get the hell out of my house and to quit obsessing over the look of utter hurt Jimmy had on his face. A trip to Faerie seemed like a damn good plan. Unfortunately, I had no idea where my house was in relation to Faerie, but I didn't care. I'd waited long enough, and I needed to save Jaeren. My grandmother had been brilliant with her strategy of asking Glabrielle for help.

Reaching out with one hand, I slid my finger through the air, ripping a hole through the space-time continuum, or at least the veil separating the human realm from Underhill. Purple liquid-mist rushed to fill the void, effectively obscuring my vision.

"You ready?" I looked over my shoulder at Dar and Yuki.

"Do you promise not to die or get hurt?" Yuki pulled her jacket closed and zipped it up.

"I don't promise, but I promise to try to not to."

"Good enough."

Dar just nodded in his canine form. He was hesitant to travel back in the elven form he had stolen from one of the guards he'd eaten. I didn't blame him. With our luck, he'd run into the guys twin brother or something and wreck our treaty.

"Let's go," I said and led the way through.

Apparently, my house was in the middle of absolutely fucking nothing in Faerie. Spinning around and looking for recognizable landmarks wasn't helping, either.

What are you doing?

"Trying to figure out which way to go. I'm completely lost."

I noticed you got lost in Walmart, too. The castle is that way. Dar looked to his right and gave a little doggy snort of laughter.

"Yeah, well. You can probably smell it or something like that. I'd know which direction to go if *I* had a super sense of smell."

Trust me. It is not always a blessing. Especially in Walmart.

"Ew. Yeah."

"He's right. It's gross," Yuki added.

"We should have brought Shea," I said wistfully, dreading the walk. "Or my car." I felt bad, I'd been in such a rush to get Jimmy out of my head, I hadn't even *considered* bringing Shea. It was probably for the best. He was half *dark* elven and even Glabrielle might not take too kindly to his presence. I didn't want him getting hurt. Ever.

"It's like a half a mile to the pub, which is the clearing. The castle itself is only about another half a mile from there. Don't forget we took the *long* way the last time."

"Yeah, yeah. I remember, Miss Goatpuncher."

"I hope he's okay. I felt really bad."

"Mean old vampire."

Someone is coming.

Dar was focused on the edge of the woods straight ahead. Looking up, I had absolutely no chance of seeing anything that far away. "What is it?"

If I knew, I would have said what was coming.

"Do you hear it or smell it?"

Hear. Wind is behind us. Probably what alerted them to our presence. Your perfume is…

"What, Dar? My perfume is what?"

"Strong," Yuki said with a chuckle. Dar just nodded.

"I hate you people."

"No, you don't. You wuv us. Especially Blue Boy."

"Blue Boy?"

"Seriously? You want me to explain? Dar. He's blue and a boy."

"That's the best you could come up with? Blue Boy?"

"Not all of us are as witty and charming as you, Boss."

"Damn right."

Elves. Should we hide?

"Probably a little late now. Maybe they know a shortcut to the castle."

"Why didn't we use that key thingy the princess gave you?"

"Don't laugh, but I'm not sure how it works. I thought about it, but I didn't want to break it. I brought it with me, though," I said and pulled it out of my pocket. It was a key that would allow me to return to the castle whenever I wanted, but without Jaeren to show me how to use it...

"Oh. I'm going to laugh. Heartily."

"Shut up, Yuki."

Finally, the elves came into view, weaving out of the forest on blue hued horses and reforming into double ranks as they approached. They were being led by a single elven soldier in chrome-like armor. He was glinting brightly in the sunlight and I had to fight the urge to cover my eyes.

Everyone behind him, on the other hand, was dressed in forest colored greens and had a nocked arrow pointed at us. They split at the last moment and encircled us.

"Uh... Hi," I called out to the glinty guy.

"Who are you?"

"I'm Dot. This is Yuki," I said and pointed at my vampire. "That's Dar."

"How did you appear in this clearing? The gate is furlongs from here."

"Uh, magic."

"You are the Witch of Cedar Falls," he said, eyes wide and a crack in his voice.

An arrow let loose, aiming directly for me. Yuki plucked it from the air. "Want me to put it in the archer?"

"Not yet," I said without looking at her. My eyes never left the elf I was talking to. At least I didn't flinch. He, however, was staring in shock in the direction the arrow had come.

The elf that had fired was nocking another arrow to his string and pulling back on it, ready to fire again. "This is for my wife!"

He let go of the string again. This time I threw up a shield and let the arrow bounce harmlessly away. The captain, or whatever he was, shook his head slowly and motioned at the other archers surrounding us. Every bow that had been aimed at us turned to the elf with the itchy trigger finger.

"Stop!" The shout had come from me, surprisingly. The only reason I knew was because my throat hurt and a clap of thunder echoed back over us, resounding from all around us. At least they stopped. I didn't want another elven death on my conscience. "Leave him be. I'm only here to see your boss and then I'll be on my way."

They might not have filled him full of elven arrow holes, but they did relieve him of his bow. Thankfully. And put him in shackles.

The captain nodded as he slid off his horse. He walked over to us and gave us a small bow of acknowledgement. "My heartfelt apologies. His wife was lost during your *last* visit, Witch of Cedar Falls."

"It's just Dot."

He nodded and gave me a strange look. "You have business with the Council?"

"Yes."

"I shall take you to the castle."

"Then I'm grateful we ran into you."

"Archer, give up your horses."

"Um. Can I just ride behind you or something? Last time I was on a horse was never ago."

"You do not know how to ride?"

"Nope."

He chuckled and offered me a hand.

"I'll just run," Yuki said, Dar echoing in agreement.

128

∞ ∞ ∞

The Witch of Cedar Falls might have been a fancy title, but it didn't get us an immediate audience with the princess. Or even a trip to the throne room. Instead, we were shown to a suite of rooms and told to wait there until we were summoned.

"Hopefully the guy with the bow will be the only one with a grudge against you." Yuki sat down on a padded chair and huffed.

"Probably not. Lotta people got hurt last time."

"Including you."

"Yeah."

I started pacing, little left to keep me occupied while we waited. And waited. The soft knock on the door stopped me from breaking something out of frustration.

Before any of us could answer the door, it opened. Without sounding racist, elves were a little hard to tell apart. Not joking. They were all thin, very tall, and breathtakingly beautiful. Even the men, which were equally difficult to tell apart from the women. Except, they didn't wear dresses. As far as I knew.

Needless to say, I was surprised that I recognized the elf in our sitting room. He was one of Glabrielle's personal guards, one of the two who had been with her when she visited me in my prison cell.

"Hi."

He bowed. "Witch of Cedar Falls, would you please follow me? Her highness wishes to speak to you."

"Since that's why we're here, definitely."

He gave me a confused look, unsure of me. "Your pets may stay here."

Yuki snarled, not that I blamed her. It's not like she was wearing a leash or anything. Then I noticed her T-shirt. It had the word "pet" emblazoned across it in bright pink letters. I chuckled and she turned her anger to me. Without a word, I pointed at her shirt.

129

She huffed but relaxed. *Guess I should have worn something nicer to meet the princess.*

We'll get you a nice collar. Maybe a harness or something.

One muzzle joke and I'll bite your ankles.

You're getting kinkier by the day...

I left my vampire blushing in her seat and followed Guard Numero Uno out the door.

Master...be careful. Please, Dar sent a trailing thought after me.

Dorothea Careful Blackwell. It's my middle name.

Okay, Stumpy.

Ignoring him, I followed the guard, expecting him to lead us to the throne room. Instead, we went up the marble steps to the second level of the castle.

"Hey," I called out to the guard.

"Yes?"

"See that spot?" I pointed to the floor. "Got stabbed there once."

He just didn't get my humor. I could tell by the disgusted look on his face. "Interesting."

We walked down the hall and deeper toward the back of the castle. The king's quarters were easy to spot, since the entrance was gilded and gem encrusted. Apparently, the princess wasn't greedy enough to have taken over the royal suite, though. We turned right and meandered through a winding corridor that ended with a much more subdued entrance. It was silver.

Without knocking, the guard pulled the door open and ushered me in with a sweeping bow.

"Thanks."

The princess was standing by the door, waiting for me. For some unknown reason, she didn't look happy to see me. "Greetings, Princess."

"Witch of Cedar Falls... What brings you to our kingdom. My brother is not with you?"

"Sorry for the intrusion," I said and sighed. "No. He is the reason why I'm here."

She feared the worst and rushed forward, grasping my arm. Elves were strong and I might have winced. "He is...gone?"

"Hopefully not for long. He's not dead, he was abducted."

Elves were also scary looking when they were pissed.

"You let my brother be captured?"

"Uh. No. It happened while I was here, buried in garbage under your kitchen."

"Pray tell."

"Maybe we should sit..."

"My apologies, please." She motioned for the sitting chairs nestled into an alcove of the far wall. As soon as we sat, she poured tea.

I took a sip, even unsweetened it was drinkable. I wasn't the fan of tea that my mother and grandmother were. Coffee or death. But, it had a floral aroma and taste that wasn't bad at all.

"What happened?" She seemed impatient now that the niceties had been followed.

"While I was in Faerie, he took the rest of my companions back to the human realm, fully intending to come back and rescue me, but he was ambushed."

"Ambushed by whom?"

"The unseleighe sidhe."

She dropped her teacup. Tea and all. It splashed over her delicate ankles and she didn't even wince. "How?"

"Long story or short story?"

"Is my brother in immediate danger?"

"No. Delron assured me of that."

"Delron of the Court of Willowmere?"

"You know him?"

"Yes. He was the one surviving member of the betrothal party they sent to propose marriage."

"Huh. He left that part out."

"I am not surprised. They are as evil as they are untrustworthy. Why do you believe my brother is safe?"

"Because they want me to marry their prince. I sent back a message that I would destroy their world if anything bad happened to him."

"That was very…"

"Brave?"

"Stupid. They would most likely slit his throat in response."

"They didn't. They tried to kill Delron…"

"Truly?"

"Rift wight poison and everything."

Her eyes widened in response. I guess she had heard of the poison. "He survived?"

"Yeah."

"But how?"

"That's not important. He's healed and living in my living room until I can rescue Jaeren."

"That is why you are here."

"You guessed it."

"You wish for a contingent of elven warriors as a show of force."

"Beautiful and smart. You should definitely be queen."

"I am barely a regent."

I frowned at her. "Whatchu talkin' bout, Willis?"

"Pardon?"

"What do you mean, you are barely a regent?"

"Upon the untimely demise of my brother, the king, the nobles of the court quickly swooped in and set themselves up as a governing council until Jaeren can be named king. I am regent, but in name only."

"Fuck."

"Pardon?"

"Fornication under command of the king. Longer story. It means bad things."

"Apropos."

"Exactly. So, no helpy?"

"Are you asking if I can offer assistance?"

"Princess, you need to come spend some time with me in the human realm. We'll get this language barrier thing fixed in a few days."

"I did not realize there was a barrier. But anything would be preferable to being a prisoner in your own castle."

"I don't know about all that. Sometimes I wish someone would lock me up in my room."

"Let me know your feelings on the matter once it happens."

"Fair enough. Well, it was worth a shot. Guess I'll just have to rescue him by my own self."

"You would still rescue him?"

"Um, yeah. I just bought him a box of crayons and everything."

"You care for my brother." She didn't phrase it as a question, and I didn't like that.

"He's growing on me."

I didn't like the small smile that crept on her lips, either.

"Then my guards and I shall accompany you. I may not be able to summon an army for you, but we will help. He is not only the only hope for our people, but for me as well."

"Uh…"

"You do not wish for my help?"

"It's not that. But…you're a princess. Won't I get in trouble for busting you out of here?"

"The Witch of Cedar Falls? The council is more afraid of you than you could possibly imagine. Plus, I do not think it is possible for you to be in more trouble. You are a king slayer."

"They pissed?" I thought I had been doing them a favor.

"Court politics. While they might not be saddened by my brother's loss, killing him was still a crime. Luckily, Captain Javrett is…an old friend."

I chuckled, catching her meaning.

"Well, I only have one other question. What can you do?"

"Do?"

"Magic? Swords? Bow?"

"Yes."

"All of them?"

"Of course. I am a princess of the realm…and a dryad. Our magic is…formidable."

I wiggled my eyebrows at her. "Welcome to the party, Princess."

Chapter 12

She looked like she only weighed ninety pounds, but damn if she wasn't stronger than a fucking bull. I was barely keeping the princess from plunging the dagger into Delron's neck. What made it worse was it looked like he would have almost welcomed the release.

"Princess! He's on our side and we need his ass to get your brother back!"

That was enough to stay her hand. She went almost limp in my arms and we fell backward, my butt smacking the wood floor of my living room and her landing in my lap. I let out a puff of air to get her hair out of my mouth.

"May I wound him?"

"Maybe later," I said and pushed her up, letting her get to her feet before I even attempted to get up off the floor. When I finally did, I rubbed my butt.

"My apologies, Witch of Cedar Falls."

"It's Dot, Princess. Just Dot."

"Your name is Dot?"

"Guess we never got to that point, huh?" I nodded. "Yes. Dot. Short for Dorothea Blackwell."

"I see. Please address me as Glabrielle."

While I appreciated the sentiment, Princess was much less of a mouthful than her real name. "Thanks Glab...rielle." I tried to shorten her name, but she made a damn face until I finished it, nodding happily at the end. I swear, her and her brother were half puppy.

We were shocked into silence by Delron prostrating himself before the princess. We *both* looked down at him.

"Princess, you have my apologies."

"Get up, cur. I do not want or need your apologies. You have utterly destroyed our lives. I will only be satisfied when your head is on the end of a sword."

"As it should be."

"No elfi-pops in my living room, please. Plus, Delron promised to help us get your brother back. Right?"

He nodded from the floor, not daring to look up at the still angry princess. "I shall. You have my word."

"I do not trust him," Glab said to me, right in front of him.

"He has nowhere else to go. And I kind of saved his life."

"You healed him from the waste water?"

They seriously needed to come up with a better name for the poison. Waste water just made me want to giggle. "Yeah. Long story."

"You have many of those."

"Long stories?"

She nodded thoughtfully.

"Yep. Nothing boring about my life."

"So I see." She turned her attention back to Delron. "Get up, swine."

"Yes, Princess."

He slowly got to his feet and when he did, Glabrielle swung, planting a nice solid right to his jaw. Even I heard the crack. He went down like a stone and didn't move.

"Guess he deserved that," I said and nodded appreciatively.

"And so much more."

"Later. We'll come up with a game plan when he wakes up. Nice hook."

"My thanks."

Your lover is here. Dar interrupted our conversation.

Which one?

Chief.

I turned around and went to unlock the door, opening it to a startled Chief. "Hey, handsome."

"Evening, beautiful." He leaned in and gave me a quick kiss before I backed away to let him in. "Heard you're buying another house."

Luckily Josie and Candace were at the book store getting the café ready to open, otherwise my planned wedding gift would have been ruined. "Shh. That's a surprise. I should have mentioned that to Herb."

"It wasn't him."

"Marge?"

He nodded. "Yep. Do you have any plans this evening?"

"Well, we were going to make plans on infiltrating the unseleighe side of Faerie and rescuing an elf. So, a little busy."

"Ah. Okay. Was going to see if you wanted to have dinner with the mayor and me."

"The attractive, cute, well meaning public servant who asks about me a lot?"

"Yeah. That one."

"Never stage an infiltration on an empty stomach, I always say."

He chuckled. "Seriously, if you can't make it, not a big deal. We'll probably be talking shop, anyway. We have the Christmas parade this weekend and a few other things."

"So, even if I don't go, you're still planning on having dinner with her?" I swallowed the little green monster.

"Why do you sound angry?"

"I'm not."

"Uh… I didn't say you were. I said you *sounded* angry. It's just work, you know. I only have eyes for you."

It's not your eyes I'm worried about. "Pshah. I know that, silly. Nope. Not angry in the least. Seriously, though. I have time. I don't mind going." *Jet propelled, wild fucking horses with afterburners couldn't drag me away.* "Glabrielle," I called over my shoulder. "Make yourself at home. And don't kill the dark elf. I'll be back in a little while. Yuki, order pizza, please?"

"Sure thing, Boss."

"Let me grab my coat," I told Chief with a smile.

"Great," he said, sounding a little worried. He had that cute little crack in his voice and put his hands on his hips.

Even with calmly walking to the bedroom, hopping in the shower, and getting dressed, we were out the door in less than ten minutes. I wasn't even going to use makeup. I'd show the mayor I didn't need it. Except for a little mascara. Eyeliner. A little lipstick, foundation, and blush. But that was it. I did it in the car on the way to the restaurant. "Where are we going for dinner?"

"Lambresco's."

"The Italian place?" Fear gripped my stomach, twisted it, and just like that I wasn't hungry anymore.

"Yeah. Cedar Falls doesn't have a lot of restaurants. You were bound to end up there sooner or later."

"I was hoping for later."

"Did you not have fun?"

"Which part? Jimmy showing me off or blowing you in the bathroom?"

"Both."

"I did. But I'm still embarrassed."

"Don't be. That was the hottest thing I've ever seen."

That just caused me to blush harder. "Thanks," I mumbled.

"Don't worry. I promise to keep my hand out of your dress tonight. At least at dinner."

"I wouldn't go that far…"

He chuckled softly. "Don't worry. I'll be with you. The food is quite good, too."

"It is. Just not overly fond of Italian."

"Me neither." He nodded for emphasis.

"Try the chicken piccata," I suggested.

"I'm allergic to capers."

"Oh. Don't try it then."

We pulled into the somewhat crowded parking lot and Chief pulled into an empty spot about halfway from the entrance. "You ready?"

"As I'll ever be."

"Good. You'll like her. She's really nice and mostly down to earth."

"Mostly?"

"You'll see."

He opened the door and held it for me, always the gentleman...when he wasn't pissed off at me. I enjoyed the moment. "Thanks, Chiefy."

"You're welcome, Dotty."

"I take it back."

The smell of tomato sauce and garlic washed over us like a wet Italian blanket. I may not have been a fan of Italian food, but the place did smell amazing.

"Welcome back, Chief," a heavily accented voice called from behind the cashier stand.

"Hey, Maria."

"I see you have company this evening." Maria smiled and then recognized me from the last time I had been in the restaurant. Her smile faltered, but then came back. "Welcome back to you, too."

"Hi, Maria," I said embarrassedly.

"Just the two of you? Or will Mr. Jimmy be joining you."

"No. We're meeting the Mayor."

"Ah, yes. She is waiting for you." She grabbed a couple of menus and led us to the back of the dimly lit restaurant. I saw the back of a blonde head as Chief turned, but he blocked my view almost as quickly.

A strange feeling settled in the pit of my stomach. "Mayor Blake, the chief and his guest are here," Maria called out. Chief was still in the way, but I saw the smile on the corner of his mouth as he reached out and shook her hand. Then he stepped aside to introduce me...

My knees nearly gave out and all the moisture evaporated from my head as the mayor turned and stood to greet me. I'd met her before. Obviously, the townsfolk of Cedar Falls had thought it wise to elect a lawyer as their mayor. A lawyer who just happened to be the very pretty cousin of the other boyfriend who was currently pissed at me. Jimmy's cousin Sherry.

"You," she said as her hand and face fell simultaneously.

"Uh, hi. Nice to meet you. Again," I said bashfully and held out my hand. She took it, somewhat reluctantly.

"You know each other?" Chief shifted his glance back and forth.

"This is your girlfriend?" The mayor cocked an eyebrow.

"She's Jimmy's cousin," I answered as if that would explain everything. Knowing Jimmy, it should have been.

"What did you do?" He immediately shifted his stance, putting his hands on his hips and narrowing his eyes at me.

"I... I screwed up. Saw Jimmy having lunch with another woman and got insanely jealous. Kinda blew up his crotch."

"You what?"

At least the mayor started laughing. "I'll take those, Maria. Thanks." She reached out, grabbed the menus, and sat at the circular table big enough for six people. Chief shook his head, sighed, and sat down next to her.

I sat a seat apart and collapsed into the seat, already dreading the remainder of the evening.

"Can I get you something to drink?"

"Beer, please."

"Chianti," I said, remembering the name of the wine.

"I'll be right back."

"Hurry, please."

She gave a little laugh and headed to get our drinks. Chief didn't even pick up a menu before rounding on me. "You blew up his crotch?"

"Yeah. You know that pleasure spell I know?"

Chief's eyes went wide and he shook his head, almost imperceptibly glancing to his side to tell me to shut up in front of the mayor. "Um...what?"

"Did you miss the part where I said she's Jimmy's cousin?"

140

"I heard you."

"She knows what her cousin is, dingbat."

"Yeah. I do. I try to ignore it. Like Jimmy needed to be any weirder than he already was."

I looked over at her and gave her an appreciative nod. "Preaching to the choir."

"So, wait. You're a witch, too?" She turned her attention to Chief.

He sighed and reached for a beer that wasn't there yet. "Not as much as the one sitting next to me, but yes." He almost looked ashamed.

"Huh. Dennis I knew about, but I'm surprised you are. Your wife?"

"Yes. She was."

"So, that wasn't a car accident?"

Chief shook his head. Things went from awkward to high school with braces and acne.

"Sorry, Bill," she said apologetically and put her hand on his arm. I managed to resist the urge to pin it there with my butter knife. Go me.

"It's okay. Dot caught the killer. After two long years."

She looked up at me and I nodded. "It was the guy who burned in the car accident on Sycamore Street?"

"And his wife, whom he shot."

"Why did he shoot her?"

"She um…slept around."

"Jimmy," Sherry said and narrowed her eyes. She was very intuitive, our mayor.

"That's not important. Dot figured it all out."

"You helped," I added with a smile.

"Well, apparently there is much more to our newest resident than just a pretty face and blowing up people's pants."

I squirmed in my seat. Thankfully, Maria brought our drinks. "*Vino* for the lady, *birra* for the *signore*."

"Thanks, Maria."

"Ready to order?"

"Actually, give us a few minutes. I'm going to see if my cousin would like to join us," Sherry said with an evil grin, pulling her phone out from her purse on the chair next to her.

I nearly spit my wine. "Uh…yeah. He's still a little pissed at me."

"That's okay. I'll make him come."

"Already did that," I mumbled under my breath. Chief must have heard me. He stopped mid-sip, beer bottle still pressed to his lips, and turned to give me a not-so-happy look. I shrugged.

He shook his head and kept drinking. There might have even been an eye roll involved.

Her phone dinged in her hand and her evil grin went to wicked. "He's on his way."

"Did you tell him I was here?"

"Of course. Not."

Oh, this bitch.

"Sherry," Chief made her name a warning.

"Oh, relax, Bill. You know Jimmy."

"Yes. That's the problem. How did I not know you were his cousin? You're more alike than not."

"What do you mean?" Sherry and I asked simultaneously.

He set down his beer and held up his hands defensively. "Sense of humor! Jeez."

"Okay. I'll allow that," Sherry said with a nod.

I just let out a breath I hadn't realized I'd been holding. I thought he meant she was perverted, too. How the hell he would have known that, I would have taken great pleasure in torturing out of him. Snarl.

"So, how long have you known Bill?" I asked, using his real name and trying not to sound like a bitch.

"Since?" She looked at Chief. "I guess about five years? When I moved back to Cedar Falls to become a lawyer here. Can't be a lawyer without knowing the cops."

Fair enough. "What made you decide to be mayor?"

She sighed. "That is one of the few things you and I seem to have in common. We both want better things for the town."

"Oh." Her answer kind of shocked me. I thought it would have been money and power. Not that anyone ever comes right out and says they want money and power, but I could tell she was being honest.

"My turn. Why are you dating my cousin *and* my chief of police?"

If she could be honest, so could I. "Because I love them both."

Her eyes widened in surprise. She even looked at Chief for confirmation. He nodded.

Good boy. He gets a nookie.

"And you're okay with this?"

"Of course."

"Not to sound rude or anything…"

"Why?" I asked the question for her.

"Yes. Why? Don't you get jealous?"

Chief chuckled. "No. That's her job," he hooked a thumb in my direction. I blushed and shut up. He wasn't lying

"That much I knew." She gave me a dirty look.

"Don't be too hard on her," Chief started to say, but stopped. Jimmy had entered the restaurant.

He looked around for a moment and finally saw us, all of us, sitting in the darker corner in the back. His face lit up for a moment before being replaced by something else I couldn't quite read. I gave him a small, sad smile as he walked over, but he was mostly ignoring me.

"What's up, guys?" He sat on the other side of Sherry, one last empty seat beside us. I felt like a leper.

"Nothing," Sherry said, leaning over to give him a quick hug. "Was having dinner with Chief and his girlfriend. Thought I should have dinner with her other boyfriend."

Jimmy narrowed his eyes at his cousin. He looked about as happy as me. "Oh. Okay."

"Was that not okay?"

"It's fine," he answered. "Hey, Bill. Dot," he said and finally looked in my direction.

"Jimmy," I answered back before downing my wine. The whole glass.

"We were just talking about how it must be awkward for the two of you to be dating the same girl," Sherry said and stared at him, wanting to see his reaction.

"Awkward? What's awkward about it? You know I'm a little different."

"That I knew. Just surprised at Bill's involvement in your little game."

"*Signore* Jimmy! Good to see you!"

"Hey, Maria."

"*Birra?*"

"Please."

"More *vino*?" She looked at me.

"Two, please."

"Oh, boy," Chief said and shifted in his chair.

"Just don't want her making multiple trips."

"Uh huh."

"You okay?" Jimmy asked, actually looking concerned.

"Peachy."

"Are you all ready to order?"

"I'll have the chicken piccata," I answered, wanting a quick escape from dinner.

"Osso buco," Chief ordered.

"Lasagna for my cousin and spaghetti for me, please."

Awww. He knows what she eats. That's so cute.

"Be right back with another round of drinks." Maria smiled and left us alone.

"Back to our conversation, you really don't mind dating the same woman as Bill?"

"No. Not at all. Don't mind the other two either."

Unfortunately, Sherry had just picked up her wineglass. She dropped it, splashing what was left across the table. Thankfully, I was far away enough to avoid getting wined and dined. "Shit! Sorry! Did you say two others?"

Oh, boy. Thanks, Jimbo. I shot him a look that spoke volumes. He shook his head at me like that would console me. I felt a single tear roll down my cheek, trying to wipe it away before anybody noticed. It didn't work.

At least it was the side of my face not facing Chief. But Jimmy saw it. "Sher," he said and started mopping up the wine with his napkin. "You need to remember something that you keep forgetting. We're not human. Things are...different for us." He blurted it out, not knowing Chief had already been outed as a witch and not caring in the slightest. It was his cousin, so I'd let him speak his mind. I was interested in seeing where he was going with it, anyway.

"But, still."

"There is no buts. She's like our queen. We treat her as such and would do anything for her."

"Anything?"

"Yep."

She looked at Chief for confirmation. He nodded as well and tipped his beer in her direction in salute. She finally looked at me with an exasperated look on her face. "How the hell did you get so lucky?"

That wasn't the question I'd been expecting. "Just born that way." I twirled the last few drops of wine in my glass. Thankfully, Maria brought me more. I slid one to Chief and nodded at Sherry.

"I'll bring some more napkins! Your food will be out shortly, too," Maria chirped and left us alone again.

"You're clairvoyant, too?" She looked down at the second glass of wine I had ordered, and her shock was even greater.

"No. I just like wine. You got lucky."

That was enough to take the edge off the conversation. Sherry started laughing. "Well, if you all are okay with it, I'll shut up."

"Thanks, Cuz."

"Your mom know?"

"Oh, fuck no. She loves Dot. And my dad doesn't have multiple partners, so…"

"Ignorance is bliss?"

"Yep."

"I wish I was ignorant. I don't know how I'm going to sleep tonight."

"Why?" She had officially piqued my curiosity.

"You have four boyfriends. I can't even get one."

"That's cuz you're too stuffy," Jimmy said with a smile and a laugh.

"Well, ignorant might be blissful, but at least I know what's going on. I hate a good mystery."

"You shoulda been a cop instead of a lawyer," Chief said with a snicker.

"I'm not *that* stuffy."

Sherry was a decent human being. Chief had been right. I sat up in my chair a little, more comfortable with the situation…and the mayor.

Of course, the front of the restaurant exploded as the angel crashed through the plate glass windows lining the front of the restaurant.

Chapter 13

"Get her out of here!" I pointed at Sherry and looked at Jimmy. "Chief, you get the rest of the humans out."

"No way. I'm staying with you."

"Chief. Not asking. Get…the…humans…out. The angel is mine."

"That's an an-an-angel?" The mayor was losing it.

"Come on, Cuz. Backdoor."

"Everybody out!" Chief's voice echoed through the restaurant. The angel turned and focused on me, taking great strides across the restaurant, her head nearly scraping the acoustic ceiling tiles overhead. She had to be at least seven feet tall. Maybe Chief was right, running sounded like a better plan.

Fight positive with negative, daughter, the goddesses voice echoed in my head.

What the hell is she talking about? I hope she can't hear me. Luckily, she didn't answer. As the angel passed, the humans either ran out the hole she had made, or headed into the kitchen, hopefully to the back door.

"Go!" I hissed the command at the others. Chief ushered Jimmy and the mayor toward the kitchen, skirting around the very angry looking celestial being.

She snarled and reached for me. "Dorothea Blackwell, you will surrender your father's mantel!"

Huh?

Negative energy, daughter. Lightning…

Then everything clicked into place. Dar's lessons on the planes of existence made a little more sense. Angels lived in the upper realms, overflowing with positive energy. Lightning was electricity. It flowed from negative to positive, the negatively charged electrons leading the path...

"*Tintreach*!" I screamed the canting, thunder resonating from my voice and then again as every outlet, switch, and lighting fixture streamed an arc of pure unadulterated blue-white fury into me and out my outstretched hand. My aim was a little off, but when you're hurling lighting, correcting your aim doesn't take much. Just a shift of the fingers. Everything outside the restaurant went dark as I channeled everything the electrical grid had to offer. I wouldn't want to be on the receiving end of Lambresco's electric bill for the month. Hopefully I fried the meter.

The heavenly being screamed in hellish agony as the one-point-twenty-one jigawatts blasted its corporeal form into cosmic dust.

I looked around the broken, battered eatery and frowned. Lambresco's was going to need some remodeling. I sighed in relief and sat back down at the table, grabbing my wine and scooping out most of the dust that had settled over the surface. The glass was perched at my lips, the liquid flowing toward its final resting place as three more angels landed in the street outside the restaurant.

"Fuck." I sighed and downed the liquid courage before getting up and heading toward the front of the battle line. There was a flash of light, and the subtle sound of a phone making a camera shutter noise, but I had bigger things to worry about. Three of them. "I should have known that was too easy."

They were peering into the restaurant, making very un-angelic faces. I saw their teeth for the first time as they snarled. They were all conical in shape and freakishly long. Their mouths were something out of a horror movie.

"You ladies picked the wrong fucking town," I said and held out my arms. Both of them. "*Tintreach*!"

My voice boomed with power and *nothing* happened. Not a damn thing. No arcs of electricity. I didn't even get a static shock. Then I realized why... My last bolt had blown the mains. There wasn't any power to be found for an entire city block.

They looked at each other, back at me, and screeched in laughter. The closest one took a bold step forward and flashed a hideous smile. The nine-millimeter slug caught it right in the forehead.

"Ha! Take that!"

Blood that looked like mercury poured freely from the wound. Chief was standing behind me, I could feel his power and yet he reached for his firearm.

What a cop.

The angel with the brand-new, shiny third eye in its forehead shook itself in anger and smiled. The bullet slowly slid from the wound and dropped to the ground in front of it.

"Chief! Get out of here," I called over my shoulder.

"Not leaving you!"

Yuki skidded to a stop in front of me. "Hey, Boss."

"Good timing."

"Blue Boy is on his way."

"We might be running away from this one." I looked at the power lines overhead. No streetlamps were flickering back to life and they didn't look like they would be anytime soon. A couple of the transformers were even smoking, completely overloaded.

"Fire?"

I tried it, the angels just started walking through the flames, their bodies completely immune. *Think, Dot*, I chanted in my head. Negative energy. Electricity and death. They were the only two forces I could think of. Maybe Yuki could hurt them. Or Dar, if he ever showed up.

The angels were done playing, each one calling a celestial sword to their now outstretched hands. The one on my left went down in a snarling ball of hellish canine fury,

Dar tackling it in his hellhound form. It couldn't swing the blade, but it was pummeling him in the arm with the pommel, Dar whining with each blow and biting down on the creature's other arm. If he let go, she would skewer him like a corn dog. Chief started firing, full bore, popping round after round into the one on the right. Yuki dove at the one in the middle, slashing with claws and spunk, but not really doing any damage either. Things had officially gone to hell.

Deal death, Daughter. The voice in my head wasn't the Lady or the Lord, but it was masculine.

Father?

Later. Deal death to your foes.

How?

Close your eyes, feel your power. Power right at your fingertips. Power I bequeathed to you…

The gem. I reached up and grabbed it beneath my shirt. Next to it was a small pouch I had put Nana's broom into. I yanked on both, breaking the chain around my neck and wincing as the clasp dug into the flesh of my neck.

The gem I held in my left hand as I pulled the enchanted twig out of the leather bag with my right, whispering, "*Dúisigh.*"

Awaken it did. There was no slow growing, or sudden transition. With a *pop*, there was a witch's broom in my hand. Remembering Nana's battle with the demon, I shook it and focused my intent. Nana's scythe had been wicked looking, the one in my hand looked like it had come from Death's hand itself. Wickedly curved and gleaming blackly in the darkened streets.

The gem began pulsing in my hand. I opened my fingers and turned my head against the red glare emanating from it. "Woah."

The angels stopped fighting and stared at the light from my hand. Simultaneously, they strode forward, ignoring everything and everyone else around them. The one with a hellhound clamped on its arm started dragging Dar across the asphalt in a drive to get to what they wanted.

Take up my mantel, Daughter.

Look. I don't know what the hell fireplaces have to do with it, but...

I could hear his mental sigh. *Mantel. Not mantle. My quintessence. My power. Take my power...*

I now understood what the gem was. Every being was made from four separate and distinct elements. Essences. The fifth was power, magic, whatever. The gem was my father's fifth essence. His godhood. How?

Make it part of you.

Ew, I thought to myself. Hopefully, he couldn't hear me.

I brought the gem up to my face. There was no way in hell I could swallow it, not without a drink. I stared at it instead, trying to get some reaction from it, but nothing was happening, nor did it feel like it would anytime soon.

"Damn it!" In my anger, I crushed it in my fist, pissed off beyond measure.

Something inside me snapped and clicked into place. The world around me took on a reddish hue, even the hand I was still staring at in frustration. When I opened it, my palm was empty. The gem was gone.

You did it, Daughter.

The angels stopped moving turned to me in confusion. Shea stepped from the shadows beside me, staring at me in adoration and completely ignoring our predicament.

"Shea?"

"I felt it..."

"Felt what?"

"You. Stepping into the shadows..."

"Great. Little busy, can we talk about this later?"

He made no other movement, didn't even nod, just stared at me like I had grown an extra head. Ignoring it for now, I turned to face the three assholes with wings. Yuki and Dar had completely stopped fighting and were staring at me much the same way Shea was. The effect was very Children of the Cornish and more than a little creepy. I focused on the angels instead. "Sorry, fucknuggets. It's gone."

They began wailing in sorrow. At least, that's what it sounded like. I could almost feel a sense of overwhelming loss from them until it turned to anger and hatred. They came at me, all at once. With my other hand free, I gripped the scythe in both hands. The first one reached me a fraction-of-a-second before the others. Without thinking, I sidestepped and brought the curved blade down over its outstretched arms, reaching for where I had been standing just a moment before. It sliced through them cleanly. Instead of gushing with liquid silver, black smoke poured from the wounds like the exhaust of a diesel engine. The aura of anger shifted into the spectrum of pain. I could feel what they were feeling, and I hoped they could feel my satisfaction.

Even wounded, it lurched at me, jaws outstretched and evil looking teeth looking to steal the flesh from my bones. It was too close to hit with the blade, so I bashed it in the face with the ebony handle of the scythe. It fell to the ground, grinding the stumps of its arms against its face in agony as the other two grabbed me from either side.

The one on my left suddenly became engulfed in shadows. Waves of frustration poured from it as it was dragged to the ground and swallowed by the street beneath us. The other angel spared it a glance as its cries were suddenly silenced and it was gone in a puff of shadow smoke. I gave Shea a silent thank you. I'd *really* show him my gratitude later.

It was a good enough diversion for me to grab it by the neck with my left hand. My intention had been to hold it enough to pull the blade through its shoulder, but the creature began thrashing in my hand. It clawed my forearm, leaving angry gouges of wet flesh as my blood poured freely from the wounds. *Its* flesh began to smoke and decay beneath my hand.

"What the fuck?" I stared in horror as it stopped clawing at my arm and began rending the flesh from its own face and neck, trying to end its own suffering. I let go and stepped back from it as it fell to the ground at my feet.

I wasn't a fan of torture, and that's what she was going through. The black welts from my hands slowly spread across the thing's neck. More black smoke poured from the wounds until the angel shoved her own fingers into the soft flesh of her neck, pulling the wound open and sucking in a lungful of air in through the hole it had made. It gurgled as silvery blood washed into the open wound, too. I stared in horror until my conscience stepped up and brought the blade of the scythe down in an overhand arc, cleanly severing her head and exploding her into another cloud of dust, ending her agony.

Well done, Daughter.

Father? Father? Aodh?

"Father?" I chanted his name over and over, falling to my knees in the middle of the street in dismay. He never answered. That feeling of despair drove everything else away.

∞ ∞ ∞

I was sitting on my couch, a steaming mug of coffee in my hand, when I finally snapped back into reality. I blinked, noticed the coffee, took a sip and looked around. Everyone but the mayor was sitting around me, staring at me in hope and worry.

"What?"

"Are you in there?" Chief stepped forward.

"Yes. How did we get here?"

Everyone took a sigh of relief. Candace got up from her spot next to Josie, pushed Yuki out of the way, and threw her arms around me, refusing to let go.

"You gave us quite the scare," Jimmy said from the loveseat across the way.

"What happened?" I started rubbing Candace's back with one hand while she sobbed silently into my stomach, sipping coffee with the other.

"You kind of lost it after you killed the last celestial. You started sobbing and calling for your father, then you kind of...checked out. Pardon the expression."

"Sherry and Chief took charge of the situation. They had the fire department and ambulances at the diner faster than you could say Hassenpfeffer," Jimmy said and smiled at Chief. Obviously impressed. "They treated the injuries from all the glass exploding." He held up his hand when he saw the worry on my face. I nodded and he continued. "Nobody was seriously hurt at all, which is a miracle."

"Thank the goddess. But... All those people. How the hell are we going to explain a fucking angel? They're going to burn us all in the center square."

Chief chuckled. "First of all, it's a circle, not a square. Second of all, we don't have to. The mayor did."

"She did?"

He nodded. "Quite well, I might add." He paused to smile at Jimmy.

"She told everybody there was a gas leak and an electrical fire. Anything they might have thought they saw, was probably a hallucination from breathing in the gas and that everybody should thank their lucky stars they weren't hurt when the electrical fire ignited it. The electrical fire also caused the blackout and the explosion blew the front of Lambresco's to high heaven." Jimmy gave me a grin.

"We probably shouldn't use that expression anymore."

"Hmm. Good point. Anyway, she covered for us."

"Me."

"You, too."

"I like your cousin."

He gave me a wry chuckle. "No more exploding pants?"

"Technically it wasn't your pants that blew up..." Everybody was looking back and forth between Jimmy and me, not knowing the story. I was happy to leave it that way. "But, no. I'm an asshole for not trusting you. I'm sorry."

Chief started clapping. I shot *him* a dirty look until everybody else started joining in. I guess I might have sort of kind of deserved that a little. Just a little.

Jimmy got up and took my cooling coffee. "I'll get you some fresh." He leaned down and gave me a soft kiss that left me sitting there with my eyes closed, staring up at nothing and grinning like a fool.

When I finally came out of my happy place, I noticed Shea, Dar, and Yuki still staring at me. "Okay, now that all that is over, what the hell is up with you three?"

Of course, they all just turned and looked at each other, not saying a word.

"Spill it. You've been like this since the fight. Shea, you said I stepped into the shadows?"

He nodded, slowly and unsurely. "Yes. I was at home…and I felt you. You were in the shadows around me."

"What about you two? You were staring at me in the *exact* same way."

"You became darkness. You were the Night." Yuki put a strange inflection on the last word.

"Night?"

"The Night." She bowed her head, reverently. Witches worshipped the goddess. I'd heard my vampire mention the Night, but never asked her about it. I wasn't so sure I wanted to. That was a conversation better left when we were alone.

"What about you?" I looked at Dar. He was in his demon form wearing jeans and a T-shirt, calmly sitting next to Shea and staring at me thoughtfully.

"You felt like home."

"Here?"

He shook his head. "You felt like a cool night standing upon the plains of Gehenna, wind in my hair, stars above me, and the thrill of a hunt. You felt like my home."

I looked down at the fae blooded personification of sunshine in my lap. "What about you, Candace? I feel any different to you?"

155

She nodded, not lifting her head. "You smell different, too."

Dar tilted his head at her statement, and shifted into his Shepherd form, wiggling out of his clothes and walking over to me. He brought his nose to my arm and started sniffing.

I'd been so wrapped up in the feeling of home, I did not notice.

"Notice what?"

Your normal smell of sunlight... It's gone. You smell like the night.

"So, the darkness in my father's gem drove out the light?"

"It is not gone, merely overpowered by what she truly is," Candace said with an otherworldly voice. She lifted her head and smiled at me. "Welcome back, old friend."

"Old friend?"

She nodded and stood, eyes glowing gold. When she straightened herself up, she lifted from the ground, arms out to her sides. "You have taken what was your father's into you. You are so very much like him."

"Aodh?"

"One of his many names, yes."

"He's still imprisoned, isn't he?"

Candace nodded sadly.

"How is he texting me? How is he speaking to me? I heard him repeatedly last night, but then when everything was over, he was gone," I said, voice cracking and tears streaming down my face.

"As I have my familiars, elements, and worshipers, so does your father," she answered and cocked an eyebrow at me, daring me to make the connection I didn't want to.

"My father is a god? A friend of yours?"

Candace shrugged and the light faded from her eyes as she settled back to the earth. She had finally told me something about my father. Something I didn't want to know. Growing up had been hard enough knowing your mother and grandmother were the most powerful witches in town. To hear that your father was so much more was…

I got up from the couch and ran to the sink in the kitchen, emptying the miniscule amount that had been in my stomach.

"Holy fuck. Your dad is the Nightbringer," Yuki said with more than a little fear in her voice.

I spit the last of it into the sink, flipped on the faucet, and rinsed my mouth out. "What do you mean?" I managed to ask through watering eyes.

"The Bringer of Night, god of the underworld," Yuki spoke reverently.

Shea nodded. "Aodh the Shadowless."

Dar shifted back into his demon form, ignoring the clothing behind him and stared. "Aodh, master of Fáil Inis. A hound-welp said to be the father of the hell hounds and barghest. No wonder you smell of home."

"Why are you all still standing? Why haven't you passed out from telling me all of this?"

Dar stepped forward and bowed his head. "Because you have taken up his mantel. It is of you we speak…"

All I could do was stare in shock at the three of them. If I'd had *anything* left in my stomach, I'm sure I would have brought the last of it up.

"No. I'm just Dot. My father can't be a god. I'm not special. I'm kind of stupid. I make mistakes all the time. I hurt the people I love. I'm a jealous, sarcastic, fuck up. I'm just a witch and not a very good one at that!"

Yuki, Shea, and Dar, Chief, Jimmy, and Josie all just stared at me incredulously. Candace was the only one who could move. She crossed the room and walked behind the kitchen counter. I dropped to my knees, expecting and needing another hug. Candace thought I needed a crack across the cheek. You could hear the slap echo off the walls of my kitchen.

"Ow." I brought my hand up to my cheek.

"No!"

"No?" This conversation was seeming very familiar. I'd had it with more than one member of my coven, but it was the first time anybody had ever turned the tides on me.

"No. You do not get to say these things about yourself. Nobody is perfect. Not even the gods."

"But I'm only half."

"And half witch. But, you're *totally* amazing. Sorry for slapping you."

"Meh. I needed it. Don't do it again," I said seriously and cocked my eyebrow at her, not really meaning it. Next time I was being a fool, I hoped she used a two-by-four.

"I am sorry!"

"Teasing, Candace."

She blushed and gave me the hug I wanted to begin with.

Chapter 14

"So, what's the plan?" Chief took a swig of his beer.

"Tomorrow morning, I'm going to rescue Jaeren and deal with the dark elves. After that, who knows. Maybe the angels are done with me now that the gem is gone." I sounded a little too hopeful.

"Who's going with you?"

I could tell from his voice that he wanted to go, but I needed him here. "Myself, Delron, Glabrielle and her guards. Shea and my familiars."

"You don't want me to go?"

"It's not that I don't want you to, Chief. It's that you can't. You're the anchor for the coven. Where I tread, you cannot follow. That way if something happens to me, you can keep everything together until somebody better than me wanders into town."

He scoffed like a good boy. "Fine. But there are two things wrong with your plan. First, there is nobody better than you. Second, you can't die."

"Um. Pretty sure I can. Not even full gods are *truly* immortal."

"That's not what I meant." He stepped forward and wrapped his arms around me. "I mean you *can't* die. It would absolutely destroy me."

"Oh." Tears slowly slid from my closed eyes as I turned my head and pressed my face against his chest.

"Not just me, Dot. It would kill everybody if we ever lost you. So be careful. Please. For all of us, not just me. But mostly me."

"I will. Promise not to purposely blow parts off, either."

"Thank you." He pulled away before I could get snot all over him. "I'm going to get going. I have work in the morning, and *you* have a houseful. Have dinner with me when you get back? Just the two of us this time. No angels, either."

"That sounds gloriously wonderful."

"Yes, it does. Get some rest," he said, leaning in to kiss me. Tears, snot, and all. "Love you."

"Love you more."

"Yeah. Don't think that's possible."

"Sure, it is. Close your eyes and think about how very much you love me. Now picture just a little bit more."

"You're a snot," he said with a chuckle, giving me one last kiss, and heading for the door.

"I'm going to head home, too." Jimmy caught my lips as I turned around.

"Aw. I thought you were going to stay?" At least, I was hoping he was. Chief was more of a one on one kind of guy. Jimmy didn't care who was around.

"I have to give my deposition in the morning. Sherry is filing a grievance with the court tomorrow."

"Ah. That makes sense. Tell her I said hi. And that I'm sorry…"

"For the angel attack? She knows you are."

"I meant everything. She's really cool, but I should have known she was if she shares DNA with you."

"Well, good luck in Faerie. Let me know when you get back and I'll share some DNA with you, too," he said and wiggled his eyebrows.

I couldn't help it, I busted out laughing. He was such a smooth talker. "Deal."

"Night, Dot."

"Night, Jimmy." He gave me a kiss that wasn't subtle, wasn't soft, and I *totally* didn't want to let him leave. "Woah."

"Yeah. I ever mention how totally kissable you are?"

"Nothing compared to you," I said and dove in again.

He pulled back with a soft, throaty chuckle. "Yeah. Yeah. Keep that up and I'm going to miss my court appearance."

I sighed. That had been my plan... I wouldn't have minded if he weren't a fireman anymore. If he never got horribly hurt again at work, I would be a happy little Dot. "Fine. Make me dinner when I get back."

He got an evil little grin on his face and leaned in closer. "Oh, I will. Then you can spend the night," he whispered in my ear before giving it a little lick. "I didn't get a chance to tell you," he continued whispering. "Dennis and Alista broke up..."

"What? Why?" I wanted to feel bad, but the shiver that ran down my spine spoke my true feelings on the matter.

"Just weren't made for each other, I guess," he answered with a chuckle.

"He okay?" This time I pulled back and asked with genuine concern.

"Yeah. Just don't think he ever got back into the relationship the way she wanted him to. That and she spent more time with her brother than him. It got old, he said."

"Understandable. Give him a hug for me. No tongue," I added with a grin.

For the first time in our relationship, Jimmy blushed. "Yes!"

He looked around to see if anyone was paying attention. They were. "Fine. You win this round, Moriarty. But the game is afoot."

"See ya later, Holmes." I chuckled and pushed him in the direction Chief had gone, watching him as he slipped out the door. I sighed when it clicked, thankful he had forgiven me for not trusting him. Jimmy was a part of my life I didn't want to live without. Ever. We were too compatible, which was rare for people who were so much alike. It was usually the opposites that attracted. Like Chief and me.

Heading back toward the living room, I stopped at the kitchen to get a glass of wine, completely forgetting that Josie's mom polished it off in a fit of Josie's mom-ishness. "Damn it."

"What is it, Lady?" Candace practically ran over.

"Nothing. I forgot we're out of wine and I never made it to the liquor store."

"Would you like me to get you some?"

"Nah. That's okay, Candace. Thank you, though. I'll just have a beer."

"I will get you some," Shea said from the couch and before I could stop him, he literally disappeared through the shadow in the corner.

"Uh… It wasn't that important," I said to the empty air. Candace just chuckled beside me.

I turned toward her. "Delron still in his room?"

She nodded and suppressed a strange look from her face. I guess she didn't care much for the dark elf. Not that I blamed her.

"And Glabrielle and her guards?"

"They are visiting the elf at the pub. They said they would be back by morning."

"Good. We'll head out when they do. I'll leave you in charge of the house. Not that I don't trust Josie."

"You just wish to have a home to return to," she said with a chuckle.

"I can hear you both, you know," Josie called from the couch. She and Dar were watching a documentary on industrial kitchen appliances. "I could make some killer coffee drinks with that."

A moment later, Shea came back through with an arm full of bottles. Three to be exact, Shea's arms weren't that big. "Here you are," he said and walked over, setting them gently on the counter in front of me.

"Thank you, Shea."

"My pleasure."

"Want a glass?"

"Please."

162

"Which one?"

"I shall leave the choice to you."

"Oh, hell no. You pick. I buy the cheap crap."

He chuckled and looked at me, half closing one eye. "You are feeling contented at the moment, the immediate danger having passed and reconciling with James. We are travelling tomorrow, so nothing too heavy... This one," he said and grabbed the middle bottle, knife appearing in his hand and deftly cutting off the waxed seal over the top. No twisty-tops for Shea.

"You guys want wine?" I called into the livingroom.

"Shit, Dar. I forgot. Hit pause," Josie said and got up off the couch, heading for the kitchen. "No thanks. I promised Dar I would make him a margarita. He's never had one."

"Where's Yuki?" I didn't ask anybody in particular.

"Shower," Josie answered absentmindedly, but apparently not absentmindedly enough not to keep tabs on where my vampire was. Not that she didn't trust her, but Candace was in the house. So, she didn't trust her.

Yuki, want some wine?

Please. I'll be out in a minute. Thank you, Lady.

What happened to boss?

I sighed when she didn't answer. "Pour a glass for Yuki, too. Please."

"Yes, Lady."

"Okay, that's it. *Everybody* listen up. Dot. My fucking name is Dot. No more of the, Lady bullshit! Everybody understand?"

"Yes, Lady," Josie said with a giggle and started the blender.

I growled, took my glass from Shea, and went and plopped my ass down on the couch next to Dar. I stared at him and narrowed my eyes.

"Hi, Dot."

"Good boy," I said and ran my fingers through his hair, scratching behind his ear. He turned his head and narrowed *his* eyes.

"Really?"

"Sorry. Couldn't resist."

"I understand the temptation, my Lady."

I huffed, but I guess I kind of deserved that one. Taking a sip of wine, I gave a little groan of pleasure. It wasn't as good as the blackberry, but it wasn't overly sweet or dry. Perfect. "This is good," I told Shea as he sat down next to me, leaving the love seat for Josie and Candace.

Josie handed Dar his margarita and sat down. Candace plopped down between Dar and I, squishing me up against Shea. Judging from his smile, he didn't mind too much.

"So, tell me what you know about my dad, now that you can."

"I knew the name from my research into my tattoos, thinking they might be connected to my shadow walking ability. They're not," he added. "Shadow walkers, themselves, are just another subspecies of fae."

"How many are there?"

"Shadow walkers or types of fae?"

"Both."

"I do not know the answer to either. Everyone seems to have heard of shadow walkers, but I have never met another in my three hundred years."

"Me, neither."

He nodded, not seeming to care. "As for fae, that number is probably innumerable, having branched off from the daoine sidhe before the schism."

"Into the light and dark courts?"

"Yes. The shadow walkers and dark courts were said to be sired by Aodh. As well as vampires, demons, and the shadows themselves. He was a prince of the daoine sidhe, and one of the sons of Lir, who was high king of the Tuatha de Dannan."

"Okay. I'll pretend I know what you're talking about."

"Sidhe legend. Irish folklore and mythos. The Tuatha de Dannan is literally the tribe of the gods. Your father is the son of the high king. *If* he is the father of demons, shadows, and vampires, it would explain your ties to myself and your familiars. And why the dark elves wish you to join them, no matter the cost. And though he is a god of the underworld, he is still daoine sidhe and probably why even Candace is drawn to you and why you can draw upon the power of Faerie," he said with a sigh.

"Daddy got around, huh?"

Shea nodded embarrassedly.

"Why do they call him the shadowless?"

"It is said that he used his own shadow to create the shadow realms."

"There's more than one?"

"There is the Land of Shadow, which is directly connected to this world. That is the one I use to travel, the one you've been to."

"And the others?"

"There are many, most of them horridly dangerous. The one directly below the Land of Shadow is Umbra. That is the realm I call the shadows from to do my bidding. They themselves are alive and sentient."

"But they obey you?"

"Yes. I thought *that* might have something to do with my tattoos, but as I have never met another shadow walker, I have not had the opportunity to find out."

Yuki had gotten out of the shower and grabbed her wine off the counter, sitting next to Josie, the only other open seat. Josie leaned away a little and Candace snickered. I was about to say something, but Candace touched my leg. "It is good for them," she whispered, so I let it go.

Trusting her, I turned back to Shea. "So, if he is a sidhe and a Twat de Dannon, how come I don't have pointed ears?"

Shea nearly choked on his wine. "Tuatha de Danann."

"Yeah. That."

"Because they did not have elven features. The daoine sidhe were eons before humans walked the mortal realms, but from the descriptions I have read, they resembled them more than the light and dark courts who were direct descendants. Just incredibly tall."

"Giants?"

"Yes. Giants that gave birth to other races of giants. Fomorians for example, who fought against the daoine sidhe quite often."

"Okay. This is hurting my head."

"Everything has to come from something. Even myths and gods."

"But it's not every day you find out it was all true."

"Very true," he answered and took another sip of wine.

I looked over Candace at Dar, he was happily sucking on his margarita and listening to our conversation. "And what do you know about him?"

"What I told you. He was king of the underworld and traveled the realms freely. Especially the lower ones. One of our major cities is named for him. He was said to be our creator and his hound the father of others."

"Yuki?"

She stopped swirling her wine and looked up at me, giving me a little shrug. "All I know is his name. I've heard it from my father. But it is the Night that all vampires invoke, and he is the name of that dark night, the creator of the vampire race. If you *really* want to know more, I suggest you call my father, just do not explain your reason."

"Why?"

"Do you wish all the vampires of the world to know that their deity had a daughter, she inherited his power and walks the streets? This place would turn into a blood sucking mecca before you could say Vlad the Impaler."

"Good point. I'll just live in ignorance. Sounds safer. And blissfully blissful."

Yuki nodded in agreement.

In fact, I'd already opted for bliss on everything to do with him. I was going to try my damnedest to try to be normal, witchy, plain Dot. It felt safer and happier with a much slimmer chance of ending up in a straitjacket and padded room.

"That's enough of that. I don't feel any different, so I'm just going to pretend it never happened."

"I do not think the gods themselves will let you do that, Master. But I wish you the best of luck." Dar took another sip of margarita, draining the last of it from the glass Josie had bought especially for them. They even had little green glass cacti hanging from the edge.

"Go slow on those. They have a kick," I warned him. He just gave me a smile.

"They are quite delicious. My thanks, Josie." He bowed his head in her direction.

"Want another?"

"Please." He stood, but she motioned him to sit. "I'll get it," she said and took his glass, draining hers on the way to the kitchen.

"Somebody's getting lucky tonight," I said and elbowed Candace, knowing the effect margaritas had on Josie. Flashbacks of The Cure concert we went to skittered through my brain.

"Dar *is* staring at you. I think you may be right," Candace said with a grin.

I turned and looked, and sure enough he was giving me a goofy grin. "Make his a half," I shouted over my shoulder.

"Don't be a spoil sport," Josie said and poured more tequila in the blender.

"Oh, boy."

Chapter 15

Dar might have been a little tipsy, but he held his own better than Josie had. He tripped only once carrying her passed out ass to bed. He practically dropped her on the mattress and Candace pulled the cover over her.

"Sorry, Candace. Guess you're not getting lucky tonight."

She shrugged. "It is just as well. She is not as tender when she is inebriated, anyway. I prefer when she is soft and gentle."

"Well, okay then. Night, sweetie," I said and kissed her on top of her head. "Come on, Dar."

"Yes, Master."

I let him go first, watching him as he walked and appreciating the way his ass rippled in his jeans. He started leaning and I reached out a hand to steady him. "Easy there, tiger."

"Yes, Master."

"Feelin' okay?"

"Ne'er better."

I chuckled. We got out of the hallway and he turned toward the couches. "Nope. Keep going straight. We're putting you to bed, too. Shea, give us a hand?"

"If you wish," he said and set his wineglass down, getting up from the couch and following us.

I was steadying Dar from behind, but Shea slipped under his arm and let him support his weight on his shoulder. "Thank you," Dar said with another goofy grin. With the blue skin, horns, and elongated canine teeth, you would think it would be a horrifying sight, but it wasn't. He was fucking adorable. But, then again, he was adorable most of the time.

"Could I use the restroom first?"

"Uh, Shea. That's all you."

He nodded and led him into my bathroom but didn't close the door. Dar was perfectly capable of using the restroom and Shea just stood behind him to keep him swaying on his feet, for which I was eternally grateful. However, I was a *little* disappointed, hoping for at least a picture of Shea undoing Dar's jeans…

Or aiming.

Shea caught me staring with a happy little smile on my face. He cocked an eyebrow at me, and I wiggled mine at him. "We should probably get you out of these jeans while you're standing up," he said without taking his eyes from me.

"You are pretty smart. That is a splendid idea." Dar was still looking down at the toilet, while nodding in agreement.

Shea let go of Dar's hips and reached around the front, feeling around for his belt. How he had known Dar had just unzipped and whipped it out was beyond me. Must have been a guy thing.

"I can unbuckle my pants if you want."

"It is okay, I do not mind." He whispered something else to Dar, but I couldn't quite catch it. Damn it.

Dar smiled and tilted his head up and then back, letting Shea fumble with the clasp of his belt. He finally pulled the ends apart and deftly unbuttoned the jean before sliding his hands across Dar's stomach and back to his hips. Slipping his hands in, he began to work the jeans over Dar's well-rounded ass and slender hips.

Dropping his hands to his side, Dar let Shea drop his jeans down to his knees. I had a glorious, unobstructed view of Dar's manhood, still soft from relieving himself. I remained very still, not wanting to interrupt the moment and very much wanting to see where it would go.

"Did you shake?" Shea asked.

"Shake?"

"Like this." He slid his hand over Dar's naked hip under his shirt and didn't stop until his fingers parted around the shaft. Slipping his fingers down the length, which seemed to be rapidly growing, he gave it a gentle wiggle over the bowl.

Holy fuck.

I was completely mesmerized. Especially when he started gently stroking Dar's cock. "Does that feel good?"

"Yes."

"Do you wish me to stop?"

"No." Dar let out a little groan and spread his legs apart a little more.

"Take your shirt off."

Dar did as he was told, grabbing the bottom of his shirt and practically ripping it over his head and dropping it to the floor. Shea turned his head and put his face against Dar's back, giving me a wicked grin before his tongue darted out and caressed the flesh by his spine. I swear Dar's cock got even bigger.

"I am going to fall over."

"You are that drunk?"

"No. My head seems to have cleared, but this feels too good."

"Would you like to move to the bed?"

"Yes."

Shea let go of him and knelt. "Step out of your pants," he said and held them down against the floor.

Pulling his legs out, one at a time, Dar turned around and Shea never moved, smiling at the eye-level erection before him. Without a word, he leaned in and gently kissed the tip.

I felt something soft, wet, and hot against my fingers. Only then did I realize I'd shoved my hand down the front of my leggings without thinking about it. Shuddering as they slid from side to side, I watched in rapture as Dar shyly smiled down at the shadow walker at his feet

Shea stood slowly, and when he was close enough, leaned up and softly ran his lips over Dar's while he caressed his thigh and cupped him in his hand. Dar pushed his hips forward, sliding his manhood through Shea's hand as he opened his mouth into the kiss.

I mewled as I shuddered, the kiss and the caress pushing me over the edge as quivering spasms ran from the wetness at my fingers up my spine.

They broke apart and turned their heads, smiling in unison as they realized what I had done. Guiltily, I blushed and sat down on the bed.

"Shall we join the Master?" Shea looked up at Dar.

"If she wishes…"

I nodded. Lord and Lady, did I nod.

They walked out of the bathroom and Dar immediately used his body to push me back across the mattress, his lips finding mine as my hands cupped his face. He tasted like cinnamon, the same as he smelled. Groaning into the kiss, I felt his hardness pressing against me, only the thin layer of my leggings keeping him from slipping inside me.

We looked over as Shea's weight settled on the bed. He had already disrobed and was simply stroking himself as he watched us kiss.

I looked at Dar and he had a hungry look in his eye as he watched the show. "He's beautiful, isn't he?"

He spared me a brief glance and nodded.

"So are you. Lie on your back."

He didn't need to be told twice, wanting to see what I had in mind. I stood, pulled off my leggings, and then lifted my sweater over my head, throwing it across the room. I'd been dying to try this since I had first pictured making love to Dar in my mind.

Throwing my leg over him, I straddled his chest. He completely forgot about Shea as I opened up in front of him. "Oh, Lady."

"Don't talk with your mouth full," I said with a smile and scooted forward until I was pressing myself fully against his lips. His hands immediately and unnecessarily pulled me in tighter as his tongue parted my folds, diving in and tasting the wetness freely flowing from me. He moaned against my flesh, sending gentle vibrations that seized my chest and forced the air from them.

Reaching down, I slid my hands over his horns like I was riding a motorcycle and held on for the ride. Shea moved around to the other side of the bed and got back on his knees, holding his throbbing cock in his hand and offering it to me. Without letting go of my handlebars, I leaned in and sucked him into my mouth.

I moved as much as I could without pulling myself from Dar's mouth. There was no place else I'd rather be. He was gentle, probably not wanting to hurt me on his sharper than normal teeth, but ravaging me with his very articulate tongue. I gasped around Shea's cock as he touched me in places that couldn't be reached with a human tongue.

I let go of one of his horns and grasped Shea, pulling him from my mouth and stroking him while I rode my familiar's face. "Oh…"

Shea leaned down and slid his hands gently over my breasts, slipping my nipples between his fingers and giving a gentle squeeze. "Is he going to make you come?"

I nodded, barely able to do that as my eyes closed against the pleasure.

"Turn around, he will be able to go deeper."

Again, just a nod as I straightened up and pulled away from Dar.

"Are you okay?"

"She is fine, just let her reposition herself," Shea said. He reached down, gently wiping some of my wetness from Dar's lips and bringing his finger to his mouth. "Such sweetness."

"I tasted the honey that Candace keeps in the cupboard for tea. They are much the same."

Shea nodded in agreement.

I blushed as I turned around, repositioning myself over Dar's face and lowering myself once again. Shea wrapped

173

his arms around me and gave my breasts a gentle grasp as he kissed my neck.

"Oh, Shea," I whispered at the intimacy of the embrace. Then Dar's tongue snaked up inside me again. Shea had been completely correct. The angle was much better, but I missed being able to hold his horns while he worked.

"Look at him," Shea whispered in my ear. "See him throbbing? He looks like he is about to explode, just from tasting you."

I opened my eyes and looked down. He was right. Dar's cock was practically rocking as his muscles contracted on their own.

"Can you reach it?"

I reached down and ran my fingers over it. His skin might have been blue, but the texture was soft and smooth. The head appeared to be a little larger than normal, now that it was freed from its foreskin sheath, but it was quite beautiful.

"Do you wish to stroke it, or do you want to watch me do it?"

"You," I managed to get the word out. I wanted to see him do more than stroke it, but I couldn't tell him with words.

He let go of me and walked around the bed while I rode Dar's talented tongue. I felt the beginnings of another orgasm, but I fought against it, wanting to stay right where I was. Looking at Shea spreading Dar's legs and kneeling on the ground in front of him wasn't making it any easier.

He put his arms over Dar's legs and wrapped his fingers around the base before sliding them up and over the tip. Fluid began dripping freely from the tip and Shea smiled as he pinched some of it between his fingers and rubbed them together. Steadily, he reached out and offered me a taste.

Curiously, I opened my mouth and his finger gently grazed my tongue. Normally, I wasn't a fan of the flavor, but the situation pushed away my inhibitions. The taste was different from that of a normal human, much sweeter without the salty aftertaste. I wanted more.

Shea chuckled as he saw my surprise and lowered his face to Dar's cock, pulling him into his mouth. Dar started breathing heavily beneath me at the sensation and promise of release. I rode Dar and Shea used his mouth and hand to milk the blue demon. Dar didn't stand a chance against the two of us and bucked his hips as he unloaded into the mouth of my shadow walker.

I couldn't hold back any more. Between the tongue inside me and the heat of the scene in front of me, I let go. Before it hit me, Shea stood and leaned forward, his lips meeting mine as he shared his treasure.

Our tongues danced as he coated mine in sweetness and I let the building orgasm wash over me like a tidal wave of pleasure. I groaned and moaned into that sweet kiss and pulled Shea into my arms, holding him tightly as he awkwardly straddled Dar beneath us.

After it started to pass, only then did I loosen my grip as I slowly sat down on Dar's lap. I lifted myself up, letting Dar free. He lay there with a dreamy look and a happy smile.

"Woah," I said. His face was *very* wet…

"You flooded me when you came," he answered with an even bigger smile.

"Your fault."

"I accept full responsibility. Would you care to try again?"

"Yeah. I'm going to need a minute before anybody touches me there," I said with a chuckle and complete honesty. I was still quivering in my proverbial boots.

"Well, I do not," Shea said and reached behind him, stroking Dar.

"What are you going to do?" I asked curiously.

"I wish to feel him inside me."

My quivers became quakes. "You're going to…?"

"You shall see. He is already hard again. Could I ask you to make him wet?"

175

I nodded and practically jumped from the bed. I knelt down and took Dar in my mouth, letting the saliva practically fall from my mouth as I bobbed my head. Dar hissed in pleasure and I felt him swell even further.

Shea looked over his shoulder and grinned. "Might I suggest something else? The lubrication would be more natural."

He didn't have to ask me twice. I stood, not caring how sensitive I might still be and pushed Dar's legs together. Straddling him behind Shea, I braced myself on my dark elf's shoulder as I reached down to guide him inside me.

The thicker head made it a little slower and I found myself having to work it in and out to get it fully inside me. Once he was there, I sat and cooed at how perfect he felt inside me.

Shea leaned back against me and I reached in front of him to play with him, but Dar's hands were already around him, stroking him softly. Instead I ran my fingers gently over Shea's stomach and chest as my lips traced soft kisses across his shoulder to his neck, his tattoos lighting up. Goddess, he was so damn beautiful. His quiet moan sent a shock of need through me and a feeling of something… possessive. *My elf.*

We played like that for a few minutes when Shea asked, "Is he ready?"

"Yes," I whispered. "Do you want him?"

Shea nodded, his breathing unsteady as Dar's hands worked their magic. I rose and almost whimpered as Dar pulled free from me, leaving me feeling empty. Shea leaned forward and scooted back a little, letting me guide Dar to his ass.

"Are you sure about this?"

Shea just nodded and slowly pushed back. Dozens of Shea's memories fluttered through my brain. Things I had missed when I brought him into the coven and relived his life in a matter of moments. Three hundred years was a lot of information to process in the span of a few minutes.

Shea was no stranger to another man's body. Or, I should say, men had been no stranger to Shea's body...

I watched in rapt fascination as the tip of Dar began to push Shea open, the ring encircling the head as Shea stopped for a moment to get used to the sensation. He was practically laying on Dar's chest with a little smile on his face. Dar wrapped him in his arms and held him until he was ready to continue. It was the most adorable thing I had ever seen. My heart was literally melting and then Shea leaned in for a very soft and very sweet kiss. My melting heart exploded in a shower of fireworks.

It began with subtle movements as Shea began to rock against him. Each time, a little more slipped inside the very content looking fae. By the time no more could go in, I had two fingers buried inside myself and was rapidly moving them, getting closer to coming again.

"That is so hot," I muttered as I watched the two of them until Shea lifted himself up, blocking my view of Dar. He turned and smiled at me as he began rocking his hips, just like a woman would if she were riding Dar.

Fingers still inside me, I used my other hand to crawl along the bed to face them. Shea's cock stood out in front of him, proud and hard, each movement inside of him causing his cock to flop forward against Dar's taught stomach muscles. On hands and knees, I continued fingering while they enjoyed themselves.

"Does that feel good?" I asked the two of them.

"Exquisite," Dar answered first, reaching over and letting his finger trace my nipple.

"I see why you like this position."

"Well, it's a little different from what I normally do, but still hot as fuck to watch."

"It has been a while," Shea said shyly.

"I know you. Been inside your head before, remember?"

He nodded. "I am going to come soon."

That kind of surprised me. "You're going to come? From having him inside you?"

"Yes. It feels incredible. You should try it."

"Maybe. Sometime. There's other places I enjoy it, though." I pulled my fingers out and stood on the bed, using my hand on the ceiling to steady myself as I stepped over Dar. Shea looked at me curiously as I squatted and sat on Dar facing him. I looked over my shoulder at Dar. "I'm not hurting you, am I?"

He just shook his head, the smile never leaving his face. I turned my head back and reached down, grabbing Shea's cock and scooting forward. Putting my legs and feet over his, I guided him into me as I slid the rest of the way, impaling myself on him.

"I want you to come inside me."

"That I can do," he said and began fucking Dar and me simultaneously.

We only held out for a minute or two. It became too much, and we were too close already. Dar grunted beneath us which started the chain reaction. I came before Shea, somehow. Already leaning back on my hands, I let my head fall back as I screamed in ecstasy, a deep guttural sound that ended on high pitched waves. I felt Shea inside me as his cock started pulsing and then a super wet feeling as it dripped from me.

He and I both rolled to our sides, gasping for breath on the mattress and smiling at each other in utter contentment. One thing was for certain, we all needed a shower.

"Please tell me you're fucking done," came a quivering shout from the other room. It was the first time I'd ever heard Yuki sound exhausted.

Chapter 16

"This is an abandoned warehouse," I said after I finished sneezing. Dust and tarps literally covered everything. You could see the dust in the air, swirling where the sunlight filtered through the broken glass windows at the top of the walls around us.

"You are correct." Delron stepped in front of me, heading toward the darkened corner on the far side of the warehouse.

"Did you expect the entrance into the dark side to be at the mall?" Yuki walked around me with a chuckle.

"Seriously? Hot Topic *never* crossed your mind?"

"Fair enough."

What is a hot topic?

I looked down at Dar in his Shepherd form. "See the clothes that Yuki wears?"

Yes?

"It's where you buy those."

She didn't find them?

He must have been broadcasting to the both of us. She turned around and flipped him off. My laughter echoed off the concrete walls around us. Everyone gave me a chastising look. "Sorry," I whispered.

Delron was waiting for us by a stairwell leading down. The rusted iron railing looked more dangerous than an actual safety measure. I looked over the edge, and thankfully it was only one flight leading down to the basement. I frowned in frustration, the sunlight filtering through the windows was enough to keep my vampiric eyes from kicking in and I couldn't see anything but the bottom of the stairwell.

"Guess this is the place."

"Not yet," Delron said and started down the stairs.

I went to follow, but Yuki put her hand on my arm, holding me back and putting herself between the dark elf and me. Shea slipped up next to me, dagger in hand, but blade hidden in the sleeve of his cloak. Dar nudged me with his nose when they were in position. I guess I was being fully escorted for the rest of the journey. It made me a little sniffly they were taking my security so seriously. Stifled, but sniffly.

"Is all well?"

I looked at Glabrielle and her two guards behind us. Giving a quick nod, I started down the stairs.

Sighing, I wish we could have postponed the trip to the dark side for a few more days. I hadn't even had a chance to talk to my mother about everything I had learned about my father. She probably already knew, but something told me she didn't know the whole story. Namely, who and what exactly he was. It was the first item on my to do list when we got back. Finding *him* was number two.

Delron was waiting for us at the bottom of the stairs, an impatient look on his face. "It would not do well to dally. There may be returning scouts seeking the portal."

"Gosh. You might have mentioned that sooner," I answered with just a hint of annoyance in my voice. At least I refrained from giving him an eye-roll.

"I thought it was a given."

"You travel to this realm often?"

He nodded.

"Why?" Glabrielle failed miserably at not sounding suspicious.

"This world interests the queen."

"Again, I would ask why?"

"She…has a trade agreement with some of the local population."

"Trading what?" I narrowed my eyes.

He blushed and wouldn't meet my eyes. "Human drugs."

"She's a fucking crack dealer?"

He nodded. "Among many others, yes."

I just couldn't wait to meet the queen. She sounded like a real fucking peach. "And what does she get in return?"

"Human funds."

"What good would that do in Faerie?"

"We are a failing people, Lady. The queen does what she can to survive. Because we are failing, we find ourselves consistently under attack. Human weapons are…very efficient."

"There are other ways."

"What would you suggest?"

I opened my mouth, but no words of wisdom were to be found. As an outsider, I had no idea what they were facing, what they'd been through, or even how to help them. Selling drugs to humans was not the answer, though. Ever. "Since I am just learning about this, I have no idea. But I will think of something and she will stop selling her poison to the humans."

He didn't say a word, just nodded. "It is no longer my concern. I will let you tell her your thoughts on the matter. I am here only as your escort."

"Fine."

He turned and headed down the corridor at the end of the stairs. Hanging yellow lightbulbs illuminated the way. I slapped one, sending it swinging as we passed beneath it, the burning I felt in my fingers distracting me for a moment. I was pissed and that never ended well. Usually for me.

"Lady?"

"Yes, Princess?"

She moved up next to Shea. "I feel I should disclose to you that this was also a practice of my brother's."

"You better be talking about Renlynn."

"I am. Jaeren would never do such a thing. Neither would I. In fact, I am not sure he was even aware."

"You stopped it?" I stopped and turned to look at her.

"I would have if I could have. Some of the nobles found the practice a good idea."

I sighed in frustration, rubbing the bridge of my nose. "Okay. We'll discuss this later. After we rescue Jaeren."

"He would be able to put an immediate end to it," she said thoughtfully. "The council would listen to him."

"If they don't, they'll listen to me."

She blanched, stepped back, and gave me a respectful nod. "If that is your will, Witch of Cedar Falls."

"The human realm is mine and I will protect it."

"As is your right." She motioned me forward, not wanting to listen to any more of my threats, apparently. I was disappointed. I was pissed and she was the only outlet I had at the moment.

Delron gave up waiting and was already halfway down the corridor, Yuki keeping pace and glancing back at us. When she realized we weren't going to rush to catch up, she grabbed the back of his jerkin and held him still. He didn't seem too happy about it, either.

The corridor made a sharp right and opened into another smaller warehouse. This one still had empty shelving filling it. Empty except for the thick coating of dust. Rows and rows of them blocked any possible view of the rest of the room. Large lights overhead glowed softly, providing a minimum of illumination. Looking up, I realized the power was still on in the building.

"She used drug money to buy the property."

"Yes," Delron answered, knowing who and what I was talking about. "As well as several of the surrounding buildings."

This just keeps getting better and better, I said to Yuki and Dar.

One step at a time. Let us retrieve your guardian. The rest can be dealt with later.

This is why I keep you around. You're pretty brilliant for a demon. And you're hot. And great in bed.

Ew. Yuki looked over her shoulder at us.

What? She is not joking, Dar answered.

I coughed to cover my laughter. Delron shot me another look. This time, he wasn't wrong to do so. As soon as I did, four elven archers stepped into the hall from behind the rows of shelving, arrows at the ready.

Oops.

"Who goes there?"

"It is I, Delron. I return with the witch."

The arrows lowered but weren't removed from their strings. They did however, step back far enough for us to pass through. I tried my best to ignore them as we passed, but they were impressive looking enough to cast them a wary glance. They all wore elven armor, but in matted black. The light around them seemed to be absorbed and not a single reflection could be seen anywhere from them.

Stealthy elfies.

Really? Yuki admonished.

You're just jealous you didn't think of it first.

No. I'm thinking about taking them out, because if we come back from Faerie in a rush, these guys will be sitting here with ample cover and nasty looking bows.

Oh. Chance we'll have to take. If a scout comes back and they're dead or tied up, I'm sure the queen would be the first to know.

Good point.

We finally cleared the shelving and the remainder of the room melted into a cave. A cave with a veil covering just like the portal under O'Malley's.

"Creepy," I said in awe. Black vines writhed all around the entrance, seemingly having their roots in the other realm. The effect was rather spooktastic.

"This is where I leave you, Lady." Delron bowed and stepped back.

"Um. No."

"But–"

"You are with me, now. If the queen still wishes you dead, she'll have to go through me first. I have no idea what is on the other side of that thing," I said, pointing at the portal. "You do. Sorry, Delron. You're stuck with us until we get back with Jaeren."

He sat deathly still for over a minute. His elven brain trying to come up with some plausible excuse. Underhill is the last realm he wanted to go back to, and I didn't blame him. Unfortunately, we needed him. He finally nodded and headed for the veil. I half expected the vines to reach out and strangle him as he tried to pass, but they ignored him. Yuki followed, Shea and I after, Dar behind me, and then our elven escort. We all passed through and I gasped at the scene before us as we gathered on the other side.

A black, twisted castle stood on a hill across a shallow valley from where we were. A narrow pathway wound through wickedly sharp stalagmites, each with a purple flame erupting from the tips. Lighting flashed overhead, illuminating the ominous looking orange sky. No sun or moon was visible, so I had no idea what time of day we had stepped into. It was a Halloween nightmare come to life. I wondered if Josie's mom could be talked into relocating.

We were standing on a ledge at the mouth of the other side of a cave. The winding pathway worked its way up the slope and ended on our left. Delron headed that way, "Stay on the path," he said unnecessarily.

It took almost half-an-hour to get close enough to the castle to see the moat of muck, bones, and fire. A rancid, burning, oily smell wafted from it, as well as plumes of black smoke. Just as I was going to ask how we were going to get across, a wet looking black drawbridge cranked open and began to lower.

That's handy. I wonder if zoning laws would allow drawbridges in Cedar Falls. The only problem was my mother could fly.

The drawbridge fully opened with a loud thud, echoing in the valley. The largest difference I noted was the lack of city around the castle. It was there and that was it. Lone spires on barren hills. Barren except for the flaming stalagmites. "Where are all the people?"

Delron gave me a questioning look.

"Dark elf families. There's no city by the castle?"

"There is no city in the realm. We live, work, and die in the castle."

"What about your families?"

"We are only allowed to breed when there is a decline in population."

"Okay. Wow. Never mind and forget I asked." The more I learned, the more I wanted to raze the castle to the ground. Seriously. The unseleighe side of Underhill was *nothing* like the seleighe side.

I held out my hand and pulled some magic into my palm, letting it coalesce into a glowing orb. The magic, at least, felt the same, both in texture and abundance. If things went south, at least I wouldn't run out of power. Letting the orb go, I smiled as it dissipated.

The wood of the drawbridge was so thick, our feet made no sound as we strode across it. I even tried stomping a few times to no avail. Taking a look over the side at the moat, I was grateful for the sturdy timbers. I'd fallen in enough shitty places in Faerie. Smoking slime moat would just be the icing on the Jell-O mold.

I fucking hate Jell-O.

When we reached the spider-shaped, silver portcullis, I lost it. I was literally standing on the bridge, laughing my ass off. Everyone looked at me, including the four dark elven guards on the other side of the grate.

"Sorry," I mumbled and wiped my eyes.

You okay? Even Yuki sounded confused.

Seriously? You don' find the fact that the most cliché thing in the universe is actually their gate? At least there's no pumpkins.

No? It's actually quite pretty. In a creepy Halloween kinda way.

I stopped laughing. Yuki's face was distorting. In fact, everything was, even the bridge below us. It started twisting and warping, but nobody else seemed to notice. "What's going on?"

"Seriously, Boss. Are you okay?"

"Suddenly not feeling so well." I tried to take a step forward, but my feet elongated, at least they looked like they did, and I tripped on the bridge, falling forward.

Dar stood and transformed, catching me in his arms. "What is wrong?"

"My vision. It's all distorted."

He looked up at Delron. "We need to get her in the castle."

"Of course. Bring her." He turned and walked to the guards, mumbling something I couldn't quite catch.

"Should I attempt to walk her back to the portal?" Shea's distorted features came into view. He was still quite lovely, in a Picasso sort of way.

"Let us get her into the castle and see if that alleviates the issue," Dar said adamantly. Shea could only nod.

Even with my distorted vision, I saw the portcullis lift as Delron approached the guards. Peculiarly, they didn't say one word to him as the giant silver doors swung inward and creaked to a stop.

"Hang on. Maybe it is the gas from the moat," Dar said hopefully.

I nodded, burying my face in his chest. Not that I was capable of speech. I closed my eyes and tried to let the feeling that I was floating go. My head felt like I drank two bottles of wine and then dropped acid. At least from the descriptions I had heard of the drug. I'd never actually tried it. I was a good little witch.

The air inside the castle was cooler but reeked of blood and rancid meat. "Oh, my goddess. Put me down."

He did and I dropped to my knees, retching on the floor of the hall, unable to stop myself. Luckily, I had skipped breakfast and what I brought up was mostly coffee and bile.

Dar, ever the gentle dog, held the few strands of loose hair back from my face and rubbed my back gently. "Are you finished? Should I try and find you a waste bin?"

"Yes. I'm done."

I groaned and stood, giving Delron an apologetic look. "Fear not, the scullions shall make it right," he told me with a grim look.

"Puking in the hallway probably won't leave a great impression on your queen, though."

"No. It will not," a rasping, mildly feminine voice called from the stairs.

Looking up, I gasped at the ancientness of her. Elves were like witches, not aging until the very last stages of life. It always signified the end for us. My grandmother was just beginning to gray at her temples and she was over a thousand years old. The dark elf in front of me looked like a dust bunny fucked a mummy. I'd had a houseplant in my room that I forgot to water for ten years. Her skin reminded me of the leaves, but instead of curled, it hung from the fine bones of her face like paper-thin scrotal flesh that had been left in the sun for far too long. She didn't belong in a creepy castle in Faerie, she belonged in a condo in Miami. She'd have fit right in.

No wonder she wants to retire. She hit her golden years about the same time Moses did. Her best friend was probably eaten by a velociraptor.

I bowed since everybody else was. I hadn't noticed because I was staring at the piece of parchment in a black velvet dress.

"Rise, witch."

I did and wobbled on my feet. Dar put a steadying hand on my lower back, without looking up from his prone position. It was enough to keep me from falling on my face and since nobody had cleaned up my yak... I was grateful.

"Refresh yourselves, I will send for you from my private chambers when you are rested and well," she said without emotion, before she turned and crept from the stairs without a sound.

"Holy shit, she's old."

"And has exceptional hearing," Delron whispered in caution. "Would you care for refreshment?"

"Water?"

He nodded and snapped his fingers. Two female goblins crawled from the walls. "Clean this up and have a maid bring water and wine to the garden."

"*Ich, vitol*," one of them mumbled and grunted, bowing low and scurrying off. It was kind of cute in a hideously ugly sort of way. Kind of like one of those hairless chihuahuas.

I must have been staring after it. Delron smirked and asked, "Have you never seen a goblin?"

I shook my head. "No. But I kind of want to give it a sock."

"I do not understand."

"Long story." I sighed. "You mentioned a garden?"

"Yes. This way, please," he said and offered me his arm. Dar growled and I shrugged in apology, preferring the arm of my naked blue demon, anyway. Shea slipped under my other arm, putting his hand on my hip.

"Take it slowly," he whispered, offering me a handkerchief from one of the pockets in his cloak. I wiped my face and motioned for him to show us the way.

He ushered us through one of many black lacquered, glass inlayed French doors at the back of the hall. When he mentioned a garden, I was expecting an Addams Family kind of garden, with snipped off rose heads and poisonous, man-eating plants. I was very wrong. Blossoms bloomed everywhere we looked, but their colors were muted under the orange, sunless sky.

"Woah," I said, impressed.

"This garden is the queen's only passion. She still visits it every day and tends to the flowers."

"I am officially impressed. It is quite lovely."

"This way," he said and followed the pathway to the center of the garden, and to the fountain which had stone benches for us to sit on. Dar immediately ushered me to the closest, and I gratefully dropped down, exhausted. He immediately began rummaging through my pack, searching for the set of clothes we had brought in case he changed forms. I was almost disappointed. He was more engaging to watch than the flowers.

Do you think you were poisoned? He interrupted my view by putting on his pants.

I shook my head at him. *No. It feels like I'm drunk and tripping.*

His eyes narrowed.

What?

Maybe you are drunk...

I haven't had a single glass of wine since last night.

From power. Magic. It happened after you called the magic of this land to your palm, did it not?

"Oh, shit. Wait! That couldn't be it. I've been to Faerie before and didn't feel like this."

"You know what is causing your discomfort?" Delron stepped a little closer after my outburst.

"Dar seems to think it might be the over-abundance of magic."

"That is quite possible? You are used to the human realm, where natural occurring magic is a rarity."

"But I've been Underhill before and didn't feel like this."

"That is because you were on the seleighe side."

"Isn't this the same plane though?"

"Top to bottom, yes. But not left to right."

Huh? "You just hurt my brain."

"How do I put this? Think of your own realm. It is mostly neutral, and everything is ordered and explainable, yes?"

"Yes."

"Now, picture your world as being mostly positive, instead of having no polarity. You have mirrors in your world. Now, assume there was another world on the other side of that mirror. Everything would be reversed, yes?"

"Yes."

"Now picture *our* side of Underhill as the world on the other side of the mirror. Magic flows differently and is negatively powered. Your body probably feels the

189

difference in the flows and is probably reacting adversely. Does that make sense?"

"Kinda sorta."

"It is the best explanation I can give. You will just have to trust me that I speak the truth."

"Oh, I do. Just not really understanding."

"Call the magic to your hand again."

I held out my hand and did as he suggested. It coalesced into a glowing red sphere, hovering about an inch above my palm. "Now what?"

"Study it. Learn from it."

I sighed, not caring much for the Zen master attitude he was giving me, but I tried to do as he said. I looked at the spinning globe of energy in my hand like it was a crystal ball. I could see my reflection on its surface, but it was distorted from the speed. Focusing on that, I tried slowing it until I was reflected more normally. Gasping, I almost dropped it, using my other hand to steady it with another push of power.

I wasn't normal Dot. My ears were much more tapered with a downward sloping straight brow, almost completely elven in appearance. Even my pupils were slit instead of round. The more I watched them, the wider they became until the black completely filled in the iris and then the whites. Opening my mouth, I gasped at the canines glinting back at me, hanging quite below my upper lip. Just as I was about to release the sphere in fear, horns sprouted from my forehead and a pair of wings, completely made from the stuff of shadows rose above my shoulders and stretched dimly against the orange sky behind me.

I shrieked and threw the magic from me, directly at the fountain in front of us. Dar covered me, expecting an explosion. Even Delron dropped to the ground and covered his head with his hands. The elves, suspiciously quiet and unobtrusive until that moment, huddled around their princess. Shea threw a sphere of shadow over the three of us and I stared in horror around Dar's shoulder as the sphere flew and just before it hit the fountain, spun to a stop and hovered.

When everyone realized there wouldn't be a massive fireworks display, they straightened themselves. Shea pulled back the shadows and Dar let go of me a fraction of a second before the sphere flew back at me, hitting me squarely in the chest and blasting me from the stone bench and into the bed of roses behind me.

"And now the power is yours," Delron's voice echoed in my head as the garden around us faded into nothing.

Chapter 17

Gasping, I sat up in the luxurious round, canopied bed and groaned. My head felt like a heard of wildebeests ran through it with a pride of lions gnawing on their asses.

"Welcome back, Boss."

I looked over at Yuki, sitting on a chair beside the bed and then glanced around the room. We were alone.

"What happened? Where is everybody?"

"Beats the hell out of me. After you got blasted with the magic, I passed out with you. I just woke up a few minutes ago and was in here with you."

"Did you contact Dar?"

"I tried. He's apparently still out, too."

Dar? It was worth a try.

His mental groan echoed how my head felt. *I am alive.*

Where? And who is with you?

He sent a mental image of an identical room to the one Yuki and I were in, Shea curled in the crook of his arm and sleeping soundly. *Awww.*

Should I try and wake him?

No. Sit tight. I'll try to find you after I find out what happened and where Delron and the light elves are.

As you wish.

"I'd kill for some fucking aspirin."

Yuki reached up and offered me her arm. "Want a sip? Might make you feel a little better."

As much as I wanted to say no, I was more than half tempted. I felt like roadkill and she wasn't lying. Her blood was potent enough to heal all sorts of ailments. "Depends. Will it make you feel any worse?" I studied her reaction.

"No," she said without hesitation. She wasn't lying as far as she knew. "I don't think I could possibly feel any worse, and I'm hoping if you feel better, I will, too."

"Okay, but just a sip."

She nodded and brought her wrist back to her mouth, opening a tear that would take a bit longer to heal than two puncture marks. She winced as she did it, before thrusting the wound in front of my face. "Hurry, before it closes."

I didn't need to be told twice. I grabbed her arm and licked across the wound, catching the blood that was about to fall into my lap. We both groaned as the blood hit my tongue and tendrils of pleasure shot from my tongue through the rest of me. I closed my mouth over the wound and bit down, my fangs piercing the flesh and making a new wound.

Fangs? Wait…what?

"Master?"

In fear, I pulled her arm away from my mouth and ran my tongue over my teeth. My canines had indeed elongated but weren't monstrous like they had been when Dar had performed the Fourth Rite. They had practically filled my mouth and left me feeling like I had turned into a saber-toothed kitty Dot. The fangs in my mouth now were much more slender, elegant, and vampiric. Turning my head, I showed them to Yuki and wasn't comforted as she gasped and slid back in the chair, nearly toppling as the legs caught the uneven stones of the floor. "What the fuck is going on?" Fear clutched my chest in an icy grip.

"Your ears, too?"

I reached up and ran my fingers over the tapered ends of my pointy little ears, shuddering as pleasant feelings ran from the sensitive flesh down my arms. The image of myself staring back from the globe of unseleighe magic embedded itself in the forefront of my brain. In a panic, I felt my forehead as I looked over my shoulders for shadow wings. Luckily, I wasn't winged or horny.

"You're turning into us. All of us."

No. You're being influenced by your father's spheres, the goddess' voice whispered into my mind.

Spheres?

Domains. Those that worship who and what he is.

Oh, boy. So, if I get that gem out of me and give it back to him, I go back to normal Dot?

Perhaps. I wish you luck, Daughter.

"We really need to find my father," I said aloud to Yuki.

"They're gone."

"What's gone?"

"Your fangs and ears. You look normal again."

"Thank the Lady. We *really* need to find my father."

"Maybe we should try to get out of here first."

"Good plan."

I slid from the bed and headed for the door, being closer than Yuki. Reaching out, I touched the handle and felt the light ward go off in my hand. It wasn't designed to hurt, just alert. Kind of like a magical doorbell. The door was locked from the outside.

"We're locked in and I just let somebody know we're awake."

"Melt the lock, or you want me to kick the door open?"

"Maybe we should just wait. Somebody knows we're awake."

"I should have tried the door as soon as I woke. My apologies, Boss."

"If your head felt like mine, I don't blame you."

"You're feeling better, at least. I can feel it."

"Yep. You should sell your blood to energy drink manufacturers."

"The FDA might have an issue with blood in drinks."

"Not if you bribe them enough."

Yuki chuckled and I sat back down on the edge of the bed to wait. Thankfully, we didn't have a long one. The lock clicked, the handle turned, and in walked something out of a wet dream. A very wet one.

Elves were, for the most part, pretty. There were handsome ones, exceptionally handsome ones, and some that make you go, *sploosh*. But they were all pretty. The one that walked into my room was fucking god-like. We're talking *sploosh, drip, dribble.* He looked like he had been carved from marble into an image of the fertility god of pillow talk. His face was a little wider than any elf I had ever seen or imagined. His jaw a little squarer, too, giving him a bit more masculine look while still being pretty *and* handsome. I think I blushed when he stopped a few feet from me and gave me a little bow.

"Lady, welcome to the Unseleighe Court of Willowmere."

His voice… It was like a cool summer breeze caressing my flesh as I danced skyclad under the moon. Of course, I was naked, or it wouldn't have been able to touch the places it was touching. I wanted to beg him to read me a 2019 Ford Flex Owner's Manual or the Apple Terms and Conditions. In French. "Uh… Hi."

He smiled and the remainder of my capacity for rational though fluttered through the barred and shuttered window. I didn't care.

Then I remembered where we were and why were here. I frowned and shook my head to shake away the ludicrously lustful lusty thoughts of lust, clouding my brain. "Where are my friends?"

He straightened and held up his hands in a peaceful gesture. "Do not fret. We placed the males in the room next to you, unsure of your relationship. I can take you to them, if you wish."

"Maybe in a minute. What about the rest?"

"You speak of Lord Delron?"

I nodded. If they hurt him in anyway while I was unconscious… "Did you say *Lord* Delron?"

"Aye. Lord Delron of the Church of Night."

"Church of Night?"

"Yes?"

"I'm a little confused. He told us he was like a herald or something. For your queen."

"Why would he say that? He does not reside in our court or realm? He is the *head* of the Church of Night."

"You're the herald?"

"Nay. The prince. Prince Elleslyn."

"Your mother is the queen?"

"That is what it means to be prince, yes." He looked up at me guiltily.

"Oh, boy. I have so many questions I don't know where to begin."

"Perhaps they should be asked of my mother?"

"No. She's kind of scary, and I want to know where I stand before I'm standing in front of her, if you know what I mean."

"I understand. May I sit?"

"Sure."

Yuki got up and offered him the chair, sitting down next to me and leaning back. "My thanks," he said to her.

He was just as graceful as I'd imagined as he sat down on the padded leather seat. I've never wanted to be upholstery before that moment, but there I was. "Where is Jaeren, his sister, and her guards?" That was a good place to start.

"Prince Jaeren, of Elfhame Autumn Glade?"

"Yep."

"I am assuming he is in their castle?" He wasn't faking the look of utter confusion he was sporting. Nobody was that good of an actor."

"You returned him?"

"We had him?"

Something was wrong. Terribly, terribly wrong. "Hold the phone. You *didn't* kidnap him?"

"Why would we do that? Their military force is much greater than ours. Should war break out between us…we would not fare well."

"No offense, but I kind of noticed that."

"None taken," he said and calmly held up his hand. "Where did you hear this rumor."

"Uh. Delron."

His eyes narrowed in suspicion. "Why would he say that?"

"To get me to come here to listen to your marriage proposal?"

"Listen to the marriage proposal he brokered with us on your behalf?"

"Huh?"

"I am assuming this is the first you are hearing of this," he said with a gentle sigh. "When I first looked upon you and saw your beauty, I knew it was too good to be true."

His words added a *splash* to the *sploosh, drips, and dribbles.* Seriously, nobody should be that good looking. But he was still a dark elf, and I trusted him about as far as I could throw him. He seemed pretty solidly built for an elf. "Why would I, a witch of the mortal realm, wish to marry a prince of Faerie?"

"Money. Power. Granted, our kingdom offers little of either."

"Got em both, don't need more."

"Then I have no answer for you. The reason is with Lord Delron, who left for the capitol as soon as you were ensconced in your rooms."

"This isn't the capitol?"

"No. We are a kingdom. The capitol of Darkenfall is where the unseleighe high king lives."

"Oh. They don't teach that in social studies. So, no Jaeren here. Where is his sister and her guards?"

"Prince Jaeren has no sister."

"Sure he does. Glabriella. She was with us when we came here!"

"I can assure you… Jaeren and Renlynn were the only two elves born of their fallen king. And I worry that you are not well."

"Why?"

"Because the four of you were the only ones who arrived here at the castle beside Lord Delron?"

"No, we weren't. There were three elves! Right, Yuki?" I turned and looked at her, afraid that she was going to say no, and that I was insane.

"My master is telling the truth. There *were* elves with us. They came to supposedly negotiate for the release of her brother."

Thank fuck.

Got your back, Boss.

They were really here, right?

Yes!

"See, I told you," I said smugly to Elleslyn.

"Then they were invisible to us," he said thoughtfully. "The question that remains is, are they still among us?" He closed his eyes for a moment and two guards entered the room. "Start patrols inside the castle. Be on the lookout for a trio of elves. Use any items granting magical sight that we have."

"Yes, my prince," they answered and left.

"Not going to lie, you don't seem like a bad guy. Why do you sell drugs to humans and not let people have families?"

He tilted his head in confusion. "What are you talking about?"

Damnit, Delron. Priest or not, I'm going to kick your ass.

∞ ∞ ∞

Watching the queen eat was not conducive to my normally healthy appetite... It was a combination of watching her gnarled, hooked fingers dragging the still moving food to her lips, the tongue that snaked out, trapping the squirming food and pulling it into her mouth, and the culmination of the sounds that sounded like porno sex that erupted from her orifice as she chewed. I swear that I heard one of the little buggers scream before she swallowed.

I let mine run away from my plate. I wasn't even a fan of sushi unless it was cooked. Moving whatevers were not on my menu. The vegetables and roasted meat, however, didn't stand a chance. Especially after I pretended it was cow. "Any sign of Glabrielle?"

I couldn't help but notice the prince was giving my Shea a small, shy smile. I cocked an eyebrow at him as he turned to me and blushed, Elleslyn shook his head. "Nay. What they were seeking in this realm is beyond me."

"She knows the gem isn't here anymore, so it couldn't have been that," I mused aloud and stared at my empty plate.

"Gem?" The queen finally spoke around a mouthful of squirmy slug with legs.

I looked up at her and ignored the legs between her teeth. Or tried to. One was still twitching. "Yes. My father's gem. It contained his power and he somehow smuggled it out of his prison. King Renlynn had it, and I was told you sent it to him. It drove him mad."

The queen gave her son a questioning look.

"I'm sorry, you said it belonged to your *father*?"

"Uh...yes."

"A red ruby the size of a child's fist?" Elleslyn continued.

"Uh...yeah."

"How could it belong to your father? That is a holy icon of the Church of Night? It has been in this realm for nearly a hundred years. Since the war between Night and Day was lost." I could tell by the anger on his face who won that battle. It was a shock to hear that it had happened in their kingdom, though.

"Here? Day fought the night *here*?"

"Yes. Tis why this cursed sky never darkens!" He pointed up in emphasis at the orange glow above us.

I just thought they were really trying to pull off the Halloween motif they had going on. "Yep. I didn't know it happened in your realm. It gets dark on the seleighe side. Why is that?"

"I assume it is because they were not abandoned by the sun and moon like we were. When day and night fought, they left as well."

The Lord and Lady. My father is night, but who is day? "I know Aodh is the god of night, who is the god of day?"

"I know not the name you have given the Night," the queen answered in her raspy tone. "The Night is naught but the Night. To give another name to the Day would make as much sense."

I nodded.

"Do you truly claim to be a child of the Night as well as a witch?"

I looked at Yuki. I'd heard her mention that another name for vampire was child of the Night. "You mean a vampire?" I asked the queen.

"Blood drinker, yes."

"Apparently, I am sometimes. But I meant that the Night is my *actual* father. He married my mother before he was imprisoned."

"Blasphemy!" The queen stood and shook in barely contained fury.

Guess I should have left that part out.

"Sit down, Lilith." A very familiar voice spoke from the shadows. Shadows that hadn't been there a moment ago. Glancing up at Shea, I nearly shot out of my seat. He was gripping the arms of his chair tightly and struggling to keep them focused.

"Help him, Daughter." The goddess' voice called softly.

I quickly got out of my chair and walked around the table, putting my hands on his shoulders. He sighed softly at the contact and immediately calmed, not struggling with his shadows. "Are you okay?" I whispered softly in his ear.

"Now," he answered and smiled.

From the shadows, two figures emerged. The Lord and the Lady gazed upon us and smiled. Every elf stood and bowed, no question who stood before them.

"Lord and Lady?" The queen shook as she stood, hanging on to the back of her chair for support.

The Lady floated a foot over the wet looking stone floor of the patio we dined upon. The Lord made no such grand gesture and stomped cloven hooves against the ground, striking sparks as he shifted from foot to foot.

"Yes, Lilith, Queen of the Unseleighe Court of Willowmere."

The queen began crying. "You have graced us once again?"

"We have never left. Our embodiments are merely hidden in the sky by the imbalance left after Night's capture."

"We thought you had abandoned us in punishment," Elleslyn said by way of apology.

"Do not be sorry. The day might have masked our presence, but thanks to the small one," she pointed and smiled at my Shea, "we were able to pass through the shadows that even daylight cannot completely extinguish."

I couldn't help squeezing Shea's shoulders in pride.

"We do not have long, the strain on the child is immense," the Lady said, sadly. The Lord gave me a wink.

"How do we fix all this?" Elleslyn begged.

"You cannot. Only the daughter of Night can free him, restoring the balance."

"I don't even know where he is," I said in futility.

"No, but you know who does."

"Day?"

The gods nodded. "Isn't that right, Aine?" the Lady's eyes narrowed as she focused on the other side of the table.

I gasped as Glabrielle slowly came into view. She wasn't sister to Jaeren, she was the goddess Day.

Holy fuckballs.

"Greetings, Brother," she said to the Lord with a little nod of her head. "And to you, wife of my brother."

"Aine, release your spouse from his prison," the Lord pleaded in anguish.

Everything clicked into place in my head. Everything. The Lord, the Sun, was brother to Day. The Lady, the Moon, was sister to Night. They sun and moon were wed, just as day and night. I also had a feeling that my mother was the reason Day had imprisoned Night…

"He left you to be with my mother," I said aloud, without thinking. *Don't piss off the deities, Dot.*

"That hag, with her fiery hair? He didn't *leave* me to be with her, she spelled him!" Day was scary when she was pissed.

"My mother might be a lot of things, but a hag…is probably one of them. *However*, she would not spell a man just to be with him!"

"What about a god?"

"No offence, but few things impress my mother. Including me. But let me get this straight, you *imprisoned* him for cheating on you?"

"No. Marriage vows are sacred, but even gods stray. No. He was imprisoned because of you."

"Me?"

She nodded.

I looked to the Lady, not really trusting Aine, or Glabrielle, whoever the hell she was. The Lady gave me a curt nod. "It is true. It was decided that any celestial who mated with a human would bear an eternity of imprisonment. Too many abominations have walked the realms."

"Any celestial?"

"Angels, demons, and gods. We were forbidden to procreate with mortals. As I told you before, even the gods answer to higher powers, Daughter."

I cast a nervous glance at Dar. Thankfully, or so I hoped, I couldn't get pregnant unless I truly wanted to. Shaking my head, I turned back to the goddess. "So, my father, whom I never met, is going to be stuck wherever he is forever?"

"Unless freed by their offspring, yes. The Powers That Be decided that would be their one chance at freedom. If the abomination they created forgave them for their very existence and worked to free them."

"Where is he?"

"That I cannot say, but the one in your hands might have an inkling. He is a scholar."

I looked down. Shea just nodded, still struggling to keep the shadows focused even with my power added to his.

"Remember the Law, Aine." The Lord's voice sounded strained.

"I know the Law! You do not have to remind me, Brother."

"We must go. Seek out your Father and this land will be healed. Fail..." The goddess was fading from sight.

I nodded in understanding.

They faded completely into the shadows and Shea cried out in relief. Glabrielle snarled at the lot of us and faded into a flash of orange hued light. I reached down and lifted Shea's chin, forcing him to look up at me. "Where?"

"Where all fallen angels go when they sire Nephelim," he answered as if I knew where the hell that was.

"Let's just say I knew the answer to that. Where in the realms would that be?"

"Tartarus," Dar answered for him.

"Like Greek mythology Tartarus?"

"The Greeks merely wrote of it. It has nothing to do with their mythos."

"Where is it?" I was looking back and forth between the two of them, wanting an answer and a fucking clue as how to end this entire nightmare.

"Remember how I told you there was no hell and that Gehenna was the lowest of the planes?"

"Yes," I narrowed my eyes at Dar.

"Technically that was true, but not completely true, either."

"Huh?"

"Allow me?" Shea asked Dar, who nodded in return.

Shea traced a sphere on the table. "Picture this sphere as every plane of existence you could imagine. The Human Realm, Faerie, Gehenna, the White Plains, the Shadow Realms. All of them, tucked nicely in layers in this ball of existence."

"Okay."

Now picture *another* sphere encircling the other. That is Etherium."

"Okay," I said and fought the urge to rub the bridge of my nose.

"Ethereum is the realm of the gods and other things you can't even begin to imagine. It has polarities, just like our realms. Top is positive, the lower is negative…"

"And?"

"At the bottom is Tartarus. If Hell had an underworld, Tartarus would be it. All of the angels, gods, devils, and demons who were to suffer an eternity of torment and anguish, were thrown into the pits of Tartarus."

"Oh. And that's where we have to go?"

Shea nodded, more than a little fear showing on his face.

"I take that back. That's where *I* have to go?"

"I'm sorry, yes. If you wish to rescue your father…"

"To hell and back."

"Precisely."

Chapter 18

"I can't believe that bitch was actually a goddess!"

"Glabrielle?" Dar wanted to clarify.

"Yes!" I dropped down on the bed in the room the dark elves had given me. After the pantheon had left, things had gotten a little more than weird. The queen looked torn between kicking me out of her realm and kissing my feet. I didn't want her sandpaper crusted chops anywhere near my toes. Elleslyn treated me the same, but even a little *more* reverently. It knocked down his hotness level a little. I didn't care for people who thought too highly of me. "Even with all those answers, I still have a million questions."

"Such as?"

"Jaeren. Where the hell is he? We came to rescue *him* and he's not even here. Why does Delron want me to marry the prince? How did my father get his gem out of Tartarus? Why did Delron give it to Renlynn? Did he know it would drive him insane? That one kind of pisses me off, to be honest. And what was Glabrielle doing in the castle, and why was she pretending to be his sister? That one pisses me off, too."

"That is a lot of questions."

"Without any answers."

Dar sighed and put his hand on my leg. "I'm sure they will come."

"First thing first. Find Jaeren and get him back."

"Even before your father?"

"Oh, that one is going to have to wait. I'm not marching into Hell until I know exactly what is going on and how to get there."

Dar smiled at me. "You are learning."

"Repeatedly getting the shit kicked out of you is a good teacher."

"So is realizing that sometimes patience truly is a virtue."

"Yeah. I suck at that."

"Let us look at this logically. Who told you Jaeren was here?" He was smiling. The bastard probably already had it figured out.

"Delron. We know this."

"So, assuming that what he said was a falsehood, the truth is that he knew that Jaeren had, in fact, been abducted."

"Yes?"

"So would it not stand to reason he would know who, if it wasn't in fact him, abducted him?"

"I guess. But now he is gone, too, so it's not like I can just ask him."

"No, but it is a place to start."

"True."

There was a soft knock at the door. Dar gave me a questioning glance and I nodded. Without hesitation, he got up and opened it.

Elleslyn was the last person I'd been expecting, but there he stood. "May I come in?"

"Of course."

He stepped into the room and shut the door behind him before crossing his wrists in front of him. "I have spoken with the queen. She wishes me to offer you sanctuary here as long as you would need."

"Tell her that I appreciate her offer, but that we will be leaving shortly."

He sighed but nodded in understanding. "I am sorry your trip here was for naught."

"It wasn't. I learned a whole bunch of things that I didn't know yesterday."

"More importantly, I am sorry to learn that your marriage interest was only feigned on the part of Lord Delron."

I blushed before finding an appropriate response. "Do you know why? Why did he want me to come here?"

"The Church of Night…is a mystery. To put it mildly."

"He was covered in rift wight poison when he came to us. Saying your mother and archers had covered him in it as a punishment."

"Waste water?"

Snicker. "Yes."

"How did he survive?"

"I healed him."

"Maybe he did it to test you. Truly, you are a daughter of Night."

"So, it seems."

"What will you do?"

"Find Jaeren. He's been gone for almost a week. Who knows how much time he has left. After that? Learn as much as I can and rescue my father."

"You would risk the pits of Tartarus for him?"

"Never met him. But, I'm not angry with him or anything. Little pissed about the powers he gave to me in an indirect manner, but I'm probably going to need them to save him."

"So brave."

"Or foolish."

He got down on one knee. "I would ask you to consider the matrimonial discussion. Truly, you are amazing, and I would be honored to call you my wife."

"Yeah. That's so not going to happen. But thanks."

"You do not wish to marry me," he answered sadly.

"I don't want to get married, period. I have too many people in my life that I love beyond measure. To commit myself to one that is not one of them… It's not written in the stars for me. I'm sorry." I hoped I let him down easy.

He tilted his head. "You have multiple lovers?"

I nodded.

"I understand. Should you find room in your heart to explore a relationship with me, you know where to find me," he said with a soft chuckle and got up off his knee. "Fare thee well, Witch of the Human Realm, Daughter of Night."

"Take care of yourself, Prince Elleslyn."

He strode out the door, giving me one more smile before he made it out the door. My loins were urging me to chase after him. I'd have to punish them later. With my fingers, in a bathtub, with images of an elf god running through my brain.

"I can smell your desire from here."

"Oh, please. That was one slab of Kobe beef right there, and you know it."

"I do not think so. There was not an ounce of fat on him and Kobe is prized for its fat content."

"When did you become an expert on steak? You were asking the differences between cuts just a day ago."

"I studied when we returned home."

"Ah. Come on. Let's go see if Shea is awake yet. I really just want to go home."

"I concur."

I knocked softly on the door to the room next to ours. Yuki had taken him to his room while Dar and I finished our dinner conversation. With the amount of energy he had expended on summoning the shadows for the Lord and Lady, it was no wonder.

Yuki answered the door and let us in. "He's still asleep," she whispered softly.

"Damn. I was hoping he'd rested enough to walk us to the gate," I answered silently.

"I am drained," Shea said softly from the bed, apparently awake.

"I understand. Do you want to wait until morning to leave? We can walk back to the gate, the old-fashioned way."

"I can get us there now, if you could provide me the power."

"Are you sure? It is no rush."

"I can do it. I wish to go home."

I leaned over him and gave him a gentle kiss as my hands found their way to his chest, settling on him and letting the power flow freely into him. Immediately, his tattoos began to glow under his fine linen tunic. "I love that," I whispered after I pulled from his kiss.

"I do as well."

"I meant your tattoos glowing. Kissing you is even better than that."

He smiled as I recharged his little elven batteries. "Can you not pull the energy from the realm? You're half dark elf."

"If I were a mage, yes. But I am a shadow walker. I would have to go there to seek power."

"Then how am I giving you power?"

"As I told you before. You stepped into the shadows. You pull power from there just as I do."

"But I'm not a shadow walker."

"Have you tried?"

"No. I've been there. That is not something I would want to do on a regular basis. I'd be too afraid of getting lost."

"If you belong there, the shadows would never let you lose your way."

"I'm good. I have you."

"Yes, you do." He gave me a smile that warmed me in all the right places. "Are you able to call a shadow to your hand?"

"I don't know. Not right now. I'm having too much fun giving you a jumpstart and touching your chest."

"You have given me enough to shadow walk to the moon. Try. Please? I am curious."

I sighed. "Fine. What do I do?"

"Hold out your hand."

I did. Knuckles up. He sighed and reached up, turning my hand over, palm facing the ceiling.

"Now, look at your hand. See the light on your palm? Picture something blocking that light with your mind. Imagine a shadow in your grasp."

I did as he said, focusing on my hand until the swirls in my palm became blurred and the color of my skin darkened. There it was, a tiny shadow looking up at me with glowing red eyes. "Now what?"

"Give it a purpose. Tell it what to do with your mind."

Find Jaeren, Prince of Elfhame Autumn Glade for me. I pictured the damn elf in my mind as hard as I could. I really didn't think it would work, but it was all I could think of. With a feeling of acceptance fluttering to me, it disappeared.

"Where did you send it?"

"To look for Jaeren."

"Lady, I don't think–"

I held up my hand. "I know, but it was all I could think of."

"Be sure to release it, or it will continue to search for the elf for all eternity."

"Aww. I'll do it now. Poor little guy."

"Do not," Dar said curiously.

"Why?"

He looked out in the hall and closed the door. "Just in case the dark ones were not being truthful, and he is, in fact, in this realm. It is better to be safe than sorry."

"Okay. Then remind me when we get back home to let him go."

"I shall," Dar answered.

"Good. Everybody ready?"

They all nodded, and Shea held out his hands. I grabbed one and Dar grabbed the other, Yuki gripping onto Dar's arm, tightly. Shea stepped into the shadows, pulling us along with him. There was a small tug at my arm, and I looked down, seeing the tiny shadow I had sent off to find Jaeren.

"You're kidding me," I whispered and stepped back, letting go of Shea's hand, purely out of instinct. By the time I looked up, they were gone, and the shadows faded around me. I was alone in the room of the unseleighe castle. I breathed a sigh of relief. Things could have gone much differently. Lost in the shadows was not something I ever wanted to be, and while Shea might trust in my power, I didn't. Not even a little bit.

The shadow caressed my finger.

"Guess it's just you and me now, Fidget." I gave a little giggle at the name I had given it. Fitting. The thing couldn't sit still for a nanosecond.

I felt it tug against my finger, urging me to follow it. Him. I don't know how I knew, but it was definitely male. Shea just lost his position as littlest shadow boy.

Fidget let go of my finger and slid under the door, leaving me no choice but to open it and exit the room the old-fashioned way. He was hovering on the other side, waiting impatiently for me to follow him. I couldn't hear his thoughts, if he had any, but I could feel his emotions.

Master?

Dar's panicked voice literally flooded my brain with worry. *I'm okay. Just got a little sidetracked.*

Sidetracked? You scared us all shitless when you did not come out the other side. Shea is screaming.

Tell him, I'm fine. That little shadow was frantic. Jaeren is here or close.

Do you wish us to return?

No. Stay there until I call.

Very well. Be safe. Do not blow yourself up.

I'll try. Keep the hearth fires warm.

Always.

He fluttered down the hallway to our left, a corridor I hadn't been down yet. No surprise there. If I had gotten close enough to Jaeren, I might have felt his presence. He might not be a familiar, but he was my appointed guardian. That bond was enough to let me know when he was near.

213

At the end of the hall was a spiral stairway, made entirely of stone and leading up and down. Half-expecting Fidget to go down, I stopped at the landing and peered up to the floor above, ignoring his emotional plea to hurry. In my experience, royals were like elevators. The higher the floor, the farther you could look down on people. No king, queen, prince, or princess would *ever* have their personal rooms on the lower floors of the castle. But, for the life of me, I couldn't fathom why they would be holding Jaeren in one of their rooms.

Elleslyn's face, story, and sweetness flittered across my brain, sending icy chills through my veins. Sure, I was a trusting person, but he had me totally fooled. His mother, not so much, but him... I *wanted* to trust him. Probably because he was so damn hot. Hot guys who were assholes *really* twerked my nerps. You're already hot, there's no damn reason to be an asshole. Unfortunately, that was often the case. I was lucky enough to have found five guys who were hot *and* sweet. Jaeren was hot, but he was a dick. He didn't mean to be, but he was.

"Okay then, Fidget Monster, I hope you're right. Or this is going to be awfully embarrassing..."

He zipped back and forth in front of my face, leaving the impression of a stern talking-to in his wake.

"Yeah, yeah. You better be right. That's all I'm sayin."

I followed him slowly up the stairs, trying to make as little noise as possible. Thankfully I had worn sensible shoes. When we got to the top of the landing, Fidget plastered himself against the wall and thinned out, turning himself into a normal looking shadow. I assumed there was someone close by and that was his most effective means of camouflage. Effective, but unfortunately left my cheese hanging in the wind. I ducked down and listened.

Footsteps softly sounded on the other side of the stone balustrade and then stopped at the top of the landing. I was stuck until whoever it was moved. After five minutes, I realized it had to be a guard of some sort. I should have known there would be sentries on the royals' floor. Nobody let people into the penthouse without a key for the elevator.

Shit.

The sound of footfalls at the bottom of the stairs threatened to send me into full panic. Until Fidget wrapped himself around me and pulled me into the wall. Then the panic *really* set in. I was back in the shadow realm, in a shadowy wall, looking into the castle. A scullery goblin, much larger than the others I'd seen, came up the stairwell carrying a mop and bucket. The guard, who had been facing the large private dining hall, turned as she reached the top. A disgusted look later, he was back to his sentry duties.

Feeling a tug on my arm, I looked down. Fidget was back in his shadowball with red eyes form, tugging on me with a tendril that almost looked like an arm. Reaching down, I ran my finger over his head to say thanks, expecting it to go through. It didn't. In the shadow realm, he had mass. "Woah. Thanks for saving me, little guy."

His eyes squinted back at me in pleasure.

"Now you have to show me how to get out of here."

He just pulled on my arm some more, so I let him take the lead. I took one step and we were by the next grouping of shadows, across from a large window in the middle of the dining area. Movement in the realm still unnerved me more than anything I had ever experienced, but not having to deal with being seen or spotted by guards made it worth it.

The next step took us to the Queen's private chambers.

Please don't be naked. Please don't be naked.

She wasn't. And she wasn't alone. She sat upon what looked like a miniature throne. Ebony wood had been carved into a semblance of a giant spider, the one that could have possibly shot the front gate out of its ass. It took up the entirety of the back wall of her suite. Elleslyn *and* Delron stood before her. Their voices were muffled, but audible.

"You *lied* to her?" Elleslyn was practically shaking with rage.

"Do not forget your place, Son. I am still queen of this realm."

"Mother, she will *destroy* this realm if she finds out!"

"You will *not* raise your voice to me. She will not find out until after you are married. I can finally rest in peace."

He turned and looked at Delron for help.

He just sadly shook his head. "I have done all I can. My only concern was getting our Lord's power to his heir. That is all he wanted, his two daughters happy and the eldest as his heir. Thankfully, it was Dorothea that was born first. The other is…unsuitable to be a god."

Two? Sisters? I have a sister?

"It was you," Delron continued, pausing to stare at the queen, "who wished the heir of Night to be *your* heir as well."

"It was the only way to ensure the survival of our realm. Even the capitol is suffering since the Night's imprisonment."

"Aye. And *that* is the only reason I agreed to help you. I have done everything you have asked, and planted all the clues for the witch to find. Now, I will take my leave."

"Take the elf with you. If she should find him here…" The queen held up her hands.

"No. I am done here."

"Lord Delron? The elf is here? Mother?" Elleslyn was practically hyperventilating. I didn't blame him. If I were him, I'd be afraid of me, too. Even I had no clue what I was capable of at the moment. The strange thing was, I wasn't as pissed off as I should be. Elleslyn was innocent. That made me happy. Delron was acting on behalf of my father, but he still needed an ass whipping for all his lies. The queen… She was toaster strudel. I was going to fry her ass and drizzle icing on it when I was done.

Ignoring Fidget, I took another step, popping into the shadows beside the throne. I was ten feet away from the trio and staring at them, trying to let the anger loose, but it

216

just wouldn't come. With a resigned sigh, I stepped from the shadows.

Exiting the shadow realm had been easier than I thought. One minute I was there, the next standing by the throne, trying not to laugh at the expression on their faces when I came into view.

Delron was the first to react. He let out a resigned sigh. Elleslyn dropped to the ground, kowtowing in my direction. The queen didn't react at all until she spoke. "It is impolite to drop eaves, child."

"Almost as impolite as lying, kidnapping, and scheming."

She nodded her head in acquiescence.

"Where is he?"

"Of whom do you speak?"

"Jaeren, obviously."

"Safe."

"You will return him to me." I didn't ask, I told.

"Gladly. Once you have married my only child."

"When Tartarus freezes over."

"You do not understand. A single command is all it will take to incinerate him. His life depends on you."

"As does yours. And his. And his." I pointed around the room at the others around her. "So does your entire realm. Make no mistake, Your Highness, if anything happens to him, I end you. I end it all. You can forget progeny, I will not marry a corpse. Do you understand me."

"You are bluffing. You would not hurt anyone who was not directly responsible. And my life is a sacrifice I am willing to make."

"Not much of a sacrifice."

She snarled in rage. "Give me your answer."

"I have given you my answer. Give me my elf or I destroy it all." To further my threat, I held out my hands, blue flame encircling both of them.

"Dorothea, please do not make the people suffer for my mother's indiscretions." Elleslyn looked up from the floor, imploringly. He truly was a prince.

"I won't. Just the people in this room."

"That I can live with."

I couldn't. "Changed my mind. Just Delron and your mother. I kind of like you."

His smile distracted me. And that was all the time the queen needed. One moment she was sitting upon her throne, the next she had half melted into it, sinking up to her waist in the seat. She gave me an evil glare and the throne began to move.

She looked like a freaking spider centaur. A spidertaur. Whatever she was, it was fucking ugly and scary. My mother wasn't the only one afraid of spiders, maybe that was why.

"Run!" Elleslyn's voice shocked me out of my spider-induced coma.

"Fuck that. Kill it with fire!" I let the flames on my hands loose, striking the queen in the chest and watching as they harmlessly spilled over her. Spiders didn't like fire. Spidertaurs on the other hand, didn't seem to be bothered by it in the least...

The queen cackled and closed the distance between us with quick movements of her hairy-assed spider legs. I shuddered and stepped back, resisting the urge to rub my arms and run in little circles, screaming.

"Magic cannot hurt her! Run!"

Oh. That explains that. Now I just need to find a really big fucking shoe.

One of her legs rose above me, striking down too fast to see. Jumping back out of pure instinct, I blinked in surprise when the tip of the leg embedded itself a half-a-foot into the stone floor in front of me.

"Will you marry my son?"

"Even though you're asking so nicely? No." I sounded brave but I was three-seconds away from shitting my jeans. Other than magic, I had no weapons, no way to fight the spider-beast trying to skewer me or agreeing to the shotgun wedding. Personally, skewering sounded like the better option of the two.

218

You command the shadows, you have the blood of demons running through you, you are the mother of the undead. Magic is only one of your many gifts, Daughter.

Silently thanking my celestial coach, I realized I wasn't as helpless as I thought I was. That was the problem with fighting. You fall into a habit, a routine, and if anything screws with that, you're screwed. As soon as I realized my magic wasn't going to save me, I froze.

But the goddess was right, I was far from helpless. I trusted my familiars and the ones around me. Shea had told me I had dominion over the shadows, but no matter how many times he told me, I still had trouble believing it. I was just Dot. Underachiever of the century, according to my mother. It took a simple act of patiently showing me how to do it, to get me to take that first step. Granted, Fidget wasn't going to be taking on any bad guys until he put a little meat on his shadow-bones, but the world was literally full of shadows.

There were three windows in the queen's suite, all situated above and behind where her throne was, before she decided to use it as an ass implant. There might not have been a sun in the sky, but there was an abundance of daylight. Aoife, or Glabrielle, had seen to that. The orange glow filtered through the windows casting shadows around it on the stone floor. As I dodged the repeated swipes of spider legs, I focused on that and not getting impaled. Picturing the shadows coalescing into forms, I called.

Stop her, I thought at them as they were forming, picturing the shadows themselves wrapping around her and subduing her spider form.

Just as in my vision, the shades lifted themselves up off the floor behind her, just like I had seen Shea do multiple times in the past. I spared her a wicked smile and stepped back as the shadows came, and came, and came some more. My smile started to fade as they began pouring from the floor like black smoke. Delron and Elleslyn, already standing apart from our battle, ran toward the door, dragging me with them as they passed me.

"Stop!" The shadows weren't listening to me.

At the entrance to the room we watched in horror as the wave of shadow lifted her, in all her eight-legged glory, and slammed her toward the floor.

Elleslyn frowned and turned his head, unable to watch.

"No!" My voice echoed like thunder just as the queen was pushed into the stones beneath her. The shadows stopped. Walking forward, I expected a splattered mess against the stones, but as the shadows parted, I saw her half in our world, half in the shadow realm. They weren't killing her, they were dragging her to their world. "Bring her back, but do not let her go," I whispered softly, and they pulled her head from the floor, their bodies a congealed mass of lightless liquid.

Her eyes were smashed closed in fear, expecting to be dashed upon the stone floor, too. When they righted her, she opened one eye and took a deep rasping breath. "I should have known better," she said, defeated.

"Let her go." The shadows pulled back, still ready to pounce and to protect me if she moved so much as a spider tip.

She curled her legs beneath her, settling the monstrous orb that was her ass against the ground. "Thank you," she whispered softly. "Death in the realm of shadows is not how I wanted to leave this world."

"Especially while wearing a big spider butt."

She tilted her head and looked at me curiously. "Pardon?"

Elleslyn coughed behind me. Delron looked like he was about to go into convulsions. "What?"

"Lady," Delron started. "Remember when you asked why there was no surrounding town? Why there were no dark elf families?"

"Yes?"

"Females of our species… They are true queens. There is but one female with multiple mates and hundreds of workers. That giant spider butt, as you so eloquently put it, is her true form…"

I turned around and looked at her, and even though she had just tried to impale me, I felt horrible. "Well, it is a *lovely* spider butt. Bet you can shoot some mighty fine webs out of that thing."

"Quite," was all she said, not knowing what else to say.

Chapter 19

"Okay, so where the hell is Jaeren?"

Delron pointed up. I tilted my head and gasped. There were literally twenty cocoons suspended from the rafters in the vaulted ceiling. "Oh."

"Shall I retrieve him for you?" The queen asked.

"Is he still alive?"

"Quite."

"Didn't suck out his guts?"

"Seleighe sidhe give me stomach pains. Too light for this dark elf's tastes."

"I see what you did there. Please. I just really want to go home."

"I think I would prefer it if you were there, as well," the queen said and stepped around the swarming shadows to start climbing up the wall.

I squatted and held my hand out to the writhing mass in front of me. There were hundreds of eyes staring back at me, but they moved like one giant monster. "Thank you. You may go home now."

I watched in fascination as they slowly began to seep back into the floor, their eyes blinking out one by one as they returned to the shadow realm. All except one. Fidget broke away and slithered up my leg and slipping into my jeans' pocket. I didn't know how the hell he fit. I couldn't even get a ball of lint in there if I tried. He would have been way more comfortable in the back pocket.

All is well? Dar's voice popped into my head.

Yes. You can wait there or come back if you wish. Just getting Jaeren and heading that way.

Shea will be pleased. He has been on edge since we would not let him leave. He had...an episode. He began frantically shaking but has been calm since a moment ago.

That might have been my fault.

What did you do?

Called the shadows.

From where?

Everywhere. All of them.

I see. I shall let him return to you for comfort. Yukina and I shall remain here.

True to his word, I felt a pair of arms wrap themselves around me as I watched the spider queen carefully untangling Jaeren's cocoon from the ceiling. Stringing it over her shoulder, she climbed back down.

"Hi, Shea."

"Greetings, Lady. I told you that you could do it."

"Yeah, yeah. Mr Smartypants," I said and turned around, giving him a quick kiss.

The queen deposited Jaeren at my feet. Shea knelt down and used his dagger to cut open the cocoon, one of the barbs on the back of the blade looking like it had been designed for such a purpose. He was half dark elf. For all I knew, it had been.

"Shea, how much do you know about dark elves?"

"Pretty much all, why?"

"You knew the queen was half spider?"

"Yes? All dark elf queens are?"

"So all female dark elves have spider butts?"

"No? Only the queens. But, females who are *not* queens are very rare. Not as rare as shadowwalkers, but rare nonetheless.

"Okay. If you have information like this, share it with me *before* we go anywhere?"

"I am sorry. I assumed you knew."

I shook my head and rolled my eyes. He was damn lucky he was cute.

As soon as the cocoon was pulled away, Jaeren started to rouse. "Dot?" My name was the first word out of his mouth.

"Welcome back. Sorry it took so long to find you."

He looked around, saw the dark elves and snarled. "Treacherous bastards!"

"Calm down. It's over," I told him, putting my hand on his chest to keep him from coming up swinging. "Let's go home."

He looked like he wanted to argue, but just gave me a curt nod. "Lady… Would you be so kind as to help me up? I seem to be unable to move…"

I looked at the queen. "It will wear off. It is the venom still in his veins. He was in stasis. Now that he is breathing again, he will regain his mobility."

I reached down and grabbed an arm, Shea grabbed the other and we hoisted him to his feet. Luckily, Elleslyn was there to catch him when his legs were unable to support him. The two of us weren't tall enough to keep him up. Even Delron stepped forward, propping the seleighe prince between them. "We shall return with you to the gate," he offered.

I nodded my thanks. It was the least they could do. "You, I'm still mad at," I said to Delron. He nodded in understanding and gave me a wan smile.

"I would do anything for your father, and now for you. I hope you realize this."

"Good. Because you're going to help me get him back."

"If it is at all possible, I will."

"Wait!" I rounded on him, jabbing my finger in his chest. "What the hell is this about a sister?"

"Heard that as well, did you?"

"Yes! Who is she? Where is she?"

He leaned in and whispered in my ear. "You know her. You've known her your entire life and treated her as who she was. How could you even doubt who she is when she shares your birthing day?"

225

I stared at him in shock as he pulled away. "That's not possible. Josie remembers her father. He was human!"

"Was he?" Delron smiled and motioned for the door.

I just stood there in shock, completely and utterly happy that Josie was my real sister. Somehow, I did know. I'd always known. Now she couldn't say shit about me wanting to take care of her, or for feeling guilty when I did. That's what sisters did. Then the thought of my father bumping nasties with that witch of a mother of hers made me throw up in my mouth. A lot. I silently vowed never to think of it again. Not even if I accidentally drank a gallon of bleach and needed to purposely induce vomiting. I'd rather die.

"Lady, may I have a moment in private?" The queen sounded even more defeated...and tired. I nodded.

"Take them to the gate for me please, Shea. I'll join you in a minute.

"As you wish. You can make it there?"

"Yes. I have a guide," I said and patted my front pocket.

"Is that a shadow in your pocket or are you happy to see me?" He made a joke. I was so proud. I grinned at him in response.

"Little bit of both." Then I looked down and noticed that you could actually see the shadow through my pocket, and it looked suspiciously like a wet spot on the front of my jeans. "It's the shadow!"

"Uh huh. I shall see you at the gate." He winked and grabbed onto Delron, pulling the four of them into the shadows.

"I shall not waste much of your time." The queen stepped from her spider body, nearly toppling over.

I quickly grabbed her, steadying her and letting her sit back down now that it looked like a throne once more. "You're going to ask me to marry your son again, aren't you?"

"No. I'm going to beg."

"Why me?"

"Because you are the very first *woman* I have ever seen him take an interest in. I do not know if it is your power, your personality, or your beauty. It might even be a combination of all of them, I do not know. What I do know is if that child of mine does not take a wife, this court is doomed."

There was something she wasn't saying. "I couldn't help but notice you stressed the word woman. Elleslyn likes…"

"Men. Yes."

"I'm sorry. Not about him liking men, but I have to refuse. I cannot tie myself to anybody. I have too many men who love me, and that I love back just as much. With that said, I do think your son is very sweet, intelligent, engaging. And kinda hot. If he is interested in me… I wouldn't mind getting to know him better. Slowly."

"That is all I can ask. I am truly sorry for trying to force you into more. I should have passed on ages ago, but until there is a new queen of the realm…"

"If people and the gods would just start *asking* instead of trying to get me to do what they want, things would be a lot better. And safer."

She chuckled, and it sounded like somebody was shaking a bag of bottle caps and marbles. *She must have a lovely singing voice.*

"That is all I can ask. You have my thanks. As well as my vow of help when the time comes to rescue the Night. I would like to enjoy one more night beneath the moon before I move on."

I stopped for a moment and looked over at her throne. "Just out of curiosity… If your son and I *ever* had children, how many legs would they have?"

"Any children are born elven. Females… They do not gain their other attributes until they have fully matured."

"Okay then. No offense, but whew."

She gave another chuckle. I really felt a driving need to get out of there before I heard it again.

"Okay, then. Be well."

"You, too. Daughter." She added with a wink.

Barf.

Fidget. Get me the hell out of here.

∞ ∞ ∞

I stepped from the shadows beside the portal, leaning against it and waiting for everybody to notice my arrival. Dar smelled me first. He scented the air and turned around, giving me a big, blue grin. "Welcome back, Master."

"Thanks. Good to be back. Shall we get the fuck out of here?"

"That's the best damn plan I've heard in a week," Yuki said and slapped the rune on the portal. The purple liquid swirled, and the warehouse could be seen on the other side. "Go ahead," I told my three. "Don't wait for me. Get Jaeren into bed."

"Thank you, *Master*," Jaeren said gratefully and respectfully. I reminded myself to give him his box of crayons when I got home. And to get him the hell home. He had his own kingdom to fix, and it sounded like it was in a bigger mess than I thought. I wasn't sure if the drug thing was true, probably not, but I didn't trust the council at all. Jaeren, I did. We'd just have to work his babysitting schedule around his kingly duties. It wasn't like I couldn't rip a hole into Faerie whenever I needed.

"No sweat. Have a bath and get some rest."

"Surprisingly, I feel like I've slept for a week."

"Surprisingly, you're right?"

"A week?"

"Yep. Told you I sucked at finding you."

"You do." He nodded for emphasis.

"Go," I said to the rest of them. Before things got ugly and he started insulting me. The gate closed behind them.

"You are staying?" Elleslyn almost sounded hopeful.

"No. But feel free to come visit me whenever you like," I told him. "I may not want to get hitched, but that

228

doesn't mean I don't enjoy your company. Come see how the other half lives."

"If you do not mind, I shall." He had the cutest damn dimples when he smiled. I fought the urge to stick my finger in one.

"Delron. You're not allowed to visit. I'll meet you someplace neutral."

He chuckled. "That is fair. Take care of yourself. If you feel the need to speak to me, send your half-elf. He has been in the capitol library. He should be able to find me from there. The Church of Night is hard to miss."

"He's been there before?"

"Yes."

"That little shit and I are going to have a *long* talk when I get home. He leaves out so much information sometimes."

"He is a scholar. They often need prompts and often assume everyone around them has the same knowledge."

"Defending him. That's the nicest thing I've ever seen you do."

"I am not a nice person," he answered with a chuckle and a bow, keying the rune and stepping through the portal.

"That goes to the capitol?"

"It goes wherever you wish to go."

"That's handy. I should put one in my house."

"You are part god. I do not think you need one."

"I've opened a portal to faerie with my hand, but nowhere else. I wouldn't know how."

"It is much the same as the gate, I would think. Merely picture where you wish to go."

"Like the capitol?"

"Have you ever been there?"

"Of course not."

"Then I do not think it possible. You would not be able to picture where you are going."

"Hmm. That makes sense. Thank you, Elleslyn."

"You are welcome, Lady. I hope to see you again."

"That is a definite. Thank you for not being a douchebag, too."

"Douchebag?"

"When you come visit, I'll introduce you to the internet. You can Google it."

"I shall."

I made a silent vow to be there when he did. I wanted to see his face. "Well, I better be going…" I looked around. He and I were alone, so I stepped forward and stood on my toes, intending to give him a quick kiss on his lips as thanks.

My lips touched his and my body tensed. He felt me go rigid and put his hands on my hips to steady me. That touch was more than enough to set me on fire.

It erupted from his palms, spreading over my tummy and headed directly south. I shuddered in his grip as my lips parted and my tongue darted into his mouth.

He moaned in surprise and tilted his head, pulling me into that kiss. His masculine scent faded as he began to smell more delicious by the moment. I wanted to devour him. I wanted him inside me and not in the good way. The burning need to *taste* him drove all the other thoughts from my brain as my lips slid off his, over the smoothness of his cheek and down the softness of his neck.

I felt him grow rigid against me as I practically climbed into his arms. My eyes rolled back as I drove my fangs into his neck and suckled the blood that sprang from the wound like a fountain of pleasure.

He held me tight as I ground against him, the pleasure from the feeding amplifying the pleasure from rubbing together, wishing I wasn't wearing jeans. I started to shake as he began groaning and lowering us to the ground. I ended up on top of him, my hips bucking as I pulled his lifeblood from his neck.

It was the gentleness of his hand, softly caressing my back that slowed my frenzy. I gave the wound one last gentle lick, instinctually knowing it would close the wound, before sitting up and giving him a smile. "Woah."

"You are a vampire?"

"No. I am what I am. Kind of like a mutt. I guess I can be sometimes, though."

"You can do that again, whenever you wish."

"I have a feeling I will. Amongst other things. You know I have multiple lovers, I would need to talk to them before we go any further, though." I found myself saying that a lot. Sighing in frustration, I vowed not to put myself in another situation like that again. Enough was enough.

"Do not worry. You are well worth the wait."

My smile got a little bigger. "Elleslyn. That is a beautiful name."

"What would you like me to call you? You have so many."

I leaned in and licked his ear. "Dot."

"Dot?"

"It's short for Dorothea."

"Short?"

"Like Elleslyn. Calling you Ellis would be short for Elleslyn. Can I call you Ellis?"

"You may call me whatever you wish."

"Mine," slipped from my mouth without thinking about it.

"That as well."

"Really?"

He nodded.

"I'm a lot of trouble."

"Again, you seem to be well worth it."

"Until next time, then." I leaned down and kissed him again, this time trying to keep it chaste, at a low simmer instead of a raging boil.

Something *clicked.* Not around us, but inside me. I felt it snap and then there was a rush of power as something broke free. Gasping into the kiss, my back arched as all the feelings of the feeding and the grinding came rushing back as I shuddered above him. The kiss broke and my cheek slid against his as I held him tightly, eyes closed and riding the moment.

When I finally caught my breath and opened them, it was dark. I thought I had gone blind until I sat up and saw the subtle glow of moonlight on his face as he stared up at me in wonder. I slid back and looked up at the sky. Stars twinkled, the moon shone, and the orange glare had finally gone.

"You..." That was the only word he could say as he slid back, stood up and held out his arms, making slow circles beneath the night sky.

Finally, he stopped and bowed again at my feet.

"Lady Night, I cannot begin to thank you."

"Are you sure it was me?" I asked hopefully. Maybe somebody at the castle found the switch...

"Of that, I have no doubt. Thank you. Thank you. Thank you. A thousand times."

"Once was enough," I said embarrassedly. It's not like I was *trying* to do it. Just got lucky.

Lucky like a goddess, a soft voice chuckled in my head.

Yeah. You're going to have to explain what the hell just happened.

You made a pact with the prince of the realm. He already worshipped you as a woman, then he worshiped you as a god. The sphere that was already your father's, truly became yours. Your powers will keep growing until you will be strong enough to save your father.

Then I can go back to being normal Dot?

You have never been normal.

Did you know I had a sister? I figured I might as well ask her while I had her on the line.

Yes.

Why didn't you tell me?

Safety. The less she knows, the better off she will be. You, as well. I am almost sorry you found out.

I shouldn't tell her is what you are saying.

She is already your sister in your heart, would hearing the truth make any difference?

No.

Then you have your answer and it came from you instead of me.

Thank you. Again.

Keep growing, Daughter. Or should I start calling you, Niece?

Call me whatever you wish. Just don't let me get out of control. I don't care for power.

Just like your father…

I felt the connection break as she moved on.

"You stopped glowing."

I opened my eyes and Ellis was sitting in front of me, cross-legged. "I was glowing?"

"Yes. And not from the moonlight."

"Golden?"

"No. With blackness."

"How does something glow black?"

"Like you. You were radiating the night."

"Must have been the Mexican food."

He gave me a strange look. "I do not understand."

"You will when you come visit me. I'll take you to Taco Bell. Then *you* can radiate darkness for a while."

"It sounds like a pleasure. You were quite beautiful."

"Maybe it wasn't the Taco Bell then. I've had some ugly radiations from that."

He just nodded like he knew what the hell I was talking about. I gave him a smile and stood up off the ground.

"Well, enjoy your darkness. I need to get home."

"Until next time, Dot." He smiled as my name rolled from his tongue like honey.

"See you around, Ellis."

I touched the rune on the gate, stepping through without taking my eyes off him and without letting go of the silly grin on my face. When I made it through, he was gone and I was staring at the mouth of the cave in the basement of the warehouse.

"Fidget, help me find my house, please."

It chirped from my pocket, the first noise it, or any other shadow I'd seen, had made.

"Awww," I said as I stepped into the shadows.

Epilogue

"So, yeah. Thanks for that." I was practically snarling over my cup of coffee at my mother. The other patrons of the diner were pointedly ignoring us and had been since we walked in.

"Thank you for what?"

"Of all the beings in the world, you had to do the horizontal mambo with a damn god. How does that make you feel?"

"Well, at the time, pretty damn good..." My mother got a dreamy look in her eye.

"Ewww. Just ewww. No."

"You brought it up, Daughter."

"We're talking about how this is affecting me *now*, not how it affected you *then*."

"You wish me to apologize for having you? I would never."

I sighed and took a sip of my coffee. "What was he like?"

"Pure intensity. He was like a lightning storm on a cloudless night. No one, mortal, immortal, fey, or god has ever made me felt the way he did."

"I have to rescue him, you know this, right?"

"You know where he is?"

"Tartarus."

"Yes. One does not simply walk into...Tartarus."

"It's not Mordor, Mother."

"No. Mordor would be a walk in the park compared to that."

"Well, no matter what. I have to save him. It's the only way to give him his power back."

"Told you, you should have given the gem to me," she said snidely, sipping her tea.

"And it would have driven you insane. Er. Insaner? Is that a word? More insane than you already are."

"There is truth to your words, Granddaughter," Nana said as she slid into the booth next to me. I hadn't even heard her come in.

"Well, if you two are going to sit here and gang up on me, I shall take my leave. I have a coven that respects me and needs my supervision."

"Only because half of them are too stupid to think on their own because all they can think about is their next tryst with you…"

"You sound homesick, Mother."

"Not in the slightest. I'm quite content here. The list of handy *men* in the area is quite large. As are their tools."

"Please be talking about their hammers. I already ordered," I said and rubbed my eyes.

"Hammers. Apropos. Especially since the last one did resemble Thor…"

"At least I know you're talking about the actual god and not that drool worthy actor they have playing him in the cinema," Mother answered. "Your Nana dated *him* before the great flood."

I couldn't help it. I chuckled. *One point for Mother.*

"At least I went to school. You were busy with the boys while they built all those triangular sculptures in Egypt if I recall correctly.

Nana evens the score.

"Well, I had to have *someplace* to bury you. Pity you escaped."

Mother for the win!

"Witch."

"Hag."

"Enough!" I put an end to their little debate, laughing. Before they blew up the diner. Or the town.

"Well, it is time I left you two. I really do need to get back. Daughter, I am proud of you," Mother said out of character. Even more so, when she gave me a smile.

"Thank you, but before you go…"

"Yes?"

"Did you know?"

She narrowed her eyes and tilted her head. "About?"

"My sister."

She sighed and sat back in the booth, looking up at the ceiling. "Yes." She looked back down at me and frowned.

"How did you find out?"

"From the high priest of the Church of Night. I was in the shadows while he spoke to the unseleighe queen."

"So, she knows as well?"

"As does her son."

"Well, at least they are a tight-lipped race. You can't tell her."

"I know. I spoke to the goddess about it. Josie is many things, prepared for any of this isn't one of them."

Nana, apparently, did *not* know. She was staring at the two of us incredulously. "He *cheated* on you?"

That is what I had assumed, too. My mouth fell open when Mother shook her head. "It was at the Imbolc Festival… We were all drunk, it only happened the one time. Your father and I had already decided to have a child… Apparently Miranda felt the same way."

I gagged. So did Nana. "You had a *threesome*… With Miranda Barton?"

"She was much thinner and much more attractive back then. And only half the lunatic she is today."

"Miranda? Barton?" It was the only words I could form, trying so hard not to open my cranial cavity and dip my brain in bleach.

"Not my proudest moment. No."

Then everything made so much more sense. "That's why you hate her. And Josie. And why she hates you and me."

Mother nodded.

"I knew it had to be something. Not like *that,* but I knew there had to be something. Oh, goddess. I'm thinking about it again." I gagged.

"Well, I'll leave you to your dry heaves. Let me know if there's anything else I can do to make you retch." She rolled her eyes and stood from the booth.

"Mom?" She stopped at my unusual address.

"Yes?"

"Stay?"

A single tear rolled from her eye and she sat back down. "You want me to?"

"Yes. Stay for a few more days. I hardly got to see you while you were here, and I do miss you."

"I missed you, too, Dot."

"Anybody need a refill?" Marge made her way back to the table. "Oh, Dot. Herb told me to tell you he has the paperwork for you in his office. You can drop the check off whenever. The total price is on the paperwork."

"Perfect. Thanks, Marge."

"No problem, sweetie."

∞ ∞ ∞

Wandering down the street, by myself, I sighed in content. It seemed like it had been forever since I'd had a moment to myself, and I was determined to enjoy it. I might have become the embodiment of the night itself, but the feeling of sunshine washing over me felt amazing. Especially in the cold, winter air.

I waved at Chief through the front window of the station. He was on the phone, or he probably would have come out to see me. I scrunched my eyes at his goofy grin as he waved back. I would see him tomorrow night, anyway. We were meeting for dinner. Tonight, was Jimmy's night. He promised me a home-cooked meal and an evening of cuddles. I intended to collect on both.

I still needed to run home, take care of a few things, and pick up a change of clothes. But, before then, I wanted to drop in on the book store and check on Jason.

The front doors, painted green, were locked. I rapped against the glass and saw him peek out from around one of the racks of books in the center of the store. His smile was warm enough to melt my heart and I stuck my tongue out at him as he headed for the door. With a twist of the lock, he pulled it open.

"Uh, sorry. We don't open until Monday."

"That's two days away? I don't think I can wait that long."

"Was there something in particular you were looking for?"

"A handsome man, in jeans. With a green apron."

"Oh! You're in luck. We just happen to have one of those," he said with a chuckle, stepping back and letting me into the warm book store.

"Holy shit, Jay. The place looks amazing." I twirled around as I walked inside, taking everything in. "I can't believe how much you got done in such a short time.

I wasn't kidding, either. Nearly all the dark wooden shelves were full of books. He had signs printed and placed above all of them, denoting genres. Everything was themed in dark forest green, except the cream-colored walls. It was everything I had pictured in my head and so much more. I squealed and launched myself at him, wrapping my legs around him and kissing him fervently.

"You taste different," he said, tilting his head when I finally let go of his lips.

"Just had lunch with Nana and my mother. That's enough to leave a bad taste in *anybody's* mouth. Might even be garlic."

He pulled me close again and sniffed my neck. "No. You even smell different."

I saw where he was going with it. "If you say I taste and smell like the night, I gonna bop you."

"No. You smell…sweeter? Taste sweeter? I don't know. Just a little different, and I like it."

"It's probably all that honey from your tongue," I said with a chuckle and set my feet back on the floor.

"Come on. Check out your office," he said and pulled me toward the back of the store.

We rounded a partition wall into the storeroom. In the back of that was a wood door with the word "Boss" emblazoned above it. I scrunched my nose in excitement as he pulled it open and ushered me in.

A mahogany desk nearly filled the room. One wall was filled with monitors that blinked with security cam footage of the entire store. High hat lights illuminated the room in a soft warm glow, not fluorescent, and it felt homey. I absolutely adored it, and the man responsible for it all.

"Jason."

"Yes?"

"It's perfect. Thank you!"

He pumped his fist in achievement. "You are so welcome."

I ran my hand over the desk and slumped into the chair behind it. "Everything is just as I imagined it. But better."

"Thank you." He grinned at me and sat in one of the chairs on the other side of the desk.

"Where's your office?"

"I don't have one."

"We can share…"

"I figured you would have me off doing bigger better things."

"Nope. The bookstore is it, for now. In the future… We will see."

"Good. I'll enjoy working here for a while then."

"Good thing. Mr. Manager."

He nodded and smiled. "Did I just get a promotion?"

"Yep. Right hand man and store manager. You'll be getting a sizeable raise."

His face darkened. "That's not necessary, Dot."

"Jason. Shut up."

He sighed but did as I said. He was worth the money, now I just needed to convince him of that. "Josie all set to open, too? Or do I need to light a fire under her ass?"

"She's set for a soft opening with a limited menu."

"Good. Starting slow is probably a good idea for her."

"Candace can handle it."

"She's not going back to the hospital?" I felt bad. I'd been dealing with so much, I hadn't had a chance to talk to either of them about their plans. Not even the wedding, which we needed to start planning.

"No. Josie asked her to quit and work at the coffee shop."

I nodded. They belonged together. "Good."

"So, do you have any plans tonight?"

I frowned. "Yeah. I'm having dinner with Jimmy tonight. Chief tomorrow."

"That's okay. I'm glad. Just seeing if you were free." I could tell by his face, he wasn't upset, but I still felt bad.

"Come here."

Without question, he got up out of the chair and came around the desk to my side. "What?"

"Sit." I pointed at the desk in front of me.

I pushed back, giving him enough room. When his butt touched the wood, I grinned at him, evilly. "Gotta break in some of the office furniture," I said with a chuckle. "You know, test its durability."

"I thought you were having dinner with Jimmy?" He asked, but he leaned back, putting his hands on the desk behind him while I scooted forward and flipped his apron up over his stomach.

"I am. But that doesn't mean I'm not hungry now." I unzipped his jeans and fished him out through the front of his pants. I *really* wanted to strip him and have my way with him on the desk, but I wasn't sure how long we had before someone knocked, walked in, or in any other way, disturbed us. It was probably better to let him keep his pants on.

I leaned forward in my chair, he wasn't hard yet, but I could fix that easily. I smiled up at him as I licked the tip. Just that was enough to make him twitch in my hand.

"What are you going to do?"

"What do you want me to do?"

"What *don't* I want you to do?"

I kissed the tip. "Do you want me to suck you into my mouth?"

He nodded.

"Tell me."

"I want you to suck me into your mouth."

"No. *Tell* me."

"Dot, suck my cock."

His words sent a shiver down my spine. It was the first time he had ever *told* me what to do, and I liked it. A lot. I closed my lips around the tip and pulled him into my mouth, using only suction.

He wasn't completely limp anymore, but he wasn't hard, either. He twitched against my tongue as I felt his condition change. I fucking loved feeling him harden in my mouth and I groaned against him as I started bobbing my head and working him with my mouth.

"Holy fuck."

I pulled him free with a soft *pop* and a gentle lick of my tongue across his opening. "You like getting blown by the boss in her office?"

"Fuck yes." He reached out and let his fingers gently caress my cheek.

"You want me to keep going?" I bobbed on his cock again, sucking him hard as I pulled him from my mouth again, waiting for his answer.

"Yes. Keep sucking."

"You want to come in my mouth?" I rubbed his tip across my lips, feeling the heat of him, the softness of his skin. And the twitching of his muscles.

"Yes."

"Yes?" I went down on him again, taking all of him into my mouth until my nose was pressed into his downy soft hair above.

"Yes. I want you to make me come, I want to blow in your mouth, and I want you to swallow all of it."

I rubbed my tongue back and forth along the underside of him as I slowly worked him free. "But you really want to fill my pussy full of your come, don't you?" If I wasn't having dinner with Jimmy, I would have let him. I might have still let him, if I were going straight there. Jimmy would probably appreciate that.

"Yes," he answered with a grin.

I took him into my mouth, just the tip and cocked an eyebrow at him. "Next time. Maybe I'll let you come all over me," I said as I sucked him back in all the way and started pumping him with my hand as I worked him in complete earnest.

"Will you let me come in your ass?"

Jason, my little sweet Jason, was getting a pervy streak big enough to match that of the master, Jimmy. I felt myself gush at the thought. I sucked him, stroked him, and did my damnedest to make him explode.

"Dot," he said almost frantically.

I forced him as far as he could go into my mouth, reaching around him and pulling him in tight.

"Fuuuuck," he said breathlessly as he unloaded a torrent of hot wetness into my throat. I let him finish before pulling away, standing, and kissing him.

For all his talk, I expected him to pull away, but he didn't. He kissed me with everything he had and I found myself whimpering into it, snuggling against his chest as he held me.

"Your turn…" He turned me around and bent me over the desk.

"Jason…"

"Shush," he said and sat down in my vacated seat.

"What are you doing?"

243

"Returning the favor," he said and worked my leggings down, followed by my panties. He stopped when they were around my knees. I let out a little moan as I felt his hot breath caress my lips, followed by his tongue.

With my legs together, he couldn't really get to my clit, but he didn't let that stop him. He dove in with all the fervor he could muster and I found myself panting as he plunged his tongue inside me. He spread me apart as far as he could and used the tips of his index fingers to rub gently beside his tongue, collecting the wetness that he was spreading all over.

When his finger tip glided over my other entrance, I hissed in pleasure.

"Somebody likes that," he said after pulling away for a moment.

"Just don't get any big ideas, mister..."

He didn't listen. The finger that was gliding gently around, began to apply pressure. I couldn't complain. It felt amazing. Especially as he started moving it in and out slowly, only going up to the first knuckle. I moaned and grabbed the other side of the desk with my hands, trying to hold myself still as pleasure spread from both holes straight through me.

"Goddess..."

His other hand let go of me, and I didn't think anything of it until I heard the drawer slide open beside me.

"Jason?"

"Shush," he commanded again as he pulled away. Something began buzzing and I felt the tip of it vibrating between my lips. I thought it was a small vibrator until he pulled it away and touched it to my ass.

"Jason?" I asked again.

He just held it there as he began licking my pussy again. Just as I was enjoying the feeling, he began pushing the well lubricated tip against me. He slowly worked it inside and I felt myself beginning to come. "Fuuuuck."

"Do you like that?"

"Yes!"

244

"I'll stop if you want me to."

"Don't you fucking dare." I found myself pushing back against it. The sensations were completely new and utterly amazing. I could feel myself spreading as the wider tip slowly slid further inside me. My hole closed around it as the bulbous tip passed through. A little bit more and I felt the flat end stop it from progressing further.

"Turn around," he said.

I lifted myself off the desk and turned, staring at him in shock and pushing my ass against the desk. "What is that?"

"A vibrating butt plug," he grinned and leaned forward, kissing my dripping lips.

"Holy shit."

"Are you going to come?"

"Lick me, please. Yes."

He stopped talking and kissed my lips once more, using his tongue to slip between them and slide upward, forcing my hood back and flicking against my clit. I exploded. If I hadn't put my arms behind me, I would have fallen backward, convulsing on the desk. As it was, I could barely hold on for the ride, and oh what a ride it was. He didn't relent with his tongue and the vibrations didn't stop. A wave of orgasms drove me insane. Finally, I couldn't take it anymore and reached out, pushing him away. "No more."

He chuckled, gave me one last gentle kiss and reached for his phone.

"You're *not* taking a picture," I warned him with a laugh.

"No. I'm shutting it off," he said and punched a button on the open app. Immediately, the vibrations inside me stopped.

"It's Bluetooth?"

"And wireless."

"That's kind of high tech."

"Yep," he answered proudly, turning it back on and off again, watching me squirm.

"Okay. Take it out. I need to go home and hose off now before I go to Jimmy's."

"Nope. It's waterproof. You can shower with it in. It's not to come out until I tell you. Oh, and just so you know, I can turn it back on and off at anytime with this," he said and held up his phone, giving it a little shake.

His commanding tone was almost as big of a turn on as the thought of going on a date with Jimmy with a butt plug that another man had put inside me was. "You're gonna give Jimmy a run for biggest perv trophy," I said in more than a little shock.

"Who do you think told me to put it there if I had the chance?"

I chuckled gently and pulled up my panties.

That's my Jimmy. And my Jason. I should have known.

∞ ∞ ∞

"So, how did the deposition go?" I leaned my head against Jimmy's shoulder. We were sitting on his couch, watching a movie while dinner cooked in the oven. Dennis was sitting in the recliner next to us.

"I still say it's fucking bullshit they fired you," Dennis added angrily.

"It went fine. Sherry doubts I will get my job back, but she thinks I'll get a hefty sum for being let go. I'm just hoping they'd rather keep me than pay."

I swallowed down my retort. I was being a shitty girlfriend. If he wanted to be a fireman, I'd support him. Just because I wanted him safe, didn't give the right to silently cheer for the end of his career. "Is that what you want?"

"To keep working? Yeah. I trained really hard to become a fireman. It's all I've ever wanted. I knew I'd have to retire one day, but I just wasn't expecting it to be so soon."

"You want me to fix the problem?"

"How?"

"Magic," I answered him deadpan. I wasn't planning on outing myself as a witch and taking credit for his miraculous healing, but I'd do whatever I could to get him back on the job. If that's what he wanted.

He beamed at me, leaning in for a kiss. "Thank you. But no. I'll stick to legal channels and see what happens. You're awfully cute for offering, though."

I snuggled closer to him and rubbed my face against his shoulder, breathing in his scent. I loved the way he smelled. I loved the way all my guys smelled. Maybe it was an effect of being their high priestess or master, but they were comforting just to be around. Even Chief with his old aftershave. I would never admit it, but I kind of missed it every once in a while.

"So how was your day?" Jimmy kissed the top of my head. "And why are you here so early? Not that I'm complaining."

I leaned in close and whispered in his ear. "I have a surprise for you."

He turned and looked at me, lifting his eyebrows. " A surprise?"

"Yep."

"Well, where is it?"

I leaned back in, nibbling on his ear. "In my panties…"

Jimmy's chuckle gave me goosebumps. I nearly snarled when someone rang their doorbell. "Hold that thought," he said apologetically, and got up to answer the door.

I looked over my shoulder and smiled at Chief as he walked in. "Hey, Jimmy."

"Bill? What can I do for you?"

"Hey, Chief. What's up?" I stood up.

"I'm actually here to see you." He paused, sighed, and gave me an apologetic look. "Dorothea Blackwell… You're under arrest." *I'm sorry,* he mouthed as he pulled out his handcuffs. If it weren't for him mouthing the apology, I would have thought he was joking. Or Jimmy was getting *really* kinky.

"What? What for?" Jimmy said incredulously.

"Don't! Don't say anything," Sherry, Jimmy's cousin the lawyer and mayor said as she walked in the still open door behind Chief. "As your lawyer, I'm strongly urging you not to say a word."

I stood there in shock.

"You are under arrest for the destruction of the thirteen-hundred block of Elm street approximately two nights ago. More specifically, the restaurant known as Lambresco's. You have the right to remain silent. Anything you say can and will be used against you in a court of law. You have the right to an attorney, which one has come forth to represent you. Should you choose not to use her services or cannot afford one, one will be provided for you. Do you understand the rights I have just read to you? With these rights in mind, do you wish to speak to me?"

I could see the emotions warring on his face. Jimmy stood behind us, yelling all sorts of obscenities at Chief, almost drowning out Sherry's voice in my ear. "Somebody took pictures in the restaurant of the battle. There is an eight by ten glossy of you throwing lighting at the front windows. The angels didn't show up on film. Tell him you understand and do not wish to speak."

"I understand. No. I do not wish to speak to you."

It will probably be a while before I do…

Bonus Scene

Enjoy this scene from Chapter 15 in Shea's point of view!

A Many Splendored Moment

To think I would actually be in the presence of an intoxicated demon... Before I passed on from the mortal realm, I expected to see many wondrous things. That *not* being one of them.

The Lady chuckled at Dar. "Nope. Keep going straight. We're putting you to bed, too. Shea, give us a hand?"

"If you wish." I set my wine glass down on the coffee table and slipped up under the inebriated demon's arm. I was much stronger than I looked and could have easily handled his weight on my own, but I also understood the importance of letting the Lady feel useful when it came to her men.

"Could I use the restroom first?" Dar's words were almost...music to my ears.

"Uh, Shea, That's all you."

I nodded and led him to the bathroom. Dorothea knew my penchant for members of the opposite sex, but my tastes were particular. Tall, dark, and brooding. Dar just happened to be all of those and so much more. I found myself oddly attracted to his smile, his laugh, and the horns sticking out from his head. I found him almost as beautiful as I found our lady.

Once we were in the bathroom, I stood behind him and steadied him as I heard the stream splash loudly in the water. At least he was not drunk enough to miss. That would have been horrifyingly embarrassing for him.

Glancing over, I saw Lady watching us with a particular smile on her face. She was enjoying the show and I couldn't help but cock an eyebrow at her. She returned my glance with a wiggling of her eyebrows. I could tell she wanted more.

"We should probably get you out of these jeans while you're standing up," I mentioned, not tearing my eyes from hers.

"You are pretty smart. That is a splendid idea," Dar replied in front of me, not knowing he had fallen into a trap.

I let go of his hips, hesitating for just a moment to make sure he was steady enough on his own before reaching around his front for his belt.

"I can unbuckle my pants if you want." The words left his lips, but I could hear the hope behind the bravado.

"It is okay, I do not mind." I leaned a little closer and whispered, "In fact…I want to."

Dar lifted his head, showing the smile in the corner of his mouth. Maybe he hadn't fallen into my trap. Maybe he dove in head first. Either way, I was not letting the opportunity pass. After a brief struggle, I managed to get the belt loose and unbuttoned his jeans. My hand slid across his stomach of its own volition, his smooth skin tingling the tips of my fingers as I brought them back to his hips and pushed the jeans down over his well-defined ass.

I worked them down to his hips and was struck by inspiration. "Did you shake?"

"Shake?" Dar sounded confused.

"Like this." I reached back around, grabbed his shaft, and slid my fingers down his length. The heat of it in my hand, the softness against my fingers… It became almost too much to bear and I fought the urge to spin him around and take him in my mouth. I settled for gently wiggling it, letting the last drops of moisture fall into the bowl. Only then did I start stroking him in front of the lady. "Does that feel good?"

"Yes."

"Do you wish me to stop?" I prayed he would let me continue. I begged that it was something he wanted, too.

"No," came his perfect answer as he groaned and spread his legs.

I wanted to see more of him. "Take your shirt off."

He obeyed almost immediately, practically ripping it over his head and tossing it to the floor. I seized the moment, rubbing my cheek against the muscled ridges of his back and giving the lady a wicked grin. He smelled divine, and I found myself wondering how he tasted. I let my tongue drift slowly across his back and wasn't disappointed.

"I am going to fall over," Dar said softly.

Concerned, I asked, "You are that drunk?"

"No. My head seems to have cleared, but this feels too good."

"Would you like to move to the bed?" *Please say yes.*

"Yes."

Letting go of his throbbing shaft, I squatted down behind him. "Step out of your pants," I said and held them for him. He obliged and turned, letting me get a good view of what I had been caressing moments before. His manhood was almost as beautiful as he was. Without hesitation, and unable to control myself, I leaned in and kissed the tip of it gently.

Sparing a smile for the lady, gently rubbing herself in the doorway, I stood and let my lips caress her demon's lips. There was no mistake, he was hers. Just as I was. Just as we all were. While my lips lingered against his, I cupped him with my hand and sighed softly into the kiss as I felt him push forward, wanting more.

The sounds of our lady's orgasm broke our kiss and we both turned to watch her come down. She blushed and quickly sat down on the bed behind her.

"Shall we join the Master?" I looked up at my new lover.

"If she wishes…"

We could almost hear her nodding emphatically.

Dar took the initiative, walking to her and pushing her back against the bed as he leaned over her, driving himself against the wetness of her leggings. They were both beautiful on their own, together they were magnificent. I quickly shed my clothes and sat down next to them, unable to keep my hand from my own member.

They both turned to watch, and I flushed in embarrassment, almost wanting to cover myself. I'd never been comfortable with people seeing me and my runes.

"He's beautiful, isn't he?" Lady asked Dar.

His smile and hungry look were all the reassurance I needed.

"So are you," she continued. "Lie on your back."

Dar didn't need to be told twice and she stood, pulled off her leggings, and lifted her sweater over her head. Without a moment of hesitation, she crawled over him and settled herself on his eager mouth, almost immediately losing herself in the sensation of his lips and tongue against her flesh. I wanted to taste her, too. My turn would come. She opened her eyes and stared hungrily at my cock in my hand. Hoping I was reading the look correctly, I moved closer to her and got up on my knees, offering it to her. She leaned over and took me in her mouth, the sensation nearly causing my release.

Dar must have had a very talented mouth. With each shiver of ecstasy he sent ripping through her, she would moan a muffled sigh around my throbbing cock. Finally, she had to pull me free, but continued stroking me with her hand while she let out a soft, "Oh."

Sliding my hands over her chest, I gave her a gentle squeeze. "Is he going to make you come?"

She nodded, unable to form words.

"Turn around, he will be able to go deeper."

She nodded and lifted herself slowly off his mouth.

"Are you okay?" the demon asked.

"She is fine, just let her reposition herself," I told him and reached down, wiping some of the lady's wetness from his lips and bringing it to my tongue. "Such sweetness."

Dar nodded. "I tasted the honey that Candace keeps in the cupboard for tea. They are much the same."

I nodded in agreement while Lady lowered herself back to his mouth while facing me. Unable to resist, I took her in my arms and let my lips and tongue play with her perfect breasts before slowly making my way up over her neck.

"Oh, Shea," she whispered

"Look at him," I whispered to her. "See him throbbing? He looks like he is about to explode, just from tasting you."

She looked down and nodded.

"Can you reach it?"

She ran her fingers over it and smiled.

"Do you wish to stroke it, or do you want to watch me do it?"

"You," she blurted.

I let go of her and moved over to him. She whimpered in pleasure while I spread Dar's legs and knelt on the ground in front of him. I wrapped my fingers around the base of him and slid them up and over the tip as fluid began dripping freely. I had been very correct; he was about to burst. I smiled as I let some of its slipperiness glide between my fingers and then offered it to Lady.

She opened her mouth and suckled my fingers, tasting Dar's sweetness. I could feel her hunger and her surprise. I chuckled and lowered my face to my friend's cock, pulling him into my mouth. Almost immediately his hips started undulating in pleasure and I used my arms over his thighs to hold him steady. Using my mouth and one hand, it did not take him long to erupt. The warm wetness flooded my mouth and I swallowed as much as quickly as I could while the lady peaked above him. Her soft moans and squeals only adding to the excitement in the room.

I stood and leaned over and kissed her, sharing Dar's bounty as the orgasm tore through her. After it passed, she slowly lifted herself from his mouth. "Woah," she said incredulously at the amount of moisture gathered around his lips.

"You flooded me when you came," he answered with a grin.

"Your fault."

"I accept full responsibility. Would you care to try again?"

"Yeah. I'm going to need a minute before anybody touches me there," she answered with a chuckle.

"Well, I do not," I said and began stroking Dar back to his full length. I wanted some pleasure as well.

"What are you going to do?" Lady asked, but she knew the answer.

"I wish to feel him inside me," I answered honestly.

"You're going to…?"

"You shall see. He is already hard again. Could I ask you to make him wet?"

She didn't need to be asked twice. She practically jumped from the bed and took Dar in her mouth. As she bobbed her head, Dar hissed in pleasure.

I looked over my shoulder at her. She had missed my intention. "Might I suggest something else? The lubrication would be more natural."

She stood up and looked very eager as she pushed his legs together and straddled him behind me, bracing herself against me as she guided him inside her. I leaned back into her embrace and let out a little sigh as she reached around me to take my cock in her hands. Dar beat her to it and began stroking me gently. The lady decided to stroke my shoulder as he did, igniting my tattoos in a flare of light. I had never felt…so wanted in my life. Nothing even came close. Not any of my previous lovers made me feel loved half as much as the two of them had in that moment.

I needed more. "Is he ready?" I asked Lady over my shoulder.

"Yes. Do you want him?"

I nodded, breathing unsteadily as Dar worked his hands over my hardness.

Lady lifted herself off him. I leaned forward and scooted back, trusting Lady to guide him.

"Are you sure about this?" She asked one last time.

I smiled and nodded, pushing back slowly and relaxing as the head of his cock spread me open slowly. I had to work myself back and forth for a few moments until I felt myself close around the head. The rest of him glided in easily, filling me, and sending pleasure everywhere as it radiated from his heat inside me.

Leaning down, I found Dar's lips with mine and melted against his chest as he kissed me back with just as much tenderness as I found my rhythm with my hips.

"That is so hot," Lady muttered behind me. I lifted myself from his chest and turned to watch her with her fingers buried inside her, fervently trying to get herself off again. I decided to give her a little show and began grinding my hips against Dar, riding him much like I had seen her do atop Jimmy.

"Does that feel good?" She asked.

"Exquisite," Dar answered first, reaching out and tracing her nipple with his finger.

"I see why you like this position," I answered her, feeling Dar drive inside me further.

"Well, it's a little different from what I normally do, but still hot as fuck to watch."

"It has been a while," I told her shyly.

"I know you. Been inside your head before, remember?"

I nodded in understanding. "I am going to come soon."

"You're going to come? From him being inside you?"

"Yes. It feels incredible. You should try it."

"Maybe. Sometime. There's other places I enjoy it, though." She stood and stepped over Dar, squatting down and facing me. She looked over her shoulder at Dar. "I'm not hurting you, am I?"

I couldn't see him, but he must have shaken his head because Lady turned and smiled at me, reaching down and grabbing my cock as she slid forward, putting her legs over mine as she guided me into her.

"I want you to come inside me."

255

"That I can do," I managed to stammer as I fucked the both of them. The pleasure was ripping through me from different directions and I didn't know which to concentrate on, which felt better. After only a few minutes, Dar was the first to break as he grunted beneath us. Suddenly, he felt much slipperier inside me as I felt his hot wetness leak out around us. Lady erupted just after. Her head fell back as she screamed in ecstasy. Her quivering orgasm was enough to bring me to the edge as I felt her squeezing me inside her, the walls of her pussy gripping my cock.

I exploded inside her, the force of my orgasm causing my own semen to rush out of her and erupt over us both as jet after jet escaped me. We both fell off Dar and collapsed on the bed, smiling at each other.

"Please tell me you're fucking done," came a quivering shout from the other room. I hadn't known that vampires could sound exhausted...

Author's Note

Reviews are important for new authors and I greatly appreciate everyone who takes a moment to leave one, even a line or two! Thank you so much for reading my reverse harem series! I'm writing away and more books will be out soon!

Follow me on Amazon to be sent updates on my new releases!

Come join my Readers Group on Facebook for news, fun, games, teasers for upcoming books, and naughty shenanigans! 18+ recommended.

Coven of the First Moon

About the Author

A late comer to the writing game, Jacquelyn had always been a fan of romance novels and lately become addicted to the reverse harem category. I mean seriously, who wouldn't? Sitting alone one night she flipped open her laptop and said, "I'm going to give this a whirl." And thus, the Lovin' the Coven series was given life. She has designs on other series as well, but only time shall tell.

As for her, she is five-foot-something, with graying hair, wicked eyes, an eager smile, and an annoying laugh. She lives at home with her dog, a cat, and that is about all she is comfortable sharing.

Other Works

Lovin' the Coven Series
(Reverse Harem- 7 book series)

First Moon
Second Blood
Third Charm
Fourth Rite
Fifth Essence
Sixth Sense
Seventh Seal

The Fox and the Hounds
(Reverse Harem – trilogy)

A Tail of Woah
A Tail of Two Kitties
The Tell Tail Heart

Other

Girlfiend (Standalone YA Paranormal Romance)
Succubus Soccer Mom (Reverse Harem Standalone)